CALCULATED ENCOUNTERS

ENDORSEMENTS

Laurie G. Westlake dials up the tension in her novel *Calculated Encounters*, sending Isa Phillips on an international hunt for human traffickers. A thrilling ride from start to finish.
—**Author Kay DiBianca**

L.G. delivers another page-turner in *Calculated Encounters*. Quirky and stubborn Isa Phillips remains one of my favorite characters, and L.G. one of my favorite authors.
—**Anne Gressett**, reader

Laurie Westlake is a top-notch writer. Her writing and storytelling abilities will keep readers satisfied for years to come.
—**Larry J. Leech II**, author, writing coach

CALCULATED ENCOUNTERS

L.G. WESTLAKE

ELK LAKE PUBLISHING INC.

PUBLISHING THE POSITIVE
Plymouth, Massachusetts

COPYRIGHT NOTICE

Cover and Interior Design: Derinda Babcock, Deb Haggerty

Editor(s): Mel Hughes, Cristel Phelps, Deb Haggerty

PUBLISHED BY: Elk Lake Publishing, Inc., 35 Dogwood Drive, Plymouth, MA 02360, 2022

Library Cataloging Data

Names: Westlake, L.G. (L.G. Westlake)

Calculated Encounters / L.G. Westlake

400p. 23cm × 15cm (9in × 6 in.)

ISBN-13: 978-1-64949-548-8 (paperback) | 978-1-64949-549-5 (trade paperback) | 978-1-64949-550-1 (e-book)

Key Words: Mafia, Italy, Spain, bounty hunter, child trafficking; romance; money laundering

DEDICATION

To the champions who've overcome.

ACKNOWLEDGMENTS

I'm grateful for you. Whether you bought, borrowed, or dug this book out of a box in your mother's attic, I'm thankful you've decided to experience the action and characters created to mirror your life—quirky, maddening, but capable of heroic feats.

Because with God, all things ... and anything ... is possible.

CHAPTER 1

Hidden in the alley's shadows, she waited.

Right on time, he appeared—the ex-member of the now defunct 96 Cartel glided under the streetlamp at the cross-section of the alley and Central Avenue.

This wasn't her first time to stalk prey. Wouldn't be the last, either.

His sluggish gate and downcast eyes let her know he was in no hurry to get to his deluxe accommodations at the Motel 66 with its half-lit, blinking neon sign at the wrong end of Central. She slipped from her hiding spot and fell in step behind him.

He didn't have a clue.

She'd come a long way from her days at a desk.

The telltale bump of a gun grip protruded from the back of his shirt, the bulk of the weapon crammed in his sagging jeans. If her target did exactly what he'd done for the last four nights, she'd have that gun in her hand and this guy wetting his pants in less than five minutes.

She wasn't the most skillful stalker, but she was an expert in the human behavioral science of scum suckers. She was also an expert in ratios.

Current percentages favored her stepping out of the upcoming altercation unscathed.

Just a few short months ago, she'd lived inside a cartel compound for several days, learning what made drug lords tick and what kept their rank and file loyal. Not many cops got the opportunity she'd had at an insider's view, and she'd walked away from the ordeal knowing one big weakness all 96 Cartel members possessed—constant insecurity.

This one had a double dose. He'd been one of the lucky ones to be released from jail because of overcrowding conditions during a worldwide pandemic called COVID-19. The five-foot-five or six-inch gangster had reentered freedom without the refuge of his old cartel and their maniac leader, El Padrino. Taking into consideration that he did not have a safety-net brotherhood to call upon, and that he probably suffered from short-man syndrome, she would use his lack of self-confidence and the element of surprise against him.

For this event, she'd chosen to wear an oversized black slicker, a wool cap, her retired black COVID-19 protection mask, and the steel-toed boots she'd bought the day she called Sergeant Caba and told him she wouldn't be returning to the Houston Police Department's white-collar crimes unit. Another lesson she'd gained from her short-term cartel life—footwear made a difference. Standard accountant navy pumps by day, and flip flops by night, were not appropriate jiujitsu footgear when fighting on the streets.

The ex-gangster turned into the unlit parking lot of his motel. Stopped. Straightened.

She pulled in the cool, dry air of the dark Albuquerque night.

Time to fly. She closed the distance. Sprang off her right foot. Aimed for his back.

CHAPTER 2

"What the …"

The 96er grabbed for her, but she jumped out of reach, his .357 Magnum now firmly in her grip. Shoving her free hand inside her slicker pocket, she pulled out her Glock. With two barrels pointed at his chest, the gangster's hands shot up.

"Hello."

"A woman?" He screwed up his face. "Why'd you take my gun?"

Another thing gang members had in common—stupid questions.

"You held up a smoke shop three streets over."

He smirked, a gold tooth shining as he tossed any chance of denying her charge to the wind. "So? So that was a hundred bucks. So what you gonna do about that, chica?"

"You're a sharp one." She stepped forward, looking him dead in the eye. "You will not go near that smoke shop again. Neither will you terrorize the owner's daughter with your foul mouth and insinuations if you pass her on the street."

He lowered his hands a little. Peered into her eyes. "I know who you are. You're that … that numbers chick that got us all busted."

"And I will do it again, only this time I'll shoot you first."

He dropped his hands and straightened up a bit. "I don't have to listen to you. Give me my gun back." Then he called her a name.

Isa slid his Magnum into her slicker pocket and held the Glock steady, aimed for his brains. She pulled out an envelope and tossed it to the ground in front of the 96er. "Take this and do something useful."

With a sideways glance at the envelope, he asked, "What's that?"

"Pick it up."

He glanced around like he didn't want anyone to see him in this submissive predicament. Once he'd determined the coast clear, he scooped up the envelope and opened it.

All manner of bad-guy composure dropped from his face. "What's this?"

"What it looks like. A prepaid tattoo removal at Tattoo You to be used tomorrow. The bus ticket is for the day after. And when you get to Mexico City, you're not to return here. Ever."

Shaking his head in disbelief, he said, "I can't get on no bus. I don't got no ID."

"It's in there."

The confused gangster dug through the envelope again. Lifted out a credit-card-sized identification.

"There's fifty bucks in there for the trip and a paper with bank account information on it. You've got $600 waiting in an account in Mexico. Only you have to show up in person to get it."

"What?"

What, apparently, was his favorite word.

"I can make five times six-hundred bills in one day." He gestured around. "There's nothing in Mexico, man."

"There's nothing for you here. No new gang is going to take you on with that 96-loser brand on your neck. El

Padrino is in jail. Your cartel is scattered. And you're on probation. One more wrong move, and you're back in the big house. I'm giving you a chance to start over. And if you don't take it, I'll hunt you down like an animal, only I won't be as accommodating next time."

"You're crazy. I ain't never heard of no woman pullin' a gun and buying a brother off."

"What's your name?" It'd be interesting to see what alias he threw out there.

"None of your business."

She racked the slide on the Glock. Put her finger on the trigger. "I'm running thin on patience tonight. Want to tell me your name before I squeeze?"

His empty hand shot back up. "Okay, okay. Be calm, chica." He looked at the ID. It looks like ..." He squinted. "Looks like I'm Alejandro."

"You learn fast, Alejandro, so absorb this. I have access to all the databases of criminal activity between here and El Paso. I'm going to be watching for every alias you've ever used and by the way, Daniel Franco, if I find out you've stepped back across the border, I'm coming for you."

From the slack position of his jaw, it didn't look like he had further comment, so she dropped her aim and said, "It's been a pleasure, and you should try visiting a church when you get to your homeland."

With that, Isabella Phillips sprinted back into the shadows of downtown Albuquerque.

CHAPTER 3

November twilight eased into town early. Through her shop's front windows, Isa watched the last persistent ray of ginger-colored light work its way across Tattoo You, a building decorated with colorful tattoo samples and some graffiti applied by local, late-night artists. Tattoo You belonged to a venture capitalist who had stopped by a few months ago to introduce himself. Blue T. Booker wore his salt and pepper beard in twin braids decorated with an occasional blue or yellow bead. Isa instantly regretted asking the twice-her-age Mr. Booker what the "T" stood for, because without missing a beat, he'd answered, "Till I met you."

She'd wanted to roll her eyes. But because her therapy assignments included demonstrating—not just considering—patience, she'd let Blue T. Booker serve up a little charm cheese, and she'd struck a bundle deal with him to remove the tattoos of any 96 Cartel members she could round up and kick out of town. So far, she'd successfully transplanted two ex-gang members, one being Daniel Franco (aka Alejandro), back to Mexico.

Always, the close of day brought on a nostalgic sensation. Closing her eyes, she remembered the first time she stepped up the curb, note in hand, facing India Magic, the abandoned Indian restaurant she'd transformed into Coffee Magic, the recklessly named coffee-and-muffin stop in downtown Albuquerque. Seemed so long ago, yet it had been just six months, one week, and three days. No. Four days. Isa opened her eyes again. The light outside faded, and the purple spider on the side wall of Tattoo You melted into the shadows.

She turned back to her office. The day's receipts wouldn't count themselves.

A car horn belting "La Cucaracha" sounded from outside and Isa glanced back to see a royal blue lowrider pull up curbside. The glitter on the fuzzy-dice mirror ornaments caught the very last of the light and that seemed, somehow, perfect.

"Maria," Isa called over her shoulder, "your grandson is here."

Maria appeared from the kitchen. "Chico!" she exclaimed, tossing her towel into the laundry bin beneath the dining room counter.

Coffee Magic closed in eleven minutes. Maria was supposed to work for thirty minutes after closing. Every day, the grandson showed up a little earlier. "Is ... is he old enough to drive?" Isa had all kinds of reservations about that boy.

Maria ripped off her apron and yelled something in Spanish,

An annoying muscle twitch struck Isa's inner right eye. "I'll finish up here. Just go."

Maria moved faster getting out the door in the evenings than she did coming in at noon.

When Isa took down El Padrino and dismantled the cartel, the gang's cook found herself unemployed and had somehow convinced Isa this was *Isa's* doing. Which it was. Sort of. So, in the providence of God, things had worked out. Sort of. But Maria had a job and Isa had a full-time dishwasher. Sort of.

From the counter, her other employee, Awena Johnson, ignored Maria's quick exit and motioned Isa over, pointing at the carvings on her cane. "Look, Daughter. There are more references to the sun as a symbol for the Light that came to the world."

Over the last few weeks, Awena had begun to explain each symbol and Scripture reference on her walking cane.

As a former forensic accountant employed by the Houston Police Department, Isa had spent ninety-nine percent of her time absorbed in spreadsheets at a desk. But it didn't take laser-sharp sleuth skills to see that Awena didn't need the cane for physical support. She carried it with her as a Christian witness of sorts. And ... as the occasional weapon. Isa had watched Awena beat off a teenage thief once. He'd made for what Awena called "an elderly woman's purse" at the bus stop. Awena had at least ten years on the *elderly* gal.

Awena's cane reminded Isa of a totem pole, but when she'd mentioned that to Awena, the old Amer-Indian gal had balked. Said totems were demonic. Said her cane, on the other hand, was an Ebenezer to her Beautiful Trail.

Sometimes, Awena wandered so far off into the spiritual atmosphere, Isa couldn't follow.

"Let's get you to the bus stop. I don't like you arriving home too long after dark."

Awena pulled a Bible from beneath the counter and flipped through a few pages. "Here, Daughter. See in Psalm 19, the sun is a bridegroom coming out of his chamber."

Isa took the book.

"The sun is a metaphor for Christ."

Isa scanned the reference beneath Awena's crooked finger. "I see."

But the day's sales receipts sat on her desk in the back. Gently, she closed the Bible. Pushed it back into Awena's hands. "I'll walk you to the bus stop."

"I walk myself. There are no more demons around here."

Early on, Isa learned that Awena found demon banishing as common as bug extermination.

"Right." Isa scratched at her head. "Thanks again for expelling those guys."

"No problem." Awena tucked the Bible beneath the counter.

"I will walk you anyway. I need fresh air before I hit the books." She pulled Awena's patched coat from one of the hooks along the wall. "Come on. We'll continue this on Monday. Or maybe tomorrow at the laundromat."

"You coming to church?"

Isa nodded.

Awena slipped her arms into the coat. "You bringing muffins again?"

"Sure." Isa chuckled. Every time she'd visited Awena's church in the abandoned washateria building, she'd brought along coffee, muffins, and her Glock—the gun hidden in her purse, of course. *Cleansed by Jesus Church* was in the middle of what people called the war zone, in the dangerous southeast quadrant of Albuquerque, and though she'd determined she didn't need to conceal and carry anymore, she made an exception when she headed to church or … hunted 96 vermin. "Perhaps I can swing by and pick you up. I don't like you walking in that area alone."

"I have my cane. It's like the rod of Aaron."

"Right." Isa nodded, slipped the store keys in her apron pocket, and headed to the front door. Flipping off the interior lights as she opened the door, the brusque, high-desert air stung her cheeks.

Awena tucked her arm into Isa's. "Even the air sings praises to the birth of the Son."

Isa nodded. "We'll have to plan our Christmas decor next week. Christmas is just six weeks away."

"No elf on the shelf." Awena wiggled her shoulders. "Elves creep me out."

"Me, too."

"We're alike that way."

"Um-hmm." The two were absolutely not alike in any way, shape, or form. Except for the elf thing.

At the bus stop, Isa hugged Awena, said good night, and turned to go back to her books.

"Isa Padilla."

Awena had never stopped using Isa's made-up last name since the two of them had been taken against their wills by the 96 Cartel. Isa had turned a bad situation to good, using the opportunity to uncover one of the cartel leader's money-laundering schemes. Awena had skillfully used her unfortunate circumstances to evangelize cartel family members and exorcise resident demons. Everything had worked out except ... except for Isa's personal war zone. Over the years, her heart had taken some hits she wasn't sure she'd ever recover from. Not only had she grown up with an alcoholic mother and perverse stepfather, she'd also married a cop who went bad and was murdered in the process. Her best friend turned out to be one of her husband's bad-cop partners. She'd been killed, too.

The battered heart in her chest pumped distrust and insecurities by the truckload to the rest of her being. That's why she visited Kevin the therapist every Wednesday at four o'clock. During recent sessions, he'd unearthed her fire-breathing dragon, discovering Isa had anger issues as well.

She might be paying Kevin the therapist for many years to come.

"Isa Padilla," Awena said again, snapping Isa back into the moment. Concern clouded Awena's face.

"What is it?" Isa raised her brows.

"You have chosen well so far."

"Chosen what?" It was anyone's guess where Awena's thoughts might lead a conversation.

"You've found your Beautiful Trail. But it will be hard to remain upon it. Beautiful Trails are never well-worn paths."

Isa tucked her hands in her pockets. "Nothing is easy." She shrugged. "I know that. Goodnight, Awena." She blew Awena a kiss and pulled out the keys.

The Saturday night bar crowd trickled onto the streets from nearby parking lots and office buildings. A truck playing "All I Want For Christmas is You" battled for air dominance with another car blaring some unknown rap tune, the bass turned to depths the human ear couldn't process. Albuquerque city streets came to life in a unique, albeit quirky, style. And the Christmas music had started too early. Thanksgiving was still a week away.

She unlocked Coffee Magic's door. Didn't flip on the lights. Didn't want the action on the street wandering in after hours.

Seeing a stray mug left on table one, she leaned across a chair to grab it.

But ... the shadow at table four wasn't supposed to be there.

She reached for the back of her jeans where her gun should have been. But no. She'd left the Glock locked in a kitchen cabinet.

A something's-not-right dread rushed up her spine. She wished like heck the shadowed shape before her eyes wasn't really taking form.

But it was. She made out a work boot on the floor.

Someone sat in chair A at table four.

He sat still. Poised like a spider waiting for its prey to enter the web.

CHAPTER 4

A memory slammed Isa's brain. Awena had claimed to see a demonic spirit back when Coffee Magic served as a cocaine and pot store house for the drug cartel she brought down. She never claimed to see spirits like Awena, but the hair on her arm stood at full attention just the same.

She slid her right foot back slightly. Crouched.

Three seconds ticked off.

"Isa Phillips."

She frowned.

She knew that voice. It belonged to the last person she expected to see—the person who'd flippantly planted the name *Coffee Magic* in her head. The person she'd fought beside and also against during that cartel week. The person she'd discovered was the best actor on the planet and had her fooled into thinking he might have been someone who cared for real.

"Well, Jay Hernandez—"

"Jacob Lahache," he corrected.

The anger issue Therapist Kevin identified awakened—the dragon hadn't stirred in weeks.

"That's right. A man of many faces and names. An undercover—"

"Bounty hunter."

Doubt took the form of a sigh. "Is that an undercover cover, or just your latest fantasy?"

Jacob uncrossed his legs. Leaned forward. The light angled across his face. He'd grown a beard. "I'm going after Sophia."

"El Padrino's wife? Pshaw." There was no point in that. Sophia's crimes were much too small for the FBI or a whatever bounty hunter. "Sophia is a bail jumper. Bringing her in won't make you a hero. She's just a scared victim. That's all. Have you been drinking?"

"You know I don't drink, and she's the daughter of a big crime boss in Italy. Rewards from the Feds and now Mexico could total $250 thousand. That's more than double my annual salary, by the way."

"I didn't peg you for an about-the-money sort of guy. But I've been wrong about a lot of things."

"Your friend Sophia just had a cousin and his wife gunned down at a wedding in Europe. The assassins hit a child nearby. Now the whole world wants her brought in."

"The whole world?" Highly unlikely. *But a child hurt?* She tightened her ponytail. "Is the kid okay?"

He waited a beat. "Last I read, he'll recover. But this has brought on some major international cries for reform along the Riviera."

His Captain America dreams had pushed him over the edge of a sanity cliff. None of this had anything to do with her. She'd taken down El Padrino, the 96 Cartel leader. That had given her a sense of recompense over the uninvited woes the illegal drug trade had inflicted on her life.

"I don't want to hear this." She started for the counter and bumped chair C at table six. Knocked it over but scrambled to get it upright.

"El Padrino didn't kill your husband."

Her breath caught as she pushed the chair under the table. "You don't know what you're talking about."

"Sophia killed him. He worked for her behind El Padrino's back. She played you the whole time."

Her inner dragon snorted.

Though she'd clearly stated she didn't wish to hear this, Jacob kept talking. "I've done some digging. She's amassing a fortune that stretches from Mexico to Italy."

"Why are you here, Jacob?" Now the dragon puffed, and it heated up her cheeks. "I've moved on. I don't need to know these things."

Except maybe she did.

"I'm here to see what else you might know about Sophia. Has she attempted contact?"

Mad. Crazed. Insane.

"You've lost your mind. No ..." Isa put her hands on her hips. "El Padrino's wife didn't bother to let me know when she jumped bail, probably because I was employed by the HPD and working undercover." She flipped her ponytail.

"She obviously trusted you."

"You just said she played me."

"I thought she might still be playing. I'm going to Italy to find out."

"Is your new wife going to let you chase an alluring but deadly female drug dealer across the world?"

Jacob lifted one side of his mouth in a sardonic smile. "There's no new wife."

CHAPTER 5

Isa had trouble prying her parched tongue from the roof of her mouth. "Wh ... what?"

"You heard me. Thanks to you, Isa, the wedding didn't happen."

She knocked against another chair while rushing to the back of her store. Flipped an overhead pendant light on. Pulled a glass from a shelf behind her and set it on the counter. She could feel Jacob's stare and assessment.

She needed moisture.

She yanked open the refrigerator beneath the counter, remembering. Remembering that Jacob used patience like a surgeon used a knife. Had a way of opening her up and exposing the toxins inside.

Like the day she'd socked him the jaw.

There was no sparkling water, no lavender lemonade. Out came the double-fudge mocha latte creamer. She poured 1.5 ounces into the glass, threw it to the back of her throat, then slammed the empty glass on the bar.

"How am I responsible for your canceled wedding?" After he'd treated her like a cancer on their only, unfortunate case together, he had the nerve to come in here and pretend she had something to do with his life?

"Thanks to you, I'm not married." He could have just announced the Dow Jones closing numbers, the matter-of-fact tone in his voice official and flat.

She absentmindedly poured more creamer and emptied the glass again.

He leaned back in his chair. Jacob Lahache made himself comfortable while she made herself sick. Spotting a carafe on the bar, she pulled it over, filled her glass, and chased the creamer with … cucumber water. "I've been here, making a life. You can't pin anything wrong with *you* on me."

"Okay. I can't totally blame you." Jacob uncrossed his legs. Rose.

Isa's eyes lifted as she followed the outline of his unkempt head raise higher and higher. Was he taller than she remembered?

He moved toward the counter in long, slow strides, maneuvering around the tables like a ghost. When he reached the counter, he leaned on it, the pendant casting a ray of light on his face.

That didn't help.

He looked more like a rugged lumberjack than the Captain America she'd battled with and against in the cartel week.

"I'll have one of those." He nodded at the carafe of cucumber water.

Isa got him a glass and poured, reminding herself that Jacob was a man with issues. Nothing more. Since she'd opened Coffee Magic's doors, she'd spotted plenty of them. Like Blue T. Booker and his delinquent taxes, or the down-and-out banker who confessed a gambling addiction over an espresso. And the 96ers she'd sent packing to Mexico.

Jacob had probably shown up to get something off his chest, and she was barista enough to handle it.

Maybe.

He sipped at his water and shot a glance at her muffins under glass. "Get me one of those and I'll start over."

CHAPTER 6

"Pistachio green tea, or caramel-glazed chai latte, or let's see …" Isa reached over and swiveled the cake plate beneath the glass dome. "Gluten-free orange marmalade with cranberries?"

"I thought you were selling muffins." He studied the plate. "No hearty banana nut?"

"No."

"No basic blueberry?"

"No."

"I'll take the caramel-glazed thing."

She got a plate and fork from beneath the counter. Passing up the serving tongs, she grabbed the muffin with her hand and dropped it on his plate. She slid it to rest in front of him before tasting the sweet glaze from the end of her thumb. "Now start over."

He didn't use the fork. Just pulled the organic paper away and shoved her prized culinary accomplishment into his mouth.

His eyes widened. "Oh, that's good." Crumbs sprinkled his plate and her spotless counter.

She crossed her arms. Did he have to sound surprised?

He chewed, nodding. "Wow, better than expected. Didn't realize accountants were good in the kitchen."

"Math and baking go hand in hand." Didn't he know that? Had he never heard one word of the dreams she'd cautiously exposed back at the cartel ranch? She almost gave in to the urge to slap the rest of that muffin out of his hand.

Therapist Kevin would call this urge a disproportionate reaction.

"I have bookwork to do. Why are you really here, Jacob?" She couldn't keep exasperation from sharpening her tone.

Whatever he had to say, she wanted it out there so she could put it in a mental box for safekeeping and take it to the next therapy session.

Jacob pushed the plate aside. "There's something I think you should know before we go on."

"Go on? We aren't going anywhere."

"Maybe you ought to listen for once."

Standard Jacob smack talk. "Where would I go with you?" He must have forgotten he'd totally humiliated her by leading her on during their undercover case, never once mentioning that he was about to be married.

"Hold on, I'm trying to give *you* some credit."

Unexpected.

She'd laugh but the knot in her throat made it impossible. If he thought he could pick the lock on her front door and wait in the dark like a thief only to throw out a thin line of flattery, he'd end up with that caramel-glazed chai latte muffin up his nose.

One side of Jacob's mouth lifted in an impish smile.

That charm had ceased to work the day she left his bedside in the hospital. She reminded herself of that.

"After spending just one week with you, I realized something about myself."

Here it came. She grabbed the counter. Poor guy. Obvious, there'd been brain damage after he'd been shot. She didn't have the teeniest bit of interest in any self-serving epiphanies he might have had.

"You see in the past ... well, that doesn't matter." He shook his head. "What matters is that after seeing you go through what you did back there on the case, I thought about stuff. I mean, you almost got us both killed just to find answers about this man you married but didn't know much about."

Isa's heart cemented over. Did he just—"What?"

"It made me think." Jacob scratched at his beard. "Did I really know who she was?"

"She?"

"Jonna. My fiancée."

The *she* had a name. "You've lost me."

"I thought, maybe I don't really know her. Or know me. You mentioned more than once that I had all these ... " Jacob shrugged. "These different sides." He leveled his gaze on her face. "It wouldn't be fair to marry a woman if I'm not even sure of who I am."

Maybe I should introduce Jacob to Kevin the therapist.

"I mean seeing you go through all that craziness because you married a man who turned out to be someone different. That taught me a few things." He set the muffin on the plate, but kept his eyes on Isa.

"Glad I could be of service."

"So I'm here to say thanks."

"You're welcome. I hope you find yourself."

His half-grin turned to a full smile. "Yeah. I'm figuring it out. Decided the FBI lanes may be a little too narrow for me."

"Hence, the bounty-hunter label," she stated.

Jacob yanked a chunk of muffin off the plate, scattering more crumbs. "Yeah. I'm trying some new things. But I still have this desire, ya know?"

She shook her head. She didn't know. Didn't want to know. Didn't want to be having this conversation.

"It's a desire to see justice. I can't get Sophia Ventura off my mind. She duped you good when she convinced you to help her escape the cartel."

"Thank you for pointing that out." The dragon took note of the insult.

"Makes you want to go after her, doesn't it?"

"No. Makes me want to make killer muffins and kick-butt coffee. That's all."

"You sound a little hostile, Isa. I think you want in on this."

She wanted to pull her hair out. Or his. "In on what, exactly?"

"I've got a plan, and I need a partner."

So now he wants a partner?

When they had worked together to bring down El Padrino, he complained constantly about her lack of real crime-fighting experience and spent most of his energy trying to move her out of his way instead of helping her solve a few money-laundering and drug riddles.

And he wanted her to join him now? Her future wouldn't include enduring Jacob Lahache's back-door insults. Nor could her stomach take the constant reminders of how much he'd gotten to her—how much he'd come to mean to her. "I have too many responsibilities here. I couldn't—"

"She's trafficking kids."

CHAPTER 7

SAHARA DESERT, ALGERIA, NORTH AFRICA

Now Chiazokam Ese knew. Without doubt, these devils would not take her to the place they'd described when bargaining with her parents.

She pulled at the thick cotton wrap around her face, hoping for relief. When Chia had, on the second day, been given the headwrap, she thought it a declaration about her captors' religion and their offense at her bare head. But now, walking through this vast place, she'd come to understand this headwrap was an offer of protection against the sun radiating wrath down upon their heads. Indeed, the kilometers of lifeless desert testified to what a displeased sun could destroy. As she and the others roasted like yams in an inferno, she considered this wasteland to be a reminder of the eternal hell awaiting the brutal men who'd abducted her, but also the living hell that awaited her on the other side of this journey.

She'd heard stories.

Brown sands stretched on forever. She feared she and the other girls would not last the distance she could see, much less what she knew to be true about the enormity of the Sahara.

Ahead of her, the caravan's leader led the way through the sands with a dozen girls walking behind. The kindest of the three captors held his horse at the back where the two youngest trailed. But the guard called Omri rode in the middle of their caravan near Chia. She could feel his distrust. Knew he'd singled her out for some reason.

With her hand, Chia shielded her eyes and lifted her head to see the sullen captor looking down at her. He pulled the wrap from his face. "Nigerian girls," he said in her native tongue of Hausa. "You are strong, no?"

She dipped her head in affirmation.

"If one of those at the back drops ..." He tossed his head in the direction of the youngest girls. "You will carry her."

Lord, Do not let that any should drop, as we will not survive if we are stacked one on top of another.

Chia affirmed him with another head dip. Though the girls were young, they were not small. Just two nights earlier, when the captors were busy with their fires and tents, Chia had asked each girl to give an account of her age. Of the two youngest, one had eleven years and the other only nine. But both had the look of preteens, the onset of their figures at hand. The other nine girls were closer to her own age. Even so, Chia was the oldest, as she would begin her eighteenth year soon.

Omri chuckled and wrapped his scarf across his weathered face once more.

Her attention returned to the front of the caravan. She saw something jutting from the sand. She squinted, studying a form through the heat waves moving across the desert floor. Getting closer, the unbelievable materialized. Beside their sandy path lay the remains of one who had not survived. Bits of hair clung to the skull, a piece of torn and faded fabric held fast to sun-bleached bone. Hide clung to a joint.

A child.

Chia's heart spasmed. She whirled around to check again on the two at the back. Lubabah, the girl of nine years, had her head down, feet dragging through the sand.

Chia started for the child, lifting her legs high to move fast through the thick sand.

Certainly, Omri would pull his gun and shoot her, thinking she attempted an escape.

But Chia ran anyway. She reached Lubabah and squatted low beside her, motioning for this one to crawl onto her back.

Omri laughed. She looked up to see him slide his gun back into its place beneath his robe.

Lubabah wiggled her way up onto Chia's back.

The girl's gangly legs hung at her sides. Chia moved forward. As God was her witness, not one of these would be left to disappear into the desert.

CHAPTER 8

Isa tightened her ponytail.

Jacob messed with her mental state now—one more reason Isa had more than garden-variety trust issues. Most folks in her life had played her for a fool.

But through therapy, she'd learned that other people's problems were no reflection on her character. Blame lay squarely in the trust-abuser's lap.

Jacob's undercover world of pretending must have created an alternate reality he now chose to live in.

"No way Sophia is trafficking kids. She's a mom. Your identity crisis has turned you mad."

"She's a rodent, and she should be exterminated."

Though that comment scratched at an old find-the-justice itch, she pushed it away, glancing at the carefully crafted muffins still under glass. Creative baking was her gig now, and she was long over the idea that Sophia Ventura had manipulated her ... just like Mac ... just like Claire. Besides, Isa figured Sophia had left town to disappear from the cartel world. Even from jail, her husband could easily order a hit. The thought Jacob might be right, that Sophia had kept up her crimes, didn't set well with Isa or her inner dragon.

Tossing back the last of her water, she shook off the urge to jump back in. The stakes were too high and Sophia no longer a concern.

It irked her he still had the power to unravel her neatly tied-up plans. "Like you said. She duped me. I'm not the right person."

"But you are."

She poured more water into her glass, her hand unsteady. "How do you figure that?"

"You're small. Look more like a teen than a grown woman."

"How flattering. But my life is headed in another direction." The backhanded compliments just kept coming, and she wasn't going to let all this nonsense pull her off the two life tracks she'd managed to get her feet on. Life track one—giving up the need for control by getting out of spreadsheet-style crime solving. Life track two—eradicating bitterness by rebuilding faith in humanity.

Okay, life-track two had been Kevin's suggestion.

Jacob looked off in the distance like he'd rehearsed his ridiculous plan in his head. "I need someone to get inside a migrant camp, ask a lot of questions, and figure who in Italy is shipping kids over."

"Get a journalist."

He leveled his eyes on her now. "More than that." Jacob Lahache leaned across his plate. "I want you to be my decoy."

CHAPTER 9

One thing Isa knew about decoys—they didn't talk. Or think. They were just hollow birds floating on a pond, hoping some real birds might take notice.

"I've got important things going on right here. I don't have time to play your dummy."

Jacob pulled off what was left of the muffin top. Eyed it closely. "You, Isa, are no dummy." He held her gaze as he finished off the last of her masterpiece. "What have you got that is more important than bringing down an international drug ring that has added humans to their services?"

Thankfully, she could always count on her innate sense of reasoning to come to her rescue. "I've got high-level financial clients I work with on the side." Blue T. Booker and his delinquent taxes weren't exactly high level, but he was going to be in trouble with the IRS if he didn't get his back taxes filed. "I'm helping with a cleanup Albuquerque campaign." Another 96er had entered her radar, and she had plans to send him back across the border. "And, I'm running the business that is producing the muffin you're stuffing in your face. I can't afford to run after some super villain you're fantasizing about."

"Hmm." He reached for his water. "Financial advisor, community advocate, and entrepreneur." He tipped the glass at her. "You're hired."

"I'm not applying."

"I'll pay you one-third of the booty."

"No, Jay ... Jacob."

"I'll pay one-third plus a little."

"One third plus a little? You mean one-half?"

"Okay, you push a hard bargain, but deal." He held out his hand for the official partnership shake, that familiar gut-wrenching grin of his in play. "I will require more than few days' work for that kind of money, though."

Isa crossed her arms to keep from slapping his hand out of the way. "I'm serious. I'm not in a place where I can jump back into crime solving right now. Not that I'd want to if I were."

"You're not in the right place? I've got good news. You're going to Spain. Who doesn't want an all-expenses paid trip to Spain?"

"Spain? You said Italy."

"I need you to follow the trafficking trail." Jacob pointed back at himself. "While I investigate Sophia's home office. You'll start in Spain. Once you hit Italy, I'll take it from there."

The temptation to be in the action pricked at her skin.

But she couldn't let her thoughts go there. Could not run after a madman with multiple personalities—some of which had major attitude problems. Tonight, he'd even admitted he didn't know himself and blamed her for it. Go figure. Jacob and Isa working together was a nightmare. "I'm sorry. I'd like to know more, but I just can't." Isa grabbed a towel from a nearby hook and started wiping up his crumbs. "I'm finding the peace I didn't even realize I needed."

His mischievous grin dissolved into the flatline hardness that characterized Jay Hernandez. He pulled a pen from the inside of his pocket, reached for a napkin, and scrawled something across it.

Replacing the pen, he said, "I get it."

Then Jacob Lahache slid off the bar stool and walked out of Coffee Magic's door.

Just like she'd walked out of his hospital room six months earlier.

Without words.

CHAPTER 10

Jacob told himself to ease up. Partnering with Isa would only present problems. He shoved his hands in his pockets, wishing he hadn't left his number on that napkin. He'd given her a chance, and she'd turned it down. As a former FBI undercover agent, he'd learned to never leave choices hanging. He credited his success to expertly maneuvering people into making decisions, keeping the game moving at a continuous pace, and heading where he wanted it to go.

Waiting wasn't an option.

It wasn't too late for plan adjustments.

There would be other ways to get inside Sophia Ventura's trafficking operations. His connections in Spain had already delivered valuable information.

A car honked at a man who'd stepped into the busy street. He wore dirty pants, a torn jacket, and his hair stuck to one side of his head.

Jacob smirked at the angry driver behind the wheel.

He'd put himself out there twice with Isa, something that didn't come easy for him.

And he'd even admitted his undercover job required him to play different roles. Slipping in and out of character without much effort was what had made him a top-notch FBI agent.

Apparently, his honesty had no effect on her whatsoever. She'd twisted up those pouty lips and flat-out refused his offer.

Ungrateful woman.

By asking her to join him, he'd also admitted she'd been more than just an okay detective when she'd worked beside him to bring in the infamous drug lord. Her crime-busting methods were unconventional and often awkward. But she brought an interesting angle to problem-solving with her financial background. As a forensic accountant, Isa saw problems from a purely logical point of view. She tied clues together in a methodical fashion. She didn't seem to want the hero spotlight like most agents he knew. She just wanted to crack the case.

The night's revelers passed Jacob in a blur. The skunky smell of pot drifted from a bar door standing ajar.

A new plan—that's all he needed. He'd still bring in Sophia Ventura. Isa wouldn't stop that train in its tracks.

He kept moving, kept thinking through the next steps.

But the mental picture of Isa throwing back creamer just wouldn't go away. She'd looked hilarious, and he'd almost laughed for the first time in weeks.

He stopped at the crosswalk signal. Crossed his arms.

Isa. What a pain in the rear.

Up the street, beneath the light of streetlamp, a man and a woman argued, voices getting loud.

"Hey!" A female voice yelled from the opposite side of the street.

A young woman—teen maybe—with spiky, bright orange hair rushed into the traffic, headed for the arguing couple. "Hey, hey!"

Glancing at the red-light palm on the crosswalk sign, then back to the couple, then to the orange-haired girl who'd made it through the cars, he reached for the gun in his holster beneath his windbreaker.

The man had the woman by the hair.

The orange-haired girl leaped from the curb to land on the back of the man, who now had the woman by both arms, shaking her hard.

Jacob's legs moved before he thought about it. He barely dodged the red Mustang pulling through the intersection. The driver threw on the brakes and presented his middle finger out the window.

Getting close, Jacob could see that the man in the scuffle appeared small, but he tossed the teenager off his back like she was a rag doll.

Something wrong there.

The teen landed on her backside but bounced right back up looking like she wanted another go.

"Stop there! Let her go," Jacob demanded when he got close enough to be heard. "Police." That wasn't a total lie. He was ex-FBI and licensed to carry.

Ignoring Jacob's command, the man drew back a fist, ready to throw a roundhouse.

"I said let her go." Jacob crouched, extracted his weapon, and aimed for what counted—the heart.

The man turned to give Jacob the death glare. That's when Jacob saw the tattoo. A spider web spread across one side of the man's face.

"That's right," Jacob said, slowly rising to full height. "Hands up."

Spiderman loosened his grip on the woman but didn't put his hands in the air.

Instead, he took off running.

Jacob pursued.

"Wait!" the orange-haired teen hollered as he passed.

Waiting wasn't an option. Waiting was *never* an option.

At the next intersection, Spiderman made a sharp right.

When Jacob got to the corner, he stopped short. Though the area was lit, Spiderman had managed to hide himself among the cars in a parking lot. Just like a spider. Crawling around looking for a dark space to string a web.

A man in a business suit entered the opposite side of the lot, head down and looking at his phone.

"Sir," Jacob signaled with his gun so the man could see he had a weapon. "Clear the area." The man looked up, did a quick about-face and moved out, but with his eyes back on his phone.

Typical.

In the split of a second, Jacob considered walking away. Maybe from it all—the gone-wrong encounter with Isa, the creepy pest lurking in the parking lot, human trafficking in Europe, his needling identity crisis ... *why not*? Nobody seemed to care anymore. Mostly the opposite. Through the new and woke cultures, crime fighters were starting to look like the bad guys.

But the luxury of considerations flew out the window when the freak sprang from the shadows to perch on Jacob's back.

What the ...?

Jacob reached behind his head to get a handful of greasy hair.

Spiderman.

Much too small to take Jacob down, his attacker jammed his clammy fingers into the veins at Jacob's neck.

Jacob coughed then tossed the gun under the safety of the truck beside him. With one step forward, he flipped Spiderman over his shoulder, and put the man's backside on the pavement.

Spiderman shrieked.

First instincts said to squash the insect, but instead, Jacob took a seat on the man's stomach.

Hissing and spewing, Spiderman mentioned Jacob's mother more than once.

"Calm down," Jacob said grabbing at flailing hands and getting scratched in the process.

When the spider moved from talking to growling, Jacob saw the man's pupils didn't look right.

The picture formed.

Meth. Meth gave people an unnatural and always unhealthy sense of nerve along with inhuman amounts of energy.

"Dude. Calm down."

The screech of a young voice came from the northern end of the parking lot. "Stop. Stop. Get off him."

Before looking over there, Jacob already knew who shrieked. She of the orange hair had followed them.

When he looked up to get a twenty on the girl, the older woman—whom Spiderman had attacked—joined the teen.

"But—" *Never mind. This is not worth the scratches on my arms.*

Spiderman stopped flailing to a look at the women.

"You some kinda freaked-out cop or what?" the young girl asked.

Jacob placed impatient hands on his thighs, eyeing the older woman. "Wasn't this guy about to hit you?"

She shoved her hands to her hips, and the younger woman answered for her. "That's my dad."

"A family outing?" Jacob asked, thinking these three made his own mom look like Carol Brady.

Spiderman told Jacob to go do something to himself that would be physically impossible.

"All right," Jacob said. If today's society didn't want intervention ... then who was he to intervene? "I'm going to get off you and you are going to slowly walk away."

Spiderman settled down.

Then Jacob looked to the ladies in waiting. "You sure about this? I could take him to the police station, and you could file assault charges."

The older woman's eyes went wide, fear flickering, like she'd lived that nightmare before.

Jacob asked again. "Your choice. What do you want me to do here?"

Eying the blue Prius beside her, she said, "Let him go."

Jacob didn't miss the hesitation. "This isn't going to end well for you ladies ... but whatever." That was the thing about being a good cop. You always knew what was going to happen and that took the suspense out of everything. With a huff, he told Spiderman, "I will seriously hurt you if you do anything, *anything* but get up and walk to the nearest street corner." Jacob got off and yanked the man up beside him. With one hand firmly around one of the spider's arms, Jacob squatted beside the truck and with his free hand, located his gun. "Now you can go. But go nicely."

Spiderman stomped past the two women and headed for the corner. The wife hurried after him. Before the daughter trailed, she looked Jacob up and down and then pronounced him a couple of nasty titles that no teenager should know, let alone be allowed to speak.

Jacob slid the gun's safety into place and tucked it back into his shoulder holster beneath his jacket. Go figure dysfunctional families.

Including his.

And go figure dysfunctional women.

Including Isa.

CHAPTER 11

The usual crowd milled around inside the former washateria. A bank of mauve dryers stacked one on top of the other sat at the west wall. The scratch-and-dent old dryers gave a yesteryear ambiance that recalled shoulder pads, fanny packs, and hair scrunchies. Isa made her way down the makeshift aisle of foldable chairs humming the theme from *Flash Dance* and stepping over capped-off plumbing pipes jutting from the floor.

Awena found the washateria the perfect place for a church to gather because Jesus, after all, was the greatest laundryman who ever lived. Isa wasn't sure that was a viable title for the Savior of the world, but hey, the ever-present scent of bleach really did offer smell for thought—Christ had, she'd finally come to understand, washed away her sins, even if she didn't fully understand why.

She put the dispenser of coffee on the folding table situated near the front of the makeshift sanctuary. Pulled out a box of twenty-four muffins and twenty-seven organic paper cups from her tote bag. She glanced over her shoulder to see Pastor Joe Tan, or P-Joe as the congregation called him, headed her way. When Isa pulled the release valve to fill the first cup, the smell of dark roast Sumatra filled the air.

Bleach and Sumatra. What a pairing.

"Good morning." P-Joe smiled, taking the steaming cup from Isa's hand. The entire washateria population flooded up to the table, reaching around Isa to grab coffee and muffins. Everyone talked at once.

Squeezing between Thomas from the homeless shelter and a new guy in dreads, Awena managed to get up next to Isa. Although usually with her hair in braids, today she'd pulled her long gray locks in a traditional *chongo* twist at the back but wore her regular broom skirt and mix-matched army boots.

Isa pulled a red-chili chocolate cupcake from her tote and presented it to Awena. "Your favorite."

Awena's almond-shaped eyes narrowed as she studied Isa's face. "Why have you made this one for only me today?"

"Because I appreciate you."

"How is it that you appreciate me today? The day has just begun, and we have only just seen each other now."

Though she'd grown accustomed to Awena's way of complicating conversations, it never got easier. "Everything." Isa reached for a coffee cup, feeling Awena's scrutiny continue. "It's my way of saying thank you for, well, for you being you."

"Something bothers Isa today."

"Why would you think that?"

"You've got the look."

"The look?"

"The look. Like the first day I saw you step up to the India Magic building looking like you had an undesirable mission." Awena got up on her tip toes and leaned towards Isa. "Plus, I saw you last night."

"Plus you saw me?"

"Correct. Plus that. In the coffee shop. You talked with a man who looked like Mr. Jay Hernandez who got married." She eased her heels back down to the floor but raised a defiant chin.

P-Joe called the eclectic congregation to order.

"I thought I put you on the bus."

"You made sure I got to the bus stop, but you did not put me on the bus. Why are your cheeks red?"

Isa touched her face as she moved out of Sister Shanika's way. The former prostitute reached for the last muffin. "Wait a minute. You didn't get on the bus?"

"No."

"Why?"

"My Bible."

Oh, brother. Here came the talking circles. "Your Bible wouldn't let you get on the bus?"

"My Bible didn't want me to leave it in the shop. I came back to Coffee Magic to get it and that's when, through the window, I saw you and Mr. Jay Hernandez talking." Awena raised one brow. "So, I watched."

"Oh." The evident *got-ya* blush in her cheeks heated up more. Which was stupid. She had nothing to hide. "Yeah, he dropped in. And his real name is not Jay Hernandez, remember? That was his undercover alias. And ... he didn't get married after all."

Frowning, Awena turned and started for the chairs. Okay, so the day wasn't off to the best start.

P-Joe's sermon covered a Samaritan man who'd found another man beaten and left on the side of the road. Isa shifted in her seat unsure if the conviction stabbing around in her chest had to do with P-Joe's message or the fact that Awena had seen her alone with Jacob Lahache.

Soon after she put El Padrino behind bars and his wife Sophia in the witness protection program, she'd made a vow to Therapist Kevin to work on her issues before getting into another relationship. She'd done something similar with Awena. More than once over after-work coffee, she and the old gal had discussed the unfortunate choice Isa had made to marry a man she barely knew. It had been Awena, not Kevin, who pointed out the fact that Isa had little relationship capital, having been raised by parents she couldn't trust. Children under the care of abusive parents missed out on all kinds of trust-building lessons that ultimately pointed to a good God who called himself a father.

So Isa had promised the two people she built trust with she'd figure a few things out before contemplating another relationship.

P-Joe was on a roll and comparing the Samaritan to the eclectic group in the folding metal chairs before him. A person seemingly cast out of society not only stopped to render aid to a beaten man on the road, but he also paid to have the man cared for.

He told the washateria congregation they should do the same.

Then P-Joe brought the congregation's attention to what modern day beside-the-road abandonment might look like.

Wouldn't you know, he mentioned drug addicts, fatherless children, the mentally ill, and the current phenomenon of human trafficking. P-Joe said people were looking the other way and ignoring the immigrant children sold into slavery right here on the streets of Albuquerque.

Isa gulped coffee, hoping no one saw her restless heart flopping around in her chest. Then, P-Joe told a story about a young Mexican boy who'd been smuggled across the border only to be sold as a slave laborer to a local agricultural operation. The boy had been rescued and needed support. Today, the church of Cleansed by Jesus would be taking up a special offering for the boy. This, everyone was told, would be in addition to their regular Sunday offering as December rent had not yet been paid.

The Cleansed by Jesus congregation shifted uncomfortably—be it the metal chairs or the financial request.

CALCULATED ENCOUNTERS

When the giving bucket reached Isa, she noted it held two fives and three one-dollar bills. With a second glance, she counted sixty-eight cents in change.

Slipping two twenties from her back pocket, she dropped them in, though she'd only intended to give one of those Jacksons today. But maybe by giving above and beyond her usual, the death-grip guilt had on her gut might loosen a little.

Instead, after church and after saying goodbye to Awena, the grip intensified.

In the forensic accounting days, the big questions of *why* had driven her to solve some complicated financial schemes, finding more than enough dirt to prove a crime, but also enough to uncover a motive. She'd discovered greed and power to be obvious motivators, but digging deeper, she'd unearthed another common denominator in the *why* everyday ordinary guys turned bad. Desperation. Desperation could change an everyday banker into a criminal, pushing an otherwise good guy across a forbidden line. The stories of a sick wife, a wayward kid in need of therapy, the need to take care of aging parents were the stories of where the little slip here and the bigger risk there of financial fraud usually began.

If Jacob was right … if Sophia hadn't jumped bail so she could hide from an assassin's cross hairs but run a syndicated crime ring in Italy, then that old familiar question needled. *Why?* Why would a mother leave the protection of the US government to move back into a criminal family business that included human trafficking?

And why am I suddenly contemplating Lahache's outrageous plan?

Dang convictions. Dang Jacob Lahache.

CHAPTER 12

ALBORAN SEA, NEAR ALMERÍA, SPAIN

"Get down. Get down in the boat!" commanded the leader called Nadir. He flattened his palm and motioned at the girls. Omri repeated Nadir's words in Hausa, slapping the coiled rope in his hand at Chia's back. The wind, the waves—it was all happening so fast. Chia flattened herself against the bottom of the boat, breathing in the rotting fish and saltwater wood. She swallowed, telling the dried dates and stale bread she'd had so very many hours ago to stay in her stomach.

On the water for the first time in her life, Chia had not realized the sea would want to toss her from this boat and swallow her in the waves. It was Omri who told Nadir and the other captor that most assuredly, the girls could not swim.

He spoke the truth.

There was never to be talking, but when they'd left the shore in Algeria, one of the girls began to cry. To soothe the girls' fears, Chia sang Akwoi Wata Geri, the wedding song of her people. Ugly Omri had laughed and asked Chia why she sang this song of marriage? When she told him that it would remind the girls that one day their Jesus would come for them, he demanded that she sing no more. Nor would she speak of this prophet whom the Americans called Jesus.

The motor of the larger boat churned the waters as it passed. The men called one to another in greeting while she and the other captives pressed their faces to where their feet should be.

When the other boat had passed, Nadir spoke to those in their boat in English, telling them in detail what would happen to the girls once they reached Almería.

Chia understood every word.

CHAPTER 13

In her office at the back of the shop, Isa made entries into the inventory spreadsheet. Twenty-four packages of twenty, six-ounce, brown, organic, hot-drink cups. She put her cursor atop the sum bar and the program automated a total. Ah, the perfection of numbers. Four hundred and eighty units counted, stacked on her shelves, and now documented.

Managing through a few step-by-step processes ushered sanity into her day and kept her thoughts from running amuck with images of justice. Or maybe revenge.

Her fingers hit the keyboard. Three hundred branded cup wraps. Two hundred and fifty biodegradable plastic cup lids. Like hot dogs and buns, food quantities ordered in bulk never matched up.

Stupid coffee-house suppliers.

Stupid Jacob Lahache.

She dropped her head back and closed her eyes. Visualized Sophia on the night El Padrino ripped his own son from her arms. He'd punched Sophia in the face so hard, Isa had come unglued. She'd lunged for the deadly cartel leader, believing she could take on the two-hundred-pound man. She'd planned to put a jiujitsu kick precisely in his chest, but El Padrino's bodyguard had stepped in her path and halted her strike.

Good times.

It was hard to believe that just eight short months ago, she was a naïve forensic accountant stepping out of her secure spreadsheet world in search of elusive answers as to why her newlywed husband had obliterated their struggling bond. It had all been lies—lies that, ultimately, cost him his life. It had cost her plenty, too. Precious commodities like trust and discernment.

Isa opened her eyes and looked back at her computer. It seemed everyone she let come beyond the walls of her carefully built barricade entered with malice in mind.

Mac had come in hoping he'd found a place to hide his secret sins. Then Claire, her best friend and crime-fighting female coworker, had done pretty much the same. Never mind her alcoholic mother who brought an abusive, psycho stepfather into her life. Isa still held that man responsible for her brother Angel's death. Her hands curled into fists at the thought of the day they took Angel off life support.

She seemed to be a magnet for fakers and haters.

Jacob Lahache had spoken truth. She was an inspiring example of what not to do and why not to love.

She should call Kevin and double up on appointments, except Kevin didn't work on Sundays.

Her down-the-hill of disparaging thoughts was interrupted by someone knocking at Coffee Magic's front door.

She stared at the backside of the kitchen door. What if Lahache had returned to try and convince her to work with him? Would she do it?

The knocking continued.

Isa pushed the chair back and started for the front, butterflies flitting around close to the heart. The thought of laying her eyes on Jacob Lahache again initiated the troublesome reaction.

She got through the kitchen door.

Blue T. Booker peered through the front door glass, a brown box in his hands.

The flitty butterflies vanished.

Of course it was Blue. She'd sent Jacob away. Probably for forever.

While she was unlocking the door, Blue was pushing his way in. "Hey, gorgeous." He winked—the fifty-second time he'd done that since they met. "I saw your car. Thought I'd bring over the files."

"Blue, look, I'm not at a place where I can—"

"No *problema*. I'm not in a hurry. Just getting all this," he raised the dusty box, "out of my office." He found a clean table for his cargo. "I think there are more records in storage. This is probably last year's stuff."

Isa blinked slow on purpose. "Probably last year's stuff? You don't know?"

He shrugged the shrug of a man who could not care less. "*Mas o menos.*"

"There's no point in me digging through half-baked files." She lifted the box top and looked in at an assortment of manila envelopes, crinkled papers, register tape, a columnar pad, and what looked like an empty vial of tattoo ink. Isa pulled out a stapler. "Blue. Really? Where are the rest of your records?"

"I love it when you say my name."

She shook the stapler at him. "You're going to have to get me more than this for us to accurately figure out what you owe."

"It's coming, *querida*. I promise." He reached out and patted the side of her head with his multi-ringed hand. "But not today. Take a break and come with me to the Second Time Around Rock Festival in Bernalillo. Guthrie Rollins will be there."

"Never heard of him."

"You've never heard of Guthrie Rollins?"

Isa placed the lid back on the box. "No ... and I have work I've got to get done today."

"Rollins is the Greg Allman of the eighties. The greatest guitar-ripping, soul-singing white boy of the century. The guy is a legend."

Isa shrugged.

"From Austin."

She shook her head.

"You never heard the song *Cry Regina*? His one hit back in eighty-four, eighty-five?"

She lifted her hands. "Not a clue."

"The man had a lick like nobody in the business. Maybe not so much anymore since he's old." He shook his head and squinted his eyes as what looked to be a memory danced across his face. "He was better live than recorded. But so were lots of 'em back then. I saw him in concert in the good old days."

"The good old days?" Wasn't all that talk of days gone by just folklore? "Chances are I missed his concert because ..." Isa tapped her chin. "Let's see ... I was a toddler in the eighties." The eighties—the image of a drunk stepfather slammed into her head. Her shoulders shuddered. "My parents weren't into rock and roll. They were into Jack Daniels."

Blue flinched.

She immediately regretted letting him in on that family fact.

His palms shot up. "You're laying down some heavy stuff today." He leaned toward her. "How about I hook you up for a nice tatt session? Nothing like writing a life statement in eternal ink across your heart. Helps you keep your feelings in the right lane."

Nice guy, Blue. Not so different from the cops she used to work with, only some of them had turned out to be the bad guys. Including the one she married. "Look, Blue—"

"You said my name again." He slapped his hand over his heart.

"Why don't you work on all this today?" Isa gestured at the box.

"Life is short, Love. Gotta move while I can." He leaned close. "Let me leave you with a little Blue T. Booker advice."

Though she put her hands on her hips and gave him her *oh brother* head tilt, inside she smiled. Blue's advice usually had something to do with chilling out, and a couple of times, she'd taken it.

He pointed at his box of disorder. "Play harder than you work ..." He pushed up the short sleeve of his T-shirt to reveal a tattoo of a long-stemmed rose held in a fist. "You should love whoever you're with. There's a song about that."

Isa squinted at the faded rose.

"And I'm the one you're with right now," Blue said, rolling his sleeve back down.

"You're old enough to be my father. Maybe even my grandfather."

He ignored the obvious. "Never heard *that* song? Heard of Crosby, Stills, Nash, and Young?"

"None of this is ringing a bell."

He turned for the door. "I'll bring more files *mañana*. Change your mind about the festival or the tatt, give me a call." He pushed through the door yelling greetings at some red-headed motorcycle mama sitting on a Harley across the street.

"Swell." Isa slid the box off the table, and headed for her office.

But she didn't make it as far as the counter before she heard the door open behind her again. She froze, afraid to turn around. Why had she let Jacob and his stupid offer to work together again hang out in her thoughts?

Pivoting slowly, she braced her heart … just in case.

A woman in a thin floral dress and beige wool coat stood just inside the door taking in the place. Something about her … familiar. A retro, Jackie Kennedy Onassis pill box hat sat sideways on her graying head.

"I'm sorry." Isa said, setting the box on the counter. "But we're not open."

"Oh my. This place smells good. Like home. Like when my little girl was in the kitchen, and we was baking up all kinds of good things." The soft accent and vulnerable, wide eyes put the anarchic thoughts of Jacob, justice, and Blue's delinquent taxes on pause.

Isa's emotions were about to swing in another direction. She sensed it. She fought the urge to count the cars passing on the other side of Coffee Magic's street window.

The woman stood tall, though bent at the shoulders. "Lordy," the woman whispered, "I wished Claire had done what you've done here. She should have left police work just like you."

There it was. *Claire.*

The woman's ebony eyes drooped as she searched Isa's face. "Somethin' went wrong with my Claire. Somethin' went bad wrong."

CHAPTER 14

MÁLAGA, SPAIN

When the door slammed, Chia rushed for it and twisted at the handle. But the man who'd thrown her inside the room had locked it.

Panic rose.

"Please." She knocked at the door, tears stinging her eyes. "What for have you put me in here?" Maybe the man had not walked away. "Where will they take Lubabah and the others?"

No one answered.

Breath stuttering, she wiped at her nose.

"Please, sir."

No sound.

She placed her ear to the door. Was he still on the other side? Or gone? Would he return?

God please, being locked away from my sisters would be worse than another beating.

"Help!" She slapped her palm to the door. "Help me! Please."

Both hands struck now. "Please! Do not leave me here. Do not leave me here."

A sob racked her chest. "No," she cried.

It was as though not even God would answer. Chia threw more emotion and power than three girls together at this single wooden door. But only silence answered.

She pressed her forehead against the door, her hand sliding down to grasp the handle one more time. Face wet with from crying, she twisted the thing, trying to wrap her mind around the situation.

Inside she knew. Back in the desert trek, she'd figured it all out. Her fate now—a slave.

What would they do to the others?

The young ones had screamed out her name when the men pulled them away from her.

Wiping at her wet cheeks, Chia straightened and turned to take in the room.

No window. A bucket in one corner, a blanket and dirty pillow in the other. A single light bulb hung from the ceiling. She slid down to the cement floor.

She and the other girls had been handed off to four new men in the alley behind the market.

One of the new men had grabbed Chia by the arm. She'd tried to wrench away, but he'd shoved her against a wall, growling in a language she could not understand, fingers pointing.

That had been the moment she'd been sold.

She examined the walls, realizing the power switch for the light bulb was not inside the room and that realization made her chest squeeze tight. Her captors were in complete control of ...

The room went black.

CHAPTER 15

"You're Claire's grandmother."

"Why, yes," the woman answered, a pleasant smile lifting the corners of her wide mouth. "And you are Isabella."

The woman held a petal-pink handbag with gloved hands. She looked like she'd come for afternoon tea in her Sunday best, only she'd showed up forty years too late.

Isa studied her own nails, knowing the next thing the woman said, she probably didn't want to hear. She'd boxed Claire into the "Traitor" column of her emotional spreadsheet. She wasn't up for reexamining that data. Not today.

Thanks to Awena's forewarning about choices and difficult paths, this encounter was no real surprise. Life continued to throw curve balls her way, with especially hard ones in the last twenty-four hours.

That's why she couldn't believe it when, out of her own mouth, came the invitation. "Would you like to sit?"

Claire's grandmother nodded. "Yes, I would like that very much."

Isa pointed to a table five. "How about some coffee? I also have tea."

"Yes." The woman stepped toward the table. "Coffee is fine, fine by me." The woman pulled out a chair, and with the grace of a noble, she sat, still clutching her handbag. "I take my coffee with one cube."

"Cube?"

The woman's eyes darted to the floor. "Forgive me, some habits live on no matter how much the culture around them don't. I believe that would be a teaspoon of sugar, if you don't mind."

Isa slid the carafe hosting the last of the Sumatra from the counter and pulled out two cups, sugar, and creamer.

Isa felt the woman's undeserved fascination as she watched Isa set the table. "My Claire, she described you perfectly."

"Did she?" Isa went back to the bar and grabbed two of the chocolate chili muffins. "And please, call me Isa."

"All right, then, Isa, and you can call me Milly."

During their after-work happy hours, Claire hadn't said much about her childhood. But neither had Isa. Ghosts from the past had a way of hanging around once you let them out of their boxes. She and Claire had mostly discussed current cases—her white-collar crime investigations and Claire's narcotics unit recon. And of course, they'd discussed their male coworkers. The two had forged a female bond in a work realm dominated by testosterone. But, evidently, theirs had been a fake bond. Claire had given in to the fantasies offered by the lucrative drug world, becoming the second person and cop in her life to turn bad.

Another reason leaving the force had been easier than expected.

Milly stirred her coffee. "You have a lovely place, Isa."

"Thank you. It's been a big change."

Milly shifted in her seat and said, "I wanted to thank you for talking with me on the phone right after Claire died. I believe I told you about her diary?"

"Yes, you did."

"At that time, I was grievin' for my girl and didn't properly express my sentiment for the loss of your husband."

"It's … okay," Isa stammered. She never knew how to respond to these expressions of respect and sorrow. Yes, she'd lost her husband, but he hadn't been much of a husband. He'd been a liar and a cheat.

"The sergeant, he tells me the same that happened to Claire happened for your husband. And I was so disappointed that I had just talked on and on 'bout Claire, never knowing you were experiencing the same things."

Isa ran her index finger down the curve of her coffee cup handle.

"I was hopin' you could tell me more. Nobody seems to want to talk about what really happened and all. I can't believe my Claire would just up and join a drug cartel. Had to be something big made her do that."

Isa didn't begin to understand it all, even when Awena continued to point out demonic forces and their tricky ways. "I've seen a lot of people do crazy things over money."

"Love of money is the root of evil," Milly proclaimed.

She'd rehashed this with Awena and Therapist Kevin and still didn't have answers. Isa redirected the conversation. "Do you live in the area?"

"I live in Galveston, Texas. Took a bus up here to find you 'cause I need your help."

Isa stopped caressing the cup handle.

"I want to know the truth about my Claire. I found papers and things in her house that make me believe what everyone is silently suggesting isn't true. At all true."

It would be rude to try another redirect. So she asked, "What is everyone silently suggesting?"

"That Claire willingly did these things. She never got a trial or opportunity to prove otherwise. I know something or someone made her do this. I got papers to prove it."

Good heavens, the woman was out to resurrect her granddaughter's reputation.

Milly kept talking, urgency in her tone. "Clare didn't just decide she'd drug-run and buy houses for a terrible man. She was ... what do you police folk say?" The whites of her eyes got big. "Blackmailed."

Isa's heart twisted. Could there be truth in what Claire's grandmother implied? Had her best friend been forced into a deadly game with the cartel?

She held a tight breath for a beat then patted the table near Mrs. Washington's gloved hand. "El Padrino has a trial coming up. Maybe some truth will come out in the court. It's best to let the law do its work."

Did I really say that?

Sergeant Caba had said the same thing to her when she told him she was going to find Mac's killer.

Back then, that phrase had ignited major irritation.

"I want you to look into this." Milly's hand slipped over to grasp Isa's.

Isa let the woman hold it. "Did Sergeant Caba send you?"

"No. Lordy no. He told me the same things you just said. 'Let the law work on it.'"

Isa closed her eyes, remembering the day she walked out of HPD with the mission to get answers.

"I can't."

Milly Washington's forehead wrinkled. "I want to give you the papers, let you sort 'em out. Don't you want the truth? For Claire?"

"Yes, but ..." Isa pulled from Milly's grasp and rubbed her forehead. "I can't be the one who ..." She looked into Milly Washington's eyes. "I can't help you. If you have evidence of anything involved with crime, you should take it to the police. Give whatever you have to Sergeant Caba."

"Caba can't know. Neither can that Lieutenant Wilson. Only you. Claire trusted you."

Memories spun around in her head. She'd misread so many things in the case. What if she'd misread Claire, too?

Isa sat up a little straighter. "I can't get involved." She scooted back her chair. "Ms. Washington, I am sorry, but ..."

The old woman's eyes pleaded. "But you got to help me. It's the right thing to do."

CHAPTER 16

Jacob tossed his duffle bag onto the bed he hadn't made in weeks. Once he got through the breakup with Jonna, he'd let a lot of stuff go. He chose instead to focus on self-discovery, like every other red-blooded American millennial had done.

The exercise wasn't going great. The only thing he'd discovered so far was he was perfectly fine with unmade beds.

He flipped the laundry basket of white socks and T-shirts over the bag. He'd pulled them from the dryer days ago. He made for the dresser to pull out his *I don't bother you, you don't bother me* black work attire.

About to open a drawer, he paused to set the family photo upright. Examined his younger siblings' smiles one at a time. They looked genuinely happy. But when he looked at his mom, he laid the picture face-down again.

His mother's confession had created quite a commotion when—with him expecting to discuss the rehearsal dinner—she'd decided then was a good time to let Jacob know he'd been living a lie for thirty-two years.

Talk about not knowing who you really are.

His engagement had not survived the catastrophe of the following weeks. Jonna had finally given up—let him go so he could get some things figured out.

After zipping up the duffle bag, he retrieved the legal documents from his desk. In went the state license for bail bonding, flight carry forms, and his dog-eared copy of the *Rights of American Bounty Hunters to Engage in Extraterritorial Abductions*. Before shoving his binder of personal notes into the end pocket of the duffle, he opened the spiral at the place where he'd written out meticulous notes for Isa and her role as his decoy.

He ripped out the three pages, wadded them up, then took a jump shot at the trash can in the corner. He would have made the shot if the can weren't overflowing.

Jacob located his backpack among the shoes, ball caps, and tennis racket at the bottom of his closet. Threw it on the bed. Pulled his gun from the nightstand drawer and emptied out the cartridges.

Truth was, he may *have* discovered a thing or two about himself. He didn't need Isa on this job. He didn't *need* any woman in his life, for that matter.

Well, there was one exception. Sophia Ventura. To get himself back intact again, he really *needed* to bring that villainess in.

Jacob double-checked the lock on his gun cabinet in the corner then closed the bedroom door, making for the kitchen. Sliding his plane tickets from the dish-covered counter, he shoved them into his backpack.

At the refrigerator, he pulled a grainy photo of Sophia Ventura and the infamous Las Zetas cartel leader, Miguel Lopez, from beneath a Scripture magnet his sister had given him two Christmases ago. The Scripture read, *And we know that for those who love God all things work together for good, for those who are called according to his purpose. Romans 8:28*

Those words *could* be true.

He studied the picture of Lopez, rehearsing the facts. The dead cartel leader's body had been found in his own home in Mexico. Shot in the head twice. Speculations in the underground world pointed at Sophia. Now, authorities from Mexico, the US, and Italy wanted Sophia in their court systems.

But he would get to her first.

CHAPTER 17

Isa smelled coffee brewing the moment she pushed through the front door thirty-three minutes later than usual.

Awena peeked through the kitchen door, scrutinizing Isa's disheveled look. "Isa Padilla, you do not look yourself this morning."

"Rough night. Sorry I'm late."

"We must work the works of him who sent us while it is day. Night is coming, when no one can work."

Isa didn't have the gumption to reach deep this morning. "Thanks for starting the coffee."

Awena started her morning routine of setting up cups, creamers, and the cake plates that had been washed the night before. "What's this?" she asked, picking up the paper Isa had inadvertently left on the counter the night before.

Uh-oh.

Isa acted like that paper was no big deal. But as it had turned out in her cartel-undercover role, acting wasn't something she was very good at. Going for the waiting aprons hanging from their assigned hooks on the wall, Isa kept it casual. "Oh, that's nothing. Just a page from a journal."

"Whose journal?"

"Hmm, let's see." Isa lifted an apron from the row of hooks—the black one with the white front pocket. "Claire. Maybe."

For an older gal, Awena's memory banks worked better than most. Except when it came to Isa's real name.

"The Claire from Houston who was killed at the hands of El Padrino?" Awena flipped the page over then back again. "The Claire whose grandmother called you after she died and wanted to tell you Claire loved our Lord?" She held the paper at arm's reach and squinted. "The Claire you have not yet forgiven?"

"Okay, yeah. That Claire." Isa slipped the apron over her head and across her tensing-up shoulders.

And of course, Awena began to read the journal entry out loud. "See to it that no one takes you captive by philosophy and empty deceit, according to human tradition, according to the elemental spirits of the world, and not according to Christ." Awena took a breath. "This is from Colossians." She pulled at one of her long braids. "Chapter, two, I think." She read on. "Lord, I have been taken captive and don't know how to get out of it."

Even though she'd already read Claire's journal page seven times, *hearing* her ex-friend's plea twisted up most of Isa's insides.

"This is a prayer," Awena whispered.

"Yeah," Isa answered, wishing she'd gotten in earlier and tucked away the diary page Claire's grandmother had given her. Milly Washington had pulled the page from her little box purse and slid it over to Isa's side of the table. Isa had left the folded page of Claire's personal thoughts lying there for two hours and four minutes while she took care of book work in the back. At last, chewing at a nail, Isa had found herself sitting at the table, transfixed by the beige paper rimmed in gold.

When she'd summoned up the courage to unfold the sheet and read, she'd checked the date Claire noted in the top right corner. Claire had penned this entry just a couple of weeks before Mac was killed. Everyone, including Isa, figured her husband Mac and Claire had worked together when they betrayed their public defenders' oath to protect ... when they worked the back alleys of a Mexican cartel ... when they accepted blood-stained money as payment.

"Isa Padilla," Awena said, pulling Isa back into the moment. "Where did you get this?"

"Claire's grandmother."

"She was here?"

Isa's brain started to throb. "Yes." She pulled the hair tie from her wrist and wrapped her hair into a ponytail. Went to the notebook at the counter and powered it up.

"The grandmother has come so you would at last forgive Claire?"

"But I have ..." Isa said, trying to make the words sound sweet even though they tasted like the bitter matcha leaves in her tea jars. "I've told you that." She pushed at the screen, opening the sales app. "What Claire's grandmother wants is for me to dig around the Houston Police Department and figure out how Claire got tied up with the 96 gangers and who else might have been involved."

Awena gasped.

"Forget about it."

"But—"

"We've got muffins to bake." Isa pushed open the kitchen door, the stain of the oily cross Awena had smeared across that door months ago still evident. It was the one door Isa hadn't painted. She'd kept the cross as a tribute, of sorts, to the days she battled cartel flesh and blood while Awena battled unseen spirits.

Awena followed at her heels, inching herself between Isa and the cabinet pantry. "Now, two people from the past have come." The old gal rubbed her chin. "Perhaps the law enforcement chapter of your life is not yet fully written."

Was that conviction or irritation that pressed into Isa's chest?

"What is it that gave you a rough night last night?" Awena asked. "Was this the offender?" She wiggled the note still in her hand.

"Okay, yes." Isa put her hands up. "I'm tired because I spent too much time exploring possible leads last night online when I should have been sleeping." Digging further into why several HPD cops might have been lured into secret cartel work seemed warranted. Her life, after all, had been greatly affected by two of those gone-bad cops.

And now, according to Jacob Lahache, there was a lot more to Sophia's story. These were the things that birthed restless nights.

"So, I dug around several HPD leader's backgrounds, and I spent way too much time looking for Sophia Ventura."

"The wife of El Padrino?"

"Yes." Here came the heat up the neck. "Jacob wants me to help him find her in Italy."

Awena shook her head, brows low over her almond-shaped eyes. "I think the storms gather at the mountain top."

"What is that supposed to mean?"

"Winds of adversity."

Isa pressed her palms deep, deep into her forehead. "Could you, for once, speak plain English?"

"The sky is gray."

Isa dropped her hands and pushed open the kitchen door, looked across the dining room and out the glass front windows of the store. "Looks sunny as usual to me."

Claire's note still in her grasp, Awena said, "Since God is sovereign and these visits are not coincidences, I'd say he's not done with your police work yet. That plain enough?"

"You think God wants me to help Jacob find Sophia and assist Milly Washington in clearing her dead granddaughter's name?"

With a quick nod, Awena said, "Perhaps there are lessons along the way." The angelic glow in Awena's eyes took on a matter-of-fact hue. "You got stuff to learn, girl."

Hands back at her head, Isa said, "We got stuff to bake, girl." She turned for the stainless-steel rack holding her mixing bowls. "Can you grab the flour?"

With a feather-like touch, Awena placed her palm on Isa's arm. "The testing of your faith will produce steadfastness which will have its perfect result."

Isa blinked back frustration.

"Evidently," Awena continued, "there is territory to be conquered."

"But I don't know what to do." Here came the outpouring—only it was words and not tears. "Follow Jacob on a wild goose-chase to Europe? Secretly investigate the HPD to vindicate Claire? Why am I being pulled from what we've created here?" She gestured with her arms. "I thought I was on my Beautiful Trail."

"The Beautiful Trail is a difficult path of discovery, not a road of comfort."

The whole week had started wrong.

Awena sighed the sigh of a teacher losing patience with the student. "I think you have already begun your journey, and you know where you are going."

"What do you mean?"

"Your actions reveal your decision."

"What—"

"The 96 Cartel member that robbed the smoke shop and harassed my friend's daughter? He's off the streets." Awena eyes made little slits in her face. "And I have a pretty good idea how it happened."

"But, how ... did ... you? I mean, how could you have known I was tracking that gangster?"

Before Awena answered, Isa added, "Never mind. I should know how this goes by now. It's like you're all seeing, all knowing."

"Only God knows all." Awena countered.

"Look, I sent that released-from-jail cartel member back to Mexico. I didn't hurt him."

"I heard."

"You have spies on the streets or is it angels keeping you in every loop?"

Awena shrugged. "I get around. And ..." she paused, grabbing the flour from a shelf. "And, you know what you are to do next and where you are to go from here."

"I can't go anywhere. I have this business to run."

"Then I shall run it for you."

CHAPTER 18

MÁLAGA, SPAIN

Chia recoiled as the sun rushed at her face. But this man she had not yet seen had hold of her wrists and pulled her down the steps, unconcerned she was blinded by the light after staying in complete darkness for hours, perhaps even a complete day and night.

When she cried out, he yanked her onto the busy streets then pushed her into a car, telling her to hush.

Just as she began to blink her sight back into focus, he pulled her from the car with never-ending threats.

He spoke English. "Do not cry. Do not yell. I will have you killed and after that, I will kill your friends who have come with you. And then I will kill your family."

Down a staircase and through several doors, he threw her to the floor in front of two men. The fat one caught her up and dragged her to a chair next to a flat and wooden table with instruments on it—a silver bullet the size of a corn cob, little vials of black ink.

"Dees not hurt much," he said in broken English.

Chia's eyes moistened.

The other man came up beside her, pushed her into the chair, and put a gun to her head.

Tears spilled and she couldn't stop them.

The short one grabbed her arm and held it flat against the wood.

Then, he brought the silver corn cob to her wrist.

CHAPTER 19

Jacob unbuckled the seat belt, maneuvered around to get the blood circulating in his numb feet. He pulled his notebook from the seat pocket. The flight to Munich had been uneventful. He knew because he'd been awake for the whole nine and a half hours.

On the bright side, the extra waking hours had given him an opportunity to figure out what he'd do without a female decoy inside the underground camp in Málaga, Spain, a major stop for transports being brought in from northern Africa. If Isa had agreed to work for him, he'd planned to get her inside an underground camp—clearing house of sorts—used for dispersing young men and women to various organizations around Europe. These organizations varied from organized gangsters to what would be considered reputable businesses. They purchased humans to use for various illegal and despicable jobs including child labor and sex trading.

Information he'd been able to assess indicated that Sophia had renamed her family's small-time syndicated crime venture to Vita Morale and had low-level grunts transporting humans in and out of Málaga.

Jacob wanted his decoy to amass facts from the grunts. Draw him a transport map that would lead right back to Sophia and her newly owned ventures and, if lucky, her headquarters. Considering she'd inherited and sold several millions of dollars' worth of real estate in the US and had managed to have the infamous Mexican cartel leader Miguel Lopez killed, she had money to invest, like most of the Italian Mafia, in diverse business ventures.

He wanted a list of them all, accounting for every dime she brought in. That would be the only way to tear apart Mafia crime completely—nab the leader then piece by piece remove all income-producing endeavors to keep other family members from taking up the lead.

With Isa's experience in forensic accounting, she would have been perfect to help him identify human trafficking money streams and beyond.

But now? He'd get a job inside one of Sophia's enterprises and do a little one-on-one detective work just like the old days ... but being careful not to run into Sophia until he was ready to take her in.

A head taller than the other passengers, Jacob knew nothing moved. He pulled his phone from his pocket and powered it up. Three text messages materialized. Two from agents inside the FBI who consistently fed him information. One text came from an unknown number.

He opened the message.

People in front of him shuffled forward.

ISA HERE. DOING RESEARCH. WHERE IN SPAIN DID YOU WANT TO SEND ME?

Jacob's upper lip twitched as a gap opened between himself and the person ahead in line. He'd done all the preliminary research and didn't need her changing her mind and messing with his.

He shoved the phone back into his pocket.

CHAPTER 20

Deboarding the plane in Germany, Jacob noted only a few people still wore medical masks. As a former undercover FBI agent, he'd been paid to read people's posture and expressions. Faces three-quarters covered made that task next to impossible.

Getting into the terminal of his next flight, he headed straight for the food court.

With two bratwursts in one hand and a coffee in the other, Jacob located a pint-sized plastic table away from the food-court crowd. Nothing like hearty meat to settle his stomach, which had been protesting the fake mash potatoes and rubber chicken he'd had on the plane.

He pulled a bottle of hand sanitizer from his backpack and lathered up. Flying around in a COVID-19 world had risks, and he wouldn't chance getting sick—especially handling the operation alone. True, his FBI connections in Rome knew of his plans, and he had kept an open line of communication with other bounty hunters in that area of the world. So he didn't work totally alone ... but likely, he was the only hunter interested in Sophia.

Which had amused one of his ex-partners back at headquarters. *She's a woman*, he'd said, shoulders pumpin' up and down in an uproar. *Going after the big, bad, and gorgeous?*

Even though Sophia Ventura spread her influence faster than the news media pouncing on a president, she was still considered small time compared to the long-standing Camorra Mafia of the southern Italian coast.

Never mind the particulars. This was about justice.

Hot coffee burned his tongue. When he stuck his plastic fork into the sausage to cut it, the flimsy utensil snapped in two. Jacob growled, picked up the juicy brat with his napkin and bit the end off.

Immediately, accumulated frustrations gave way to the sweet and spicy flavors of smoked meat. The whole world looked better with a brat in his hand.

Jacob slipped his phone from his pocket feeling better than he had in two days.

He opened Isa's earlier message and studied it again. Did he want her help or not? What he really wanted was ... he pushed that romantic and irrational thought out of his head. Women were known to change their minds. Maybe he could let her dig around ... on a platonic basis, of course. He typed:

MÁLAGA. PORT CITY, MAJOR HUB FOR TRAFFIC. LOOKING FOR LEADS TO VITA MORALE.

Maybe it took one crazy woman to figure out the moves of another.

CHAPTER 21

Crazy. The idea that Isa would just hand over her budding coffee venture to all-things-out-of-the-box Awena and prickly Maria while she chased criminals around Europe sounded ludicrous. Insane.

Yet she'd texted Jacob after Coffee Magic's lunch crowd thinned, hoping to get a little more information so she could, at least, make this ridiculous consideration with a few more facts.

Isa exited and locked Coffee Magic's front door. A twilight gust sent the day's milder temperatures scurrying for the foothills on the east side. She pulled her jacket together and zipped it up, glanced back through the glass door and into the shadows of her life-long dream. Baking for profit.

Though she loved the baking and brewing and loved the little coffee shop family she'd amassed, the pull to see justice served remained. Seemed to be part of her DNA.

That revelation just might be a payoff for the hours she had sat in Kevin's grey-plaid chair. He'd told her people worse off had sat in that seat. Made her feel a little better.

She dug around in her purse for her phone, because for the first time ever, she hadn't slipped her cell into its home—the side pocket.

Rereading the text Jacob had answered at 2:30 that afternoon, she bit her bottom lip.

So he *had* wanted her to go to Málaga and find leads to a Mafia called Vita Morale. How would she penetrate the underground trafficking markets of Spain? He'd mentioned her being a decoy, and exactly what did that mean?

Still outside her front door, she dialed his number.

The call went to voice mail.

She disconnected. Texted:

COME TO THE COFFEE SHOP TOMORROW AND LET'S TALK. MUFFINS ON ME.

Phone back in her purse's side pocket where it belonged, she headed for the parking lot. A forensic graph took shape in her head as she passed a tourist-looking couple who, hand-in-hand, gawked at the turquoise, hand-painted low-rider with a sunrise on the hood, bouncing up the street.

It's Albuquerque, she'd wanted to explain, but she kept walking, focused on her mental investigation chart. The first column she would need to fill with potential evidence including facts from interviews. She'd probably be interviewing prostitutes on the streets or inside a migrant camp.

That thought spurred a sense of anticipation. Though interrogating a prostitute would probably be a night and day difference from interrogating a nervous banker, she felt sure her experiences with ex-prostitutes at Cleansed by Jesus would be helpful. If there was one thing she'd learned about human nature in the washateria, it was that all people loved muffins. As long as she brought the goods, she could converse with just about anyone.

The next section of her graph would be the examination results. Binary data and percentage estimates.

Third, she would document the root causes of the actions—her favorite part—the *why* behind the crime.

Reporting was the fourth section of her typical chart, presenting evidence to the court as an expert witness. She wouldn't be presenting evidence to a court, but to Jacob.

Crossing the parking lot and pulling more spreadsheets from her memory banks, she almost didn't notice the unusual couple walking towards her. Unusual appearances usually indicated unusual behaviors. The man had a spider web tattooed across one side of his face and the younger girl had hair the color of a crosswalk monitor's vest. But what was most notable about the girl was the scowl on her face as she stomped straight for Isa.

Isa quickly patted her purse down and located the outline of her Glock. Slowly, she unzipped her purse. Stopped, feet apart and all senses on alert.

"Hey," the girl said, getting close.

Isa held her position and didn't bother to respond.

"Hey," the girl repeated, getting a couple of steps ahead of the man with the web tatt.

The muscles in Isa's neck and shoulders contracted.

"You run that coffee shop?" The girl asked.

This. Is. A robbery. Probably they thought she'd be loaded with cash after a day's work and wanted her purse. No way. Not with her Glock inside. She got her hand in her purse and Glock out of it by the time the girl was five feet in front of her. She didn't aim the gun but held it between her leg and the purse, hoping it didn't show.

Still the orange-haired teen noticed. "Hey," she stated, pointing at the gun. "What's wrong with everybody around here?" She threw her hands in the air. "Crap, Lady, I was just going to tell you to be careful. There was a crazy white guy in the parking lot two nights ago and he jumped my dad here." She tossed her orange hair toward the man with the web-face.

"Oh." Isa slipped her gun back in her purse.

"You should park closer to your store," the young girl said as she and her dad walked on past, "People in this town are crazy."

CHAPTER 22

With a decaf herbal tea on her nightstand and the computer in her lap, Isa created a document titled "Houston Police Personnel." It wouldn't hurt to create this file for Milly Washington and let her decide what to do with it. That would be it. Create the file and pass it on. With over five thousand officers employed, it would take her days to document every single one of them. So she started with the top brass and wrote the names and titles of Chief Evans and his two executive assistant chiefs. Barnes, a guy who'd been with the force for a millennium, it seemed, and Janice Zucker, a no-nonsense investigator who'd worked her way to the top. From there, the captains numbered in the double digits. She could only name four. HPD employed nearly two hundred lieutenants, and Isa only knew two by name. Lieutenant Breck Jamison and Lieutenant Todd Wilson. Her boss, Sergeant Caba, who oversaw her detective financial crimes unit and Mac and Claire's homicide detective unit, answered to Wilson.

Milly Washington didn't want Isa talking to Lieutenant Wilson about Claire. She highlighted his name.

Another hour passed with Isa searching and documenting titles and names. She'd only made her way through one-third of the entire HPD. She spent the next thirty-minutes delving into Todd Wilson's personal, but public, information. Most notable was the obituary on his wife—she'd died three years ago while Isa still occupied the forensic accounting office. Why hadn't she known? She didn't recall Caba ever saying anything about it.

And Caba? There would be no reason to dig around on her old boss. No way he had anything to do with Claire and Mac being bought off by El Padrino.

Caba might have been the closest thing she ever had to a father figure the four years she worked under his watchful eye. He'd believed in her without wanting anything more than a job well done. He'd probably be the only man who gave her hope because most in the male species left a path of destruction behind.

Patting her hand around on the comforter, she located her phone and checked texts. No response from Jacob. Since she'd asked him for a coffee discussion a lengthy six hours ago, perhaps he'd changed his mind. Maybe after *seeing* her, he remembered some of the bungling mistakes she'd made as she felt her way through her first-ever undercover job.

First job? When she quit the force, she intended her first undercover job would be her last undercover job. But the truth was, her heart had skipped around the walls of her chest when Jacob talked of justice—of bringing Sophia back to the US for a proper trial.

She reached for the now room temp tea. Sipped at it, too involved in thought to get up and nuke it in the microwave.

Awena was right, as always. Isa had known two days ago she should and probably would work with Jacob to finish the job. If her undercover work with El Padrino and the 96 Cartel had transpired under Sergeant Caba's watch, he wouldn't consider the case closed until they had the biggest eyewitness and possible offender back in custody.

No, the job she'd started with the drug cartel wasn't finished. The major takeaway she'd extracted from the 96 affair was nestled in God's sovereignty—her purpose. While locked in a room in El Padrino's cartel castle, she'd read the verse that had now become her anthem.

And we know that for those who love God all things work together for good, for those who are called according to his purpose.

God had a purpose in her playing a part in the 96 Cartel takedown, and if the case wasn't closed, that meant her purpose in this had not come to a close either. It didn't matter if Jacob had changed his mind—the Lord had used him to invite her back into the fray.

And the Lord had also given her a loving and responsible person to oversee her business while she wrapped up the case.

She pulled at her ponytail. Maybe *responsible* wasn't the right word, but whatever.

She could hear Queen's "We are the Champions" build in the background of her thoughts ... this was her moment.

Isa closed her laptop, humming Queen's song.

She pumped her fist a couple of times then retrieved a sheet of stationary from the nightstand drawer. Penning a letter to Milly Washington, she explained she wanted to help but wouldn't be able to do much more than send a list of police personnel Milly could look into.

Then, Isa looked at ticket costs for flights to Spain.

And sang the song *sotto voce* ... as she made her arrangements.

CHAPTER 23

Focus returned. With his stomach full and an empty seat beside him, Jacob had managed a catnap on the flight between Munich and Naples.

Now, in the back of a yellow Fiat—whose Daytona 500-wannabe driver hit the curves so fast Jacob dropped his phone twice—he felt ready. Except for his scratchy throat.

Unlike the standard brown stucco of New Mexico, Naples's buildings were bright colors of yellow and red. And unlike the culture of most Americans, the people of Naples did life outside and on the streets, not through their phones and stuck in cars on a highway.

The breath-of-fresh-air scenery didn't stop him from tightening his grip on the phone, though. He planted his feet on the floorboard and read through a string of emails from the FBI attaché office couched inside the American Embassy in Rome. The flow of information was spotty, but having been a badge-carrying federal agent before, he figured the appointed overseas agents would trust him more than the typical rough and trigger-happy bounty hunter. Most *bona fide* agents didn't want common rogue criminal trackers meddling in their cases. But Jacob was being treated like he still belonged to the brotherhood, and he anticipated the boys in Rome would continue to pass on legit intel.

He'd sent the Rome guys an email asking for a list of properties or businesses Sophia's Vita Morale owned near Naples. With knees nearly in his chest, Jacob used his right thumb to scroll through the larger-than-expected list they'd returned. Sophia had snagged a lot of properties in a short amount of time. That, or her family had managed to hang onto some land, despite their faltering syndicated crime efforts. Small but agile baby gangs and sub-Saharan human trafficking rings had risen in the area, winning turf wars against the established Mafias. Times were changing for everyone, even the instituted crime families of Italy.

Looked like Sophia knew how to play on a game board of shifting rules and players, however.

Jacob identified a restaurant in the inventory. It was near the apartment he'd rented in the Forcella neighborhood known for gang activities. Perfect.

When the cab driver pulled to the curb, Jacob looked up to see a mother and child, both masked, reaching for the back passenger door handle.

"No, no," he said banging on the back of the driver's seat. "I said I'd pay extra to ride alone."

The driver threw his hands around in exaggerated motion and reeled off some sharp Italian words.

But the woman and child climbed in next to Jacob.

The kid had dark hair and round eyes and a red sucker stuck in his mouth. The woman, in a skirt and leather jacket, had shoulder-length dark hair. She nodded at Jacob as she maneuvered the toddler next to him.

Jacob exhaled some frustration and slipped his phone back into his pocket.

The woman and the driver exchanged more Italian. They looked at him, then they looked in opposite directions.

Great.

The cabbie hit the narrow and freshly wet streets fast.

"You're American?" The woman asked, accent heavy and volume muffled by the mask.

He nodded.

"Tourist?"

Wouldn't you know he'd get a talker? A talker with a toddler.

The kid held up his sucker for Jacob's scrutiny.

Jacob nodded at the child, acknowledged the woman with a glance, and said, "Yeah."

"You will love Naples," she said. "Everyone should visit sometime. I can't say I've been anywhere like it. This time of year is especially beautiful. Have you seen the nativities around town?"

Oh great. A tour guide. No, nativity excursions didn't make the list. "Nice old city, but I hear there's crime." He pushed back into his seat. "I hope that's not the case."

The cabbie shot him a stern look in the mirror.

"I've been mugged before," he added with a shrug.

The little gasp behind her mask was almost undetectable. But it was there. "Well ... you should be safe, but it depends. How long are you here and where are you staying?"

What was with the chit chat? To stifle the conversation, he opened his eyes wide, shook his hands and using a frantic tone said, "But a guy at the airport said there are gangs everywhere!"

She must have told the driver she'd had enough already because after she muttered a few Italian words, the cab pulled to the curb, and mother and child exited the car.

She gave Jacob a long, quizzical look before shutting the door.

Jacob leaned across the back seat to watch her as they pulled away from the curb. She gathered the kid up to her hip and started walking.

He almost felt guilty that his abruptness had encouraged her exit ... until he sat back up and found the red sucker stuck to his khaki Carhart jacket.

Yeah, he probably deserved that. He extracted the sucker and handed it up to the cabbie. "I think this belongs to you."

The history of Naples passed in a blur—old architecture and ancient parks lining the streets. A tourist attraction controlled by Mafia, Naples had become an oxymoron. Maybe. He wasn't entirely sure if he had the appropriate word.

It just didn't get more human nature than this, though. Despite the graffiti, the traffic, and the grit of this city, Naples offered some of the most spectacular views and historical sites in the world. His last trip to this area had been a quick one, but he'd never forgotten the vivid picture of good and evil so closely coexisting.

Jacob pulled out his phone again.

Now to deal with Isa. Holding his breath for a few second-guessing seconds, he considered Isa's text. During their brief time of working together in Albuquerque, he'd silently chuckled his way through showing her the ropes only to watch her tangle herself up in them. Why he found her escapades compelling, he hadn't figured out, but knew this had been an unspoken factor in his post identity-crisis breakup with Jonna. He couldn't marry a woman knowing another one had captured his attention, even if it had been brief and unintentional.

The hesitant breath he'd held finally blew past the questionable moment. He quickly texted a reply to her invitation to come over for coffee and discuss his case.

Thanks for the coffee invite to discuss, but I'm going in a different direction now. I'm already on location in Italy. Later.

CALCULATED ENCOUNTERS

The cab slowed at a round-about. He typed the word oxymoron into the google search bar.

A figure of speech in which apparently contradictory terms appear in conjunction. Example: fuzzy logic.

Isa was an oxymoron if he ever knew one.

CHAPTER 24

Holding her sore wrist, Chia eased down onto the bare mattress. The tiny room had four bunks with a mattress on the floor. The other beds had sheets or blankets and pillows thrown about. Atop the mattress on the floor was a girl asleep or passed out ... or possibly dead.

She'd never seen a drunk woman before. In her village back home, there were only two men who drank alcohol excessively, and they would sleep in the road or in the back of a family's house. The others in her village had scorned the men, but not her mother and father. They had seen to it that her family prayed for the men during morning prayers. Once, Chia left a bottle of soda next to one of them so that when he woke, he would not be thirsty. The soda had been a gift brought back to her when her father returned from his travel to the city.

She wanted to shake the girl on the floor mattress but didn't know the house rules. When the man who'd taken her to get the tattoo brought her to this house, he said it was where she would live for now.

That's when she'd asked him if this house would be where the other girls who traveled with her would be. He had only said she would know plenty of girls now.

Chia flinched when the door opened. The woman who stepped into the room was not unlike many of the older

Hausa women back home. Most were well-fed and carried ample flesh and curves on their bones. The woman held a half-eaten African green pear in her hand. "Come," she said in English.

Glancing back at the still-motionless form on the floor mattress, Chia wished she had a soda to leave next to this girl. "Please God, do not let it be that this girl is dead or that I should find myself alone on a mattress someday," she whispered as she followed the woman out of the room. Until that night in the dark cement room alone, Chia had never slept without her sisters next to her—or the young girls on their desert journey.

Chia followed the woman down a long hall.

"I am Nasha," the woman stated, setting her pear on the desk in the middle of room. A man sat on one side of the desk, sharpening a knife.

Chia nodded.

"Sit down." Nasha pointed at the empty chair next to the man. "This is Tem. Starting today, you will work with Tem, and you will work with me."

Chia's heart almost leapt from her chest. "It is true then?" she gushed. "I am to work as a maid?" She placed her hands on her face. "I thought you had lied to my mother and to my father when you brought me to this place, and that I would not be working as a housemaid in the way they negotiated for me."

"Is that what you thought?" Tem chuckled, studying the end of his knife.

"You're going to work, but you will not serve in some fancy hotel," Nasha said, her head shaking back and forth.

"This is well for me." Isa patted her chest. "I am pleased to work in your home."

This time Nasha was who laughed. "Girl, you are a simple one, I see." She lumbered to the oversized chair on the other side of the desk. "That tattoo tells everyone that you belong to us now. You are our property to rent, sell, or trade."

Chia looked down at the ink-black stripes across her wrist and frowned.

Nasha opened a file on the desk. "These are your identification papers that we have paid for. It was not cheap for us to bring you into this country."

"But that is what my father has paid for," Chia countered, the truth dawning again. "He paid for my transport."

"No, he paid for *part* of your transport. We have covered your many additional costs until now, and we will continue to pay for you to eat and sleep and walk about protected in a place where thieves and killers hunt young girls every day."

A lump formed in Chia's throat.

"So, this is how you will work." Nasha picked up the pear. "You will do as I say, and all will go well for you. Once you have earned the money you owe, you will be free to work as a maid with others, or in a hotel if you like. But you will not speak of our agreement to anyone or tell of where you live. Then things will go good for you."

The man Tem leaned forward and pointed his knife at Chia.

"I understand," Chia said, barely able to hear her own words above the buzzing in her ears. She swallowed hard to make the lump go away. "But may it be I work with the other girls that were brought over with me?"

Nasha glanced at Tem, who shrugged. Then she shrugged, too. "I know not of other girls. I only care about those who were brought to me. Soon you will begin work in a gentlemen's club on the other side of town, and Tem will take you there and pick you up. Until then, you will be here with me. But you must remember ..." Nasha shoved the last of the pear flesh into her mouth, licking at the green residue on her fingers. "If you think it is good for you to try to run away or try to disobey my orders, then things for you will go very bad."

CHAPTER 25

Isa's impatient foot tapped the floor twenty-one times before Awena finally answered the shop phone. "Coffee House."

"Awena, it's me ... and our name is Coffee Magic."

"I don't like the word magic. Makes me think of fetishes and medicine charms."

"But it's our name."

"It is a weak name."

Isa pushed her morning hair out of her face then slid further down into her chair. "I'm going to be late. You can cover for me, right?"

"I told you already that I would run our shop while you hunt for God."

"I will be hunting for Sophia Ventura, actually."

"Whatever you say, Isa Padilla. But I must go to make the blue corn muffins."

"We don't serve blue corn muffins."

"We do now." Awena hung up.

Isa pulled the phone from her ear and stared at the screen as if she waited long enough, she might get another result. With her eighteenth, no, nineteenth sigh of the day, she scrolled to read Jacob's text for the thirteenth time.

He had dismissed her.

He'd tried to do that before.

Unsuccessfully.

Isa inched the yellow note pad over and picked up her fine-point mechanical pencil. Drawing a line down the center, she divided the page into two sections. At the top of the first half, she wrote *Pros* and over the second half she wrote *Cons*. Working her way down the page she numbered the blue lines to ten.

At number one under Pros, she wrote, *The cartel job isn't finished after all. I need to finish it.* Under Cons, she penciled, *Jacob can't make up his mind if he wants my help or not.*

Line two under Pros—*There are no coincidences, only the sovereignty of God.* Cons: *But God clearly led me to open Coffee Magic.*

She tapped the eraser at her lip. Why would God change his mind just when they had gotten the shop up and running?

At line three Pros, she wrote—*Awena could manage the shop.* At line three Cons she wrote: *Awena could manage the shop.*

Line four Pros—*Plane tickets bought and hotel in Málaga, Spain, booked.*

Pencil twirling between her fingers, she read through her half-written page.

At sigh number twenty, she ripped the page out, wadded it with both hands, and got to her feet.

On her way to the airport, Isa tossed the paper in the trash.

CHAPTER 26

Jacob studied the menu. From what he could make of the pizza selection, Bambino's didn't offer their pies with meat toppings. Further down the list of options, he found a calzone with salami and wondered if the cook in the back could add a little ham to beef up his lunch.

But the impatient employee threw up his hands and went back to the kitchen. Jacob wiped at his nose with the back of his sleeve.

Waiting for whatever would come next, Jacob surveyed the restaurant. At this midafternoon hour, a handful of customers littered the dining room—the pandemic had hit Italy especially hard. Word from the American Embassy said local Mafias had taken advantage of the crippled tourism and offered to financially prop up struggling independent restaurants. What unsuspecting business owners never realized, however, was that once their personal ventures became income sources, greedy Mafia types would not likely let go of the revenue stream even if debts were repaid. Entrepreneurs would be paying off mob bosses for the rest of their lives.

The waiter returned with a man he'd pulled from what looked like kitchen duty. Flour covered the young man's apron.

"Sir, you want to order something different from the menu?" The kitchen worker asked in a thick eastern European accent.

This time, Jacob pointed at his selection. "The calzone with the salami—can I get ham on it?"

"Ah ..." The kitchen guy glanced over at the frowning waiter before choosing his answer. "I think perhaps yes."

"Can you make that a lot of ham?"

"Perhaps yes."

Jacob thought he heard the words *fat Americans* as the waiter stomped off.

The kitchen guy gave Jacob a half-grin, which was a good sign concerning meat consumption. "Where are you from?" Jacob asked.

"I am from Ukraine. And you are American, no?"

"Right. But I'm relocating here, thinking Naples is a good place for me at least for now. Just went through a nasty divorce and lost my job back in the pandemic days. I'm looking to make a fresh start." He shrugged, working to look like an American in need of a friend though in reality, that was the last thing he needed. In the search for his true self and also for renegade fugitives, the fewer folks involved in his life, the better.

"I know, yes," the cook answered. "I get your order to the chef now. You gonna love the calzone." He kissed the tips of his fingers Italian style.

"Hey," Jacob said before the kitchen guy got away. "What's your name?"

"Marko." Marko gave a quick bow, bypassing the almost-gone tradition of a handshake or kiss on the cheek.

Meeting an immigrant working in the targeted restaurant was the best thing that had happened in days, save for the brats in Germany. Immigrants could be a wealth of insider information as they had little loyalty to the established culture or to deep-rooted community traditions. He'd seen an example of long-time loyalty with the woman in the cab.

For the most part, immigrants were transient and had little to worry about protecting.

Jacob leaned back and smiled, wanting to appear carefree. "I'll be looking for some temporary work while I figure out if Naples is right for me. I love the free health care." He flashed a smile. "And the babes." He nodded at the girl in the blue dress at the hostess stand.

Marko put a big, goofy grin on his face. "Yeah, the women here, they look like cash."

Jacob furrowed his brow. "Cash?"

Marko scratched at a cheek. "She looks like ... like ..."

Jacob literally saw a light bulb switch on above Marko's head. "She looks like big money."

"She looks like a million bucks?" Jacob asked.

"Yes, yes. The babes here, they look like millions of bucks."

"Is Bambino's hiring? I'm willing to do dishes, bus tables, whatever."

"I only work here a couple of months," Marko said. "But I ask the boss."

"Got a piece of paper?" Jacob asked.

Marko dug around in a pocket and extracted a lunch ticket. Jacob pulled out a pen and wrote on the back. "This is my US number, but I'll be getting a local phone soon. I won't turn off this phone for a few days, so call or text me when you find out."

Marko shoved the paper back into the pocket of his apron and nodded with a grin. But when the front door of the pizzeria opened, and two rough-looking characters stepped in, Marko, head down and eyes on the floor, hustled back to the kitchen.

The men blew right by the cute hostess, who avoided making eye contact as well.

The two disrupters had similar characteristics. Could be brothers. Same build, dark hair cut close to the scalp, and the tail ends of tattoos peering out from trench coat collars. The shorter of the two kept his right hand inside his coat, the signal to employees and patrons alike—he carried.

Bingo.

Mobster activity, and Jacob was just getting started.

The guys at the embassy had given him one heck of a hot tip.

The two thugs walked between a couple of empty tables and towards the back. Before disappearing into the kitchen, the taller one turned to scan the few patrons who chose to ignore the disruption.

Except Jacob. He didn't ignore anything. He twirled his pen between his fingers, eyeing the gangster who returned his stare.

Now here was something that did not disappoint. First day, and he was eye to eye with and step one into what he'd come for.

CHAPTER 27

Travelers moving about inside the Albuquerque airport still wore masks, which was fine by Isa. The short-term COVID-19 pandemic had, surprisingly, instilled long-term health precautions she found reassuring. Even after vaccination, the population still had a 52.3 percent chance of contracting a full-blown case of COVID. As a rule, airports were hubs for disease dispersal.

Considering it was Thanksgiving day, however, the crowds were thinner than they could have been.

Isa sanitized her hands and dug her phone out of the oversized satchel she'd bought to carry must-haves: an identification wallet, a money wallet, a fresh change of clothes, and a toiletries case of three bottles plus toothbrush and toothpaste all at the exact four-ounce size. Her satchel also hosted her laptop, three cashew crunch bars, an apple, and a Twix bar. During her first episode of undercover work, she'd learned a thing or two. Like not carrying her real identification around in her purse. And also keeping a change of clothes on hand. Even though the odds of a second abduction were on the low side, one never knew when one might be forced into overnight situations or, as it happened with El Padrino, kidnapped.

The only thing her handy new satchel didn't have? Her fingernail file, which she'd uncharacteristically forgotten, and her Glock.

Carrying a Glock on a plane provided challenges she couldn't quickly overcome.

She stared at the phone while rolling her bottom lip around under her top teeth. Likely, if she texted Jacob now, he'd insist she *not* fly to Spain.

She was way past the stopping point.

Earlier in her apartment, she'd made a few phone calls to the handful of good cops she still knew at HPD to learn that yep, Sophia Ventura had jumped bail and headed to Italy. The woman she'd tried to help escape the cartel had headed right back into crime.

She put her phone back into her purse.

The announcement to Jacob could wait until her London layover.

CHAPTER 28

Isa hailed a cab outside her three-star hotel, which, as it turned out, wasn't really three-star. Seemed Spanish hotels used different measurements from the US when rating their accommodations.

But it would do.

On the ride through *Paseo de Parque* of Málaga, the cab passed spectacular Christmas light displays that arched over streets and sidewalks. Blue lights blinked from park trees, and Christmas trees made of wire and lights flanked coliseum-styled buildings. And the outdoor, bustling Christmas market—complete with green and red lit palm trees—was unlike any Christmas wonderland she'd seen. Illumination and celebration filled not just the air but every corner of Málaga. Once, Isa rolled down the window trying to breathe in the holiday spirit and the mouth-watering aromas from the street food vendors—prawns fried with fresh garlic and spicy chilis. For a moment, the cab ride felt like a vacation. But it wasn't. Gathering intel for human trafficking didn't do much for the holiday spirit, which was okay by Isa. There were no Christmas plans waiting for her back in Albuquerque.

After ten minutes or so of the Christmastime awe, the cab found a highway. Two minutes later, they pulled down a dismal-looking street where the shoddy buildings speckled among the old stately structures of Málaga looked out of place—almost ominous. "Is this the right place?" Isa asked the driver when he pulled over to the curb.

"You wanted a place to buy a knife?"

"Yes."

"You won't find those in the tourist areas." Tapping at the console and head turning to scan the area, he announced his fare.

While Isa quickly worked the exchange rate from Euros to US dollars through her head, his tapping picked up speed.

She handed him a twenty.

He motioned for the curb.

Isa edged out and the cab driver gunned the gas before she had her purse adjusted on her hip.

The quote-unquote knife store held a resemblance to what she thought an underground ammo bunker might look like. Dim lights, windows half-covered, and a narrow door that indicated large-sized people were not welcomed.

Doubtful the place was open, she half-heartedly twisted the doorknob, glancing over her shoulder to get a twenty on the rough-looking characters outside a bar across the street.

The door swung in.

Boxes and crates made a pathway to an old-style glass case or what might be the sales counter at the back. Atop the counter, a wooden rack of pocketknives set off to one side. Two antique, colonial-era swords hung on the dingy wall behind the counter. Unclear what, exactly, vending took place here, she was sure of one thing—someone had a major case of hoarding.

Wafting through the earthy smell of mold and cardboard, Isa also got a whiff of pipe tobacco and of something not being quite right.

She flashed back to India Magic and the first day she stepped inside her surprise inheritance that had been an Indian Restaurant but was then used by the 96 Cartel for drug storage. That memorable day, she'd been hit by the odd scent combinations of curry, strawberry Shasta, and wet rat. The wet rat, according to Awena, had been a major indicator of demonic activity. Isa guessed demons must leave pellet droppings behind, too, because India Magic's floor had been littered with them.

Always one to learn from life's lessons, she spun for the exit. Intuition was something she cultivated these days.

But a rustling from a stack of boxes stopped her mid-step.

Inching back around, it took a minute to pinpoint him among all the debris, but there he stood on a stepladder, hand in the top box.

He spoke, but in a Spanish that didn't quite resonate with her ear. The accent, the verb conjugation, were slightly different than the childhood Spanglish she'd grown up with.

"Do you speak English?" Isa asked.

"Oh, American," he replied, the previous accent gone. He hopped off the ladder. "Yes, I lived in LA for years."

Isa breathed lighter. "That's great. I wasn't sure my brand of Spanish would work here."

The man, bowed in the legs and a good nine or ten inches shorter than she, waddled up. Head tilted back, he squinted one eye and gave her a quick study.

"As an American, the fact that you even try to speak any language other than English is a good start. You lost?"

"I don't think so." She scanned the place. "I was told you sell knives, and I thought this would be a good place to purchase a can of Mace."

"Mace?"

"Pepper spray."

"Oh." He squinted the eye again, glanced at the front door. "Why pepper spray?"

"I'm new and alone." Probably shouldn't have mentioned the alone part.

"If you stay in the tourist areas, you'll be safe."

"Well ... I don't plan to be in the tourist areas."

"New and alone. Not a tourist? What brings you to the seedy part of Málaga?"

"I'm working on ..." Her alias as an international freelance reporter wasn't feeling right among the mystery boxes and dark corners, even though something, something about this guy felt safe. If she was an official undercover cop looking for an informant, he'd fit the profile. So, she went with her original alias. "I'm working on a story of sorts."

His posture stiffened. "Reporter?"

Instincts correct. She was now an official threat. She tried to back pedal. "Only curious really. Looking at ..."

"Culture?"

Isa shook her head.

"Christmas celebrations, then. Visiting the Belenes Nativity? Or our world-famous Christmas markets? Or the city's holiday lights?"

"Uh, no ... it's more like," Why couldn't she find a placid word? "It's more like human interest."

"Human interest in what?"

Thoughts were not loading up fast enough. And it felt familiar. She could say some pretty stupid things under pressure.

Need to tread lightly here.

"Where some particular humans are?"

"What humans, exactly?"

"Girl humans."

106

He frowned. "I don't sell girls here." He pointed at the door. "You should go."

"No, it's not like *that*. I'm doing a story on ports of call for human traffickers."

His blond brows lifted with alarm. "You should have stayed in America. There's plenty of dirt for a good story there." He pointed at the door again. "Like I said when you came in. *You're lost.*" He squinted. "And you should go."

Rewind, Isa.

"Look. I've said too much. Forget the story stuff. I came for Mace—a way to protect myself while I'm in the area."

"I can't help you." He started for the front door. "And we are closed."

"Hang on a second," she said reaching for the back of his shirt. "I ... I." She dropped her hand just short of grabbing his collar. "I won't tell anyone where I bought the pepper spray."

He stopped, his back still to her.

"If you'll help me out, we can both forget I was here."

The man waddled back around to face her. "You radiated 'suffering advocate with a cause' when you came in. Professional journalists have been killed trying to expose what you're digging around in. You should go home."

"It's not that simple." Isa bit her bottom lip. Raised hopeful brows.

"You in some kind of trouble?" he asked.

Maybe the little guy had a big heart. She wanted to trust him and his wide blue eyes. "No. But there are a lot of girls who are."

He kneaded around on his cheeks like he had a thought baking. Then he waved his hand about. "Forget it. You're wasting my time, little fish. There's an ocean of sharks out there." He thumbed at the door. "Now beat it."

"I'm looking for someone in particular—"

The blue eyes narrowed. "Somebody's daughter?"

"No, no, I'm not here on a rescue mission. I'm looking to connect a few dots to someone living on the other side of the Mediterranean."

"A ring? You think you're going to expose a trafficking ring?" He shook his head like that thought needed to be tossed into the Mediterranean. "It doesn't matter if you're looking to connect dots to Antarctica. News that you're looking to expose someone will make it across Europe in a matter of minutes. You'll be stopped. And I'd prefer it not be on my turf when it happens." Now his hands were on his hips like he was done—really done.

Isa lifted her nose. Sniffed. "What's in all these boxes anyway?"

"Time for you to go."

"Look, I don't want to get you or any bystanders in trouble." Sucking in a deep breath, she then let out the truth. "My husband was murdered, and I'm looking to expose his killer."

"Oh no!" He put his hands in his hair. "Don't tell me any tear-jerking tales." He waddled to the front door, and just when Isa thought he'd open it and order her out, he flipped the deadbolt.

"You're totally alone, right?"

She nodded.

"Nobody is going to come around looking for you?"

"No one has followed me," she reassured him. "I'm on a solo mission."

"I am called Pepe," he said making his way past her. He headed for the back of the store. "Stay here," he ordered just before disappearing behind a door. "And keep away from the windows."

CHAPTER 29

With every step, the blister on his right big toe stung. And he still had a dozen or more blocks to walk to his apartment.

What a day.

Just an hour after Jacob finished off his pepperoni and ham-laced calzone and was back in his apartment, Marko had called his US phone to say Bambino's could use help and to come back to the restaurant immediately. Suspicious, yeah, but Jacob had heard that a lot of the food industry personnel hadn't returned to work after the COVID-19 scare. Italy had been hit especially hard and tourism was down. Workers would, naturally, be hard to find. Made nabbing a job at his targeted spot easier than expected.

So when he showed back up, Marko had shown him all the new-employee ropes. From dishwashing to bussing to waiting a table of obvious Americans. He'd spent the next five hours on his feet.

He hadn't been even remotely prepared for the brutality of the food industry. In his six years of undercover FBI work, he'd taken the roles of several professions, but never a waiter. He hoped the waiter gig wouldn't last long. His feet couldn't handle it, and his head ached. People had major attitudes when it came to their chow, and more than once, he'd been tempted to shove a slice of pizza pie up a customer's large nose.

Aware more blisters formed with each excruciating step, he pulled the new and buzzing burner he'd bought on his way back to Bambino's from the front pocket of his jeans. The undercover work moved so quickly, he'd hardly had time to get a burner and tuck his US phone away in the apartment safe before his first pizza shift had begun.

Marko's text read,

TOMORROW SHIFT STARTS AT 8:00. PREPARE TO WAIT ENGLISH-SPEAKING TABLES AGAIN.

The new hiking boots he'd bought before this trip just needed some break-in time. No way he'd consider spending big bucks on another pair.

And once he found Sophia and determined how he'd extract her, then he would deliver the female mob boss to the FBI agents at the American Embassy. Or, he might rent a private plane and fly her back to the US if the Italians made a play for her. Either way, it couldn't happen soon enough, because his feet and his head wouldn't be able to endure the waiter and busboy job for long.

At his apartment door, he leaned in and listened for unusual sounds while extracting his key from his jeans.

All clear there, nothing but the sound of little cars blowing their horns from the street outside.

Jacob unlocked the door. Stepped in.

First thought to hit—he'd entered the wrong apartment.

Second thought—he'd forgotten to pick up the place before he left. Which wasn't unusual.

But he was pretty sure he hadn't dumped his clothes on the floor.

Reality commenced.

He'd been ransacked.

CALCULATED ENCOUNTERS

The Murphy bed he knew he'd put up in the wall was down and the bedding all over the floor.

The kitchen fridge door stood ajar. Three Coke cans lay on the floor.

Stretching low to step over clothes thrown about, he got to the bathroom. Gently pushed the door open with his boot. Peered inside.

Empty.

He yanked the shower curtain to one side. The small window above the bath was shut and locked from the inside.

Jacob made his way back across the living area and to the single closet. The safe door was askew, and the safe just one big empty square space where his US phone and gun had been.

Jacob hustled to the window over the kitchen sink and scanned the street below.

Mobsters moved fast. This job wouldn't take the months and months of prepping and relationship building like his jobs back at the US southern border. Nope, he'd already identified gang activity and the gang activists had already identified him.

Interesting. Would have considered it entertaining if his feet didn't hurt and his head wasn't stuffy.

As the night took charge of Naples outside the window, he knew his intruder could be watching from anywhere out there.

Jacob surveyed the streets.

Looked like his intruder would not be bothering with shadows or hiding out in a car.

Under the streetlamp at the corner, the gun-toting, shorter of the two lookalike brothers he'd seen in Bambino's earlier leaned against the lamp post, face turned upwards to Jacob's window.

Jacob grimaced.

The man saluted, turned, and walked away.

With no sign of forced entry, someone must have let the slick-haired mobster into Jacob's studio. The empty safe staring back at him let him know that *same* someone had been given a master code which meant whatever syndicate crime ring ruled this area had ties to his apartment building and manager.

The call to come to work had probably been a scam to get him out of the apartment building so the search could take place.

He'd hit paydirt.

The FBI's suspicions that Bambino's was run by a local mob were dead on. And the mob was likely to be the one he wanted to infiltrate—Vita Morale.

He pulled the checkered curtain across the window. Took in the mess he had no intentions of cleaning up tonight.

If Vita Morale had a tech wizard, it wouldn't be long before they could unlock his phone and read everything in there. Thankfully, his phone was programmed to wipe clean after four hack attempts. And maybe, just maybe, Isa or his contact in Spain hadn't texted again. He'd have to make some calls on the burner and shut his real phone account down.

If he went to his supposed job tomorrow, one of two things could happen: he would walk into Bambino's cleared as a potential recruit for organized crime, or he would walk into a trap with the mobsters knowing who he was and what he wanted.

He stooped to pick up the Coke can. Peered into the fridge. The intruder had taken the hunk of ham he'd bought at the corner market.

He slammed the fridge door.

Stepped over some clothes and plopped down on the bed.

He didn't have any idea what he would walk into when

he showed up at Bambino's tomorrow. But he'd be ready. Right after he got off his feet for a while.

CHAPTER 30

When Isa left the, ahem, knife shop, Pepe locked the door behind her.

The streets outside came alive as the day bedded down. Twice as many people milled about and music blasted from a store a few doors down. All cities had their share of seedy areas, and from the looks of this street, she was in the middle of Málaga's.

Legs and cleavage on display, girls gathered in small groups while the boys made catcalls in passing. From behind the wheels of cars, middle-aged slime bags pulled to the curb next to the girls like they were pulling through a KFC drive-through.

The red-light district teamed with life that wasn't really life at all. Not life to the fullest as God had promised those who followed him—but life that never reached satisfaction, a wicked cycle of filling emptiness with momentary pleasures. Tempted to cover her eyes and cry, she knew if she didn't face the problem, the job she'd come to do wouldn't get done.

Looking back, Isa could clearly see that while her Savior didn't pluck her out of the insane circumstances of her dysfunctional family, he had given her an element of protection and amazing coping skills through mathematic calculations. The columns upon columns of imaginary numbers and mental equations had kept her from going mad while she hid from her stepfather in her bedroom closet.

Isa pulled her phone from her purse, glanced up at a man in a grey hoodie who pushed past her to rush on. She looked back down at the phone to check for a response from Jacob. During her London layover nine hours earlier, she'd sent him a text telling him she wasn't researching online anymore. Her fingers hadn't wanted to cooperate when she'd typed in the part about what she *was* doing.

Flying to Spain.

Closing one eye, she prepared herself for his response.

But there was none.

Swiping through her list of texts again, she double-checked. A message from Awena said that a box had arrived from Milly Washington. She'd put it under Isa's desk still taped up.

Yeah, right.

Awena also wrote that Maria had added sopapillas to the baked goods menu.

Oh, brother.

But not one texted word from Jacob.

Slipping her phone back into her purse right next to the new can of Mace, Isa started for a group of three girls gathered at the closest corner. Time to start inquiries. Ask a few questions—an initial introduction to get friendly and establish some trust with local workers.

From down the street, a couple of male teens on a motor scooter slowed as they passed. They seemed to make fun of the girls and the taller of the three women pumped a fist at the cyclists.

The scooter sped up.

The guy on the back pointed at Isa.

Before she could make sense of what was happening, the driver swerved into the curb right next to her.

Isa stepped aside instinctively, but still not putting all the dots together. Otherwise, she would have clung to her purse while executing a jiujitsu kick.

In the span of three seconds, the kid on the back reached out and slid her purse right off her shoulder.

"Hey!" she said getting her hand on the bag as the strap ripped from her shoulder.

The two-wheeler wobbled.

She yanked hard. "Stop that!"

The nabber pulled at her purse while the driver punched the gas.

The purse snapped from her hand.

"Hey!" she screamed, taking to the street. "Give that back!" Her feet couldn't hit the cobblestones fast enough.

A taxi driver dodged her, laying on the horn.

The thieves rounded the next corner.

Slowing after another horn blast, Isa looked behind to see a red Ferrari, the driver yelling something about Isa's *madre* as he threw his hands up.

Isa threw her own hands up but stepped out of the way.

Icky neighborhood. And Mace gone.

"That is why you shouldn't carry a bag here."

Isa whirled around. The three ladies she'd seen at the corner formed a semi-circle around her. "Those chicos ... they lifted two purses this week already," one said, her accent unrecognizable.

"But I have never seen a woman chase a thief." The girl in the short, short skirt said, offering Isa a high five. "What would you have done if you caught them?"

The other two laughed, and Short Skirt leaned closer to Isa. "Did he get all your money?"

Isa patted the secure pocket that hung from her neck and beneath her shirt. Thank God she'd put her identification and the money she'd need for the night in a traveler's pouch hidden beneath her navy T-shirt. "No."

"Passport?"

Isa shook her head.

"American." The tall girl seemed delighted. "Are you a tourist?"

"Of course," Short Skirt said. "That's why the bandits went for *her* purse. She put her eyes on Isa's navy windbreaker and blue jeans. "You can no walk around here alone looking like American tourist."

"Actually," Isa said, "I'm not a tourist."

"You a cop?" Short Skirt asked.

"I'm a journalist."

As if Isa had just announced she had a fresh and mutated case of COVID-19, all three girls took a giant step back.

"Wait. I'm … uh … working on an international story about working women and how they survive. I'm not here to get anyone in trouble."

"What kind of working women?" The tall one asked, her dark scrutiny intense.

Isa rolled her shoulders. "Okay. I'm here to find out how girls end up working the streets. Like …" She shrugged.

The tall one pointed at her. "A snitch! Don't talk to her." She grabbed Short Skirt by the elbow and pulled her away.

"Please … wait …" Isa pleaded as each turned her back and walked away. "I just want to understand."

They kept walking.

Isa's hands went to her hairline. Fruit from the first night on the job? Zero. No info. No Mace. And now, no phone.

Isa eyed Pepe's closed door.

CHAPTER 31

After Isa knocked three times then pounded a couple more, Pepe finally unlocked and cracked the door open.

"It's you."

"It's me."

"I thought I told you to never come back here. I can't have a reporter seen hanging around my place. I've got customers, you know."

"My purse got stolen with the pepper spray inside. I need another can."

He gave the width between them another inch. "Already? You've got troubles already?"

"These two guys ... on a motor bike. I was distracted by a group of African girls down the street."

Pepe pulled the door open and squinted that one eye. "I knew you were trouble."

"Please?"

He stepped aside, scowl planted, and locked the door behind her.

He hustled over to some crumpled papers lying near an open box and started stuffing them back inside. Seems he didn't want to chance she might sneak a peek.

"What *is* all this stuff, anyway?" She couldn't help herself.

"None of your business." He folded the top of the box.

"You're right," she said. "It's none of my business."

Pepe turned for the back of the shop. "I only have one can of the spray left. You can't lose this one. And it will cost you double." He halted. "Oh, wait." He looked back at her. "You probably don't have any money now that your purse is gone, do you? You probably expect me to give you the spray and money for a cab back to your hotel. You probably thought I'd be a sucker for a sob story."

"Uh, no. You don't seem like a sucker to me."

"I'm not, you know."

"I know."

"So how are you going to pay if you don't have purse anymore?"

Isa pulled out the pouch beneath her polo. "I didn't lose all my cash. This is not my first rodeo."

"Rodeo? You ride broncos, too?"

"Never mind."

He waved for her to follow him.

She did. "So about those local working-class girls out there. They don't want to talk to me."

"No one is going to talk to you. I thought I made that clear."

At the door to his back room, he signaled for her to wait again.

Again, Isa looked around. What on earth was he hiding in all the piled-up boxes?

Pepe reappeared with another can of Mace in hand.

"So ..." She pulled out a twenty and tucked the pouch back down her shirt. "What would it cost for some information? I'm not convinced you can't help me get started."

Pepe took her twenty. "I didn't figure you for the type to offer bribes."

"I need to make headway on this article."

"Why?"

"Because girls like those," she pointed over her shoulder, "are bought and sold like commodities. I think what's happening outside your door is criminal. No. It's evil. And people like you look the other way."

Pepe's finger shot up in the air. "You don't know what you are—" he stopped. Looked long and hard, his blue eyes flickering.

Isa braced.

But instead of a verbal assault, his face drooped.

"I'm getting too old for this."

Maybe true. The short man had gray at the temples and deep crow's feet around the eyes. "You're never too old to help someone out. I promise not to mention your name."

"I've almost quit twice. But it is proving harder to get out than it was to get in."

"Get in what?"

"Over my head," he said, waving her off.

She liked him. Didn't know why, but with a little prodding, he really could be her informant. "I think you want to help me out. I hear there's a migrant camp that's selling girls."

"No camp I know of."

"Look. We both know there are proven traffic lanes coming in and out of Málaga. Maybe you've heard of some place where the children are gathered?"

Shaking his head as if he wanted to jiggle the thought away, he mumbled, "I'll be sorry for this." He pointed at her. "I'll point you in a direction, but don't come back here crying when things don't work out."

She nodded slowly, biting her lip. Probably everyone one on this side of Málaga knew someone in a trafficking ring. People living in hoods knew things, and one was about to share with her.

"You're craftier than you look, which can work in your favor," he said.

Did everybody pass around insults like a case of COVID?

He turned for the counter at the back. "Aren't you a journalist?" he asked, wobbling up to the taller-than-his-chest counter. He pulled out a pen and paper from beneath the counter. "I've got a couple of things you'll wish you'd written down." He glanced back at her. "Then our business is finished."

"Of course. You won't see me again."

Back outside on the sidewalk, a man with close-cropped white hair, a sharp chin and donning a long trench coat, stepped past her, his eyes steeled straight ahead. She scooted to the nearest light post and got behind it to watch the man and his regulated steps. He stopped at Pepe's door. Pulled out a key and let himself in.

CHAPTER 32

Isa read the street address to the cabby again. "Club Exóticas," she said, folding the paper she'd written the address on. She liked Pepe but thought it best not to push anymore about his career choice. She had managed to convince him to recite his cell number—in case she needed to call, although she doubted he'd given his actual number. He probably felt pretty safe handing out a number because she didn't have a phone.

"Club Exóticas," the cab driver announced, pulling beside a line of parked cars at the curb. He held out his hand for the fare.

Isa's upper lip developed a twitch. In a foreign country and about to step into a seedy part of the culture—what was she thinking? Sure, she'd worked with some lowlife characters during her short stint as an undercover drug investigator with Mexican cartel. And she'd hunted down some of the old 96 gang to send them packing back to Mexico. But this? Could she handle what she was about to willingly step into?

Probably not.

She looked into the cab's rearview mirror, making eye contact with the driver. "You ever been in there before?"

"Club Exóticas? Lady," he said in broken English, "I got a wife and kids at home. I never even been on this street before."

Great.

Just a few days before Coffee Magic officially opened, Awena had flipped through her Bible, reading out loud the stories of her personal heroes. At that time, Isa had never even heard of some of the names—Deborah, Hannah, Sarah. Awena had compared Isa's shooting a drug lord in the knee to Jael, a biblical woman who'd hammered a tent stake through some guy's head.

One brave step at a time. Isa put her hand on the door handle.

It had been the story of Esther that completely engulfed Isa, though. She'd watched Awena's face as she read how Esther put everything, *everything* on the line to save her people.

The women in that bar were Isa's people. Girls who'd been deceived and used. Lied to and pawed. Innocent and undeserving of their awful circumstances.

She pulled the handle, and the door opened.

Since the day Awena had introduced Isa to Esther, she'd read the story fourteen times.

"If I perish, I perish," Isa quoted Esther, climbing out of the cab and stepping onto the street, wondering where her courage had run off to.

Then watching the cab pull away, she wondered why she hadn't asked him to park around the corner, give her fifteen minutes, meter running, then pull back around and pick her up. And why she hadn't asked the cabbie if they could stop and let her buy another phone on the way.

Stupid scooter thieves.

She faced Club Exóticas.

Eyed the windowless stucco building.

Didn't initial steps always prove challenging? Even in white-collar crime spreadsheets? Pulling this information column to line up with that set of facts and placing dates and timelines into the crime timeframe were truly the trickiest maneuvers in her crime-fighting days—which were not so long ago. But many times she'd been here, standing before the giant, speculating about what she would uncover.

Only most of her giants were financial institutions hosting one or two lost-their-way brokers and not sex clubs full of lawless flesh consumers.

Crime was crime, and now was the time to get started. She adjusted her windbreaker's collar, realizing a bouncer parked on a stool outside the skinny black door watched her.

She swallowed back her nerves and took those first steps through the cars and toward the bouncer, telling herself she was Esther headed for the king's court.

The bouncer appeared underwhelmed with her arrival. He looked her up and down then contemplated the parking lot once more.

She asked if she could go inside.

He crossed his arms, which were the size of railroad ties. Didn't say a word.

CHAPTER 33

"My brother is in there," Isa pointed at the door. "I need to talk to him."

The big guy didn't budge. Practically yawned.

A couple of men ... no, creeps ... walked up behind Isa. They must have communicated telepathically because the bouncer stood, opened his palm, and accepted a sum of cash with zero words exchanged.

The two customers disappeared behind the skinny door.

Isa eyed the bouncer again. "It will only take a moment."

He settled again on his stool and went back to his parking lot watch.

Another man-creep eased up, greased the bouncer's palm, and slipped through the door like a snake. Again, verbal exchanges didn't happen.

"Fine." She reached inside the collar of her T-shirt, pulled the travel pouch out and withdrew a $50. She held the folded bill between her index and middle fingers. "Now can I go in?"

The stone man took the bill and shoved it in his pocket then held out his hand.

"More?" Isa asked. "Are you kidding me?"

He shook his head.

She raised her brows.

He pointed at the front pocket of her jeans.

"Fine," she repeated, and yanked the six-ounce can of Mace she'd thought she'd hidden well beneath the loose T-shirt. "You win."

Pocketing her pepper spray, the bouncer nodded at the door.

CHAPTER 34

Once inside the dimly lit entrance into the club, Isa encountered another bouncer. Only this one didn't ignore her. He sat beneath a single beam of overhead light, like he was an orator on a stage, and made it clear he knew she was there. He visually dissected every inch of her body.

Her insides shuddered, but she managed an "Hola."

He answered in English. "Hello. You making a food delivery?"

Guess it was better than asking her if she was Fedex.

"I'm looking for my brother, and I need him to come back to the hotel with me. He said he was coming here last night. He didn't come back to our room all day. Maybe he's still here."

The man tilted his head as if considering her story. She went with it.

"He has our money with him. I need to buy a sandwich or something."

"You American?"

Was it always so obvious? "Mexican," she answered, hoping the distrust of a possible American journalist ... or food delivery girl ... would help get her through the door.

"Interesting," he remarked, leaning back against the wall. "Why have you and your brother come to Spain?"

She steeled a haywire nerve. "Opportunity. We're looking for work."

No way could she make herself any more vulnerable than this. She'd practically said, *I'm available for whatever.*

The doorman pushed off the wall and stepped to the other side of the small room. Isa had neither seen the desk in the shadow nor the silhouette sitting behind it. As her eyes adjusted to the dark, the form of a woman took shape. Sable hair fell to the shoulders that framed a full face. The woman wore a dark blouse beneath a business jacket and had a cellphone in her hand.

The woman and the doorman looked at each other for a long, uncomfortable moment.

More of Isa's nerves got unruly.

Finally, the woman glanced back at Isa. Isa couldn't see her clearly but noted a small nod of her head.

"We're going to help you find your brother," Mr. Grease Hair said. "Come with me."

Here we go.

Isa followed him through a door. Loud dance music thumping with heavy bass echoed down a hall. At the end of icky-carpeted hall, the doorman pushed the silver lever on double doors.

Isa had never been inside a gentleman's night club before.

Probably wouldn't be stopping in again because things looked creepier than the carpet. The flashing lights over the dance floor revealed a half-naked woman between flashes. She didn't seem embarrassed to be pulling Napoleon Dynamite moves. But it didn't seem to matter. No one watched her because there were plenty of half-naked women at the tables with the ... ahem, gentlemen customers.

Gag-inducing nausea commenced, and she hadn't been in there for even four minutes.

The doorman stifled a laugh.

She didn't need Awena to know demons filled these airways.

"He in here?" the doorman asked, leaning close with brows raised as if he cared.

She shook her head. No way could she conduct undercover interviews about trafficked girls in this seedy scene. Evidently, you had to remove portions of clothing to get a conversation.

She shook her head.

"So ... your brother's not here?"

Isa couldn't figure why he seemed so awfully pleased with himself. "I don't see him. I should go."

"There's another room."

"I'll just wait for him outside," She hated that she couldn't take it. What had she expected anyway? Girls ready to chat over tea?

"This way," he said moving across the room.

Probably, he wasn't leading her out the door. Probably—because they weren't going back the way they'd come.

Before she could politely protest, he had her by the arm.

Politeness no longer an option, Isa screamed.

CHAPTER 35

"Quiet down," the greased-up guy said, pulling her toward the back of the room.

Isa resisted, pulling her right leg back for a jiujitsu kick.

In the dark, she caught his shin.

He grunted but twisted her arm behind her back. She flipped around, slapping for his face with her free hand. Expected one of the gentlemanly customers to come to her rescue.

No one in the room was on their feet except the awkward dancer under the strobe light. She, at least, had her hands on her hips, glaring at the altercation.

That's it. With her arm wrapped up behind her, she couldn't get enough distance between them to leverage another accurate kick, so she head-butted under the chin.

She felt his teeth jar.

And his anger mount.

And somehow he had her up off her feet and heading through a set of brocade curtains. She twisted and punched all the way through.

He dropped her on the floor, and Isa scrambled to her feet, hands up and left leg forward. It was on.

On!

Greasy Hair rubbed his chin, backing toward a sofa where two teenage girls—one with Asian features, one with the coloring of an Arab, sat on a dingy crushed-velvet blue sofa.

"Want more?" Isa asked, eyeing the girls.

But the girls looked as scared as she had been back in the days of the hiding closet, counting dust bunnies while her stepfather roamed the house calling her name.

Without further thought she took command. "Come with me," she ordered the girls.

Anxious, both girls flipped their heads to check Greasy Hair's response.

Something or someone moved behind her.

An arm seized her by the neck.

One of the girls gasped.

Isa tried to wedge her flat palms up between the smelly arm and her neck.

A rag came over her face.

She twisted her head left, then right, then left again, shoving hands up, up.

A metallic taste filled her mouth.

She gave up on getting her hands around the arm at her neck and grasped at the rag over her face. She got one eye cleared well enough to see Greasy Hair on the floor, about to secure her legs.

Her eyesight went fuzzy. Then her feet were off the ground.

She bucked, or at least thought she bucked. It was hard to tell as her body stopped responding to commands.

Did this happen … or was she dreaming?

Her brain wouldn't put the events in order. She fought but hit nothing. Yelled but heard silence.

Everything went black.

CHAPTER 36

Jacob walked an alternate route to his 8:00 a.m. shift. Standard procedure when expecting the unexpected. From this day on, unless he wanted to be followed or set a trap, he'd alter every trip to and from his new job.

When he opened the door to Bambino's, there sat the mob brothers at a bare-top table. As anticipated.

When the shorter brother, in no hurry, methodically got to his feet and pulled out his gun, he showed Jacob that everyone understood this to be the inevitable encounter. He moved to the other side of Jacob.

Still in his seat, the tall one said, "My cousin Londo doesn't think we should trust you, but I told him, 'Hey, we gotta give the guy a chance.' Things could, you know, work out in our favor."

So they were cousins, not brothers, proving the fact that all gangsters hosted some identical genetic code.

Jacob, sending the same message of expectancy, shrugged. "I like favors." Even though his big toe still throbbed, it felt good—felt right to be back in the imposter zone, an odd space in his life where the ending always justified the means. It was true this philosophy ran counter to his Christian black-and-white ethics, but in law enforcement, he operated in the various shades of gray.

Jacob stretched his arms forward, letting the guy with the gun know he couldn't be rattled. "So if that's Londo ..." He thumbed towards the tall one. "Then who are you?"

"Mike," he answered, a wry smile snaking up at the corners of his mouth.

The relating began. With a little show of camaraderie and a large dose of confidence on Jacob's part, Mike had transformed from dominating thug to game player. Game players loved to volley their wills back and forth with opponents. That strategic flaw bought Jacob valuable time—time that would result in more opened doors.

"Mike, you got my phone and my friend?"

Mike ran his finger down the bridge of his straight nose. "Maybe, but—"

Marko busted through the stainless steel, swinging door, saw Jacob between the two mobsters, turned and went right back through the doorway before the door had the chance to swing back shut.

Jacob chuckled. "Looks like Marko's been in my shoes before. Has he joined *la famiglia* yet?"

Mike jutted his chin into the expectant air. "It's true we're a big clan. We've got members in all kinds of places. But let's talk about you, bro."

Jacob's heart warmed. They wanted to be brothers. "I'm brother Bob." Jacob grinned.

"So you wanna play wise guy?" Mike clearly loved the banter. He pulled Jacob's phone from his trench coat pocket. Held it at arm's length and tapped the screen with his thumb. "The contact you've initialed 'IP' says he's headed for Spain and not researching online." Mike put the phone back in his pocket. "Researching what?"

He hoped like heck that the fake smile still plastered to his face masked the fact that his heart plummeted to his stomach.

Isa had texted while the cousins had possession of his phone.

Had they gotten an expert to hack his cell, or was the message she'd sent just showing up as a screen alert? And. And ... Isa had flown to Spain? He restrained himself from extracting Londo's gun from his hand and digging his phone out of Mike's pocket so he could text Isa to keep her too-little-too-late backside in Albuquerque. She wasn't needed now.

Hard as it was, he held composure tight. "You think I came all the way to Naples to flip pizzas? Everybody knows there's money here—new outfits taking over. I've left small time drug running in the US and come to Europe looking for action, man. And it's looking like this is my lucky day."

"Who is 'IP'?" Mike wasn't going to let the phone issue go. Nor was Londo, who moved in closer.

How he explained away Isa's text would either get him beaten at best, killed at worst, or invited into the world of Italian Mafia.

He steeled his jaw. Ran through a couple of mental options.

If they'd truly gotten inside his phone, then his cover was blown. And of course if Sophia were to receive an alert, it would be a matter of seconds before she figured he and Isa were coming for her.

She'd have a hit put out before he could leave Naples.

Jacob pressed his fingertips together, raised one brow. "IP was a partner in crime, kind of like you and Londo here. I sent him to Spain to get rid of him. You see, I'm the one with the brains, and he's the screw-up. He'll never make it without me, and he'll get himself killed for all I care. But I'm standing here ready to get adopted. I want a big," he spread hands apart, "big family."

The competitive smirk on Mike's face melted into a frown. "You're gonna have to come up with a name and a better explanation than that."

That remark told him they hadn't been able to hack the phone yet. Had simply read the screen's abbreviated texts. "Name's James Hawkins. And you won't be sorry we met. I'm good at coverups. You'll probably get a promotion for bringing in a loyal guy like me."

His frown falling deeper, Mike stood, slipping Jacob's phone from his pocket again. He asked, "Password?"

"Give me the phone and I'll open it for you."

Mike slid his eyes to Londo, who shook his head.

"I don't want you reading my love letters, okay? What self-respecting man wants other men seeing his babes or reading his black book ... if you know what I mean? Plus, I give you my standard password, how do I know you won't be hacking into all my life?"

"Open it up," Mike said, and tossed the phone to Jacob.

Fast on his feet but also in his head, Jacob stepped forward to catch the phone, let it fumble around in his hands for a couple of seconds, then dropped it to the floor.

Just as Mike bent for it, Jacob smashed it. Not with a step, but with a stomp. The stomp just happened to be with the toe-sore foot and Jacob grimaced.

The screen splintered in a thousand directions.

"Oh, ouch." He bent over and picked it up. He shook it, little pieces of glass flitting in the air. "Well, look at this. I'm going to have to get a new phone."

Now Mike's gun was out and pointed at Jacob.

"Look," Jacob said, not wanting to oversell, but wanting to get past the initial vetting process, "I know you're recruiting. After the pandemic, nobody's got jobs, local joints are dying, and this is the time smaller clans are making their moves. You guys are propping up locals and loyalty with financial loans. You can't pull power out of the Camorra's hands with just a few guys on the street. I had my family's contacts in that phone. I can't take chances with you guys having my heart in your hands. So, if a phone is going to stop you from bringing me in, then I'll go find another mob to join."

"So you want a piece of action?" Mike asked, getting nose-to-nose with Jacob. "Everyone starts at the bottom."

"Okay," Jacob answered.

"And you ever pull a stunt like that again ..." Mike pointed his gun at the phone still in Jacob's hand. "You won't be working with us anymore, 'cause you'll be in a casket."

"I know the ropes," Jacob answered. "But I don't just work for anybody. I need to know who I'm working for at the top—how solid and how big is this venture?"

Mike pulled his thin lips against his teeth, narrowing those beady eyes.

It was Londo who stepped up beside Jacob and answered, "You ever heard of Vita Morale?"

Jacob nodded. "Got a woman at the top, right? No thank you." He shoved the broken phone into his front pocket. "I'm outta here." He saluted the cousins. "You won't see me again."

"She's the daughter of a big-timer who died a few years back." Londo sounded like he wanted to convince himself more than Jacob. "And she's legit. She's pulled the family back together after her second cousin nearly took it down."

"Shut up," Mike said to Londo. "You talk too much."

The idea that he'd struck so close to Sophia within just a couple of days on the job sent a surge of electric pulses through his veins. He was back on the job and succeeding. If he'd known he could walk into a pizzeria in Naples and make immediate connections, he would have never asked

Isa to join him in the first place. Sending her to Spain to uncover a human traffic trail had been a lack-of-confidence, spur-of-the-moment, terrible decision.

He glanced between Londo and Mike. "So you guys …" Jacob said, nodding slowly, " … are in with the family." He grinned. "Well now, I don't see that I have a choice here. If I'm working directly with family, then I'm in." He glanced over at Londo, who'd started to look both prideful and pleased. "So when do I get my gun back, Cousins?"

"What? you think I'm going to pull out a contract for you to sign? You'll get what's yours when you prove yourself. So today, you prove yourself here." Mike faced the kitchen. "Marko," he yelled.

Marko reappeared through the swinging door. "James Hawkins is gonna help you out today. Show him the real ropes. Okay by you, Marko?"

Marko nodded, smile spreading.

Jacob gave himself a mental congratulatory pat on the back. He was in. But he'd have to make sure Isa was out. Definitely out.

CHAPTER 37

Wet with dew, Isa couldn't quite figure out how she'd awakened in a springtime field in the beginning of December.

Voices. Vowels she'd never heard.

Her back ached. Legs wouldn't adjust.

Lids fluttering, she managed to get one eye opened.

She wasn't in a field. What took shape just a couple of feet from her was a wooden frame of some sort, a blanket or pillow stuffed beneath it.

A bed. She lay on a floor. She wasn't covered in dew. But sweat—acrid, musty sweat.

She rolled over to her side and tried to prop up on her elbow. She just ... couldn't ... get her arm to ... cooperate.

Ankles and bare feet stepped between her blurred vision and the bed frame.

A pair of knees dropped beside her. Next came hands, wrists, and slender arms. Stretching out beside her, the girl's face finally appeared. Full pink lips beneath a prominent nose. Almond-shaped eyes nestled in rich mocha-colored skin.

A strong and steady hand grasped Isa's shoulder. Held there.

As Isa got her other eye open, the anxiety of not knowing where she was or why she couldn't move melted into the background. With the angelic being lying beside her, she felt the sensation she'd always wondered about but had never experienced—the peace that surpassed all understanding.

She wanted to drift back to the spring field and sleep some more.

But the girl shook her shoulder.

An image of men holding her down, a rag over her face, blurred in and out of Isa's memory. Had she been hurt? Had this angel beside her come to usher her to heaven?

Am I about to die?

As if reading her mind, the angel spoke. "I am Chiazokam Ese," she said with a noble accent.

Trying to pull her lips apart, Isa wasn't sure she could unglue her tongue from the roof of her mouth.

"I am going to help you up to sit," the angel said. "It is best you try to stay awake for now."

The girl got to her knees, slipped her arms beneath Isa's, and lifted Isa with ease. "I am called Chia," she said, leaning Isa against a wall.

The room went aslant, but Isa made out bunks on either side of her. She looked down to see her legs on a bare, striped, and stained mattress.

"You were brought here last night, and now the hour has passed midday. It is time for you to drink water." Chia reached up to the bed beside them and slid a water bottle from behind her pillow. Putting the bottle to Isa's lips with one hand beneath Isa's chin, Chia filled in a puzzle piece for Isa's scrambled brains. "They drug the girls they bring in from the streets."

Water ran down Isa's chin. But she kept her eyes steady on Chia's, letting her know to try again.

Lifting the bottle, Chia pressed it again to Isa's lips. "I was brought over from my own country, and I have not been drugged yet. They know I will not run, for I have no place to go."

This time, Isa managed to get a few sips into her mouth. She swallowed, and though it burned like crazy, she nodded for Chia to give her more.

With water making its way through her veins and fried brain, clarity began to take shape. Isa rocked to adjust her hips and straighten her knees.

Patting her chest to locate the pouch holder which held her passport, money, and the note she'd written down, she wanted to cry when nothing was there. But she couldn't produce tears.

Her jaw ached.

Chia set cross-legged next to her. "You must never drink that," she said pointing to a cup on a beat-up dresser against the wall. Beside the cup was what looked like a sandwich—one with curled-up crust. "When they do not have time to deal with you, they put a drug in the tea. This drug, it will make you sleep for the whole of day. Nasha will bring it for you to drink."

Isa frowned. Nodded to let Chia know she understood.

"They are thieves. Robbers of children. Even young boys."

Isa straightened against the wall as her memory cleared up.

"After they brought you in, they gave you an injection, here." Chia pointed at Isa's upper arm. "Now drink more," Chia said, placing the bottle into Isa's limp hand. "You try. You must. Then I will pour the poison into this bottle and flush it in the toilet down the hall, then refill the water from the faucet."

Isa glanced at the cup on the dresser. Moved her lips around looking for moisture. "Why?" she managed to squeak.

"Because you must pretend to be sluggish from the drugs." Chia cupped her hand around Isa's, helping her tighten her grip on the bottle. "But you must stay fully awake. It is the only way you will escape."

Moving a strand of hair from the middle of Isa's forehead, Chia tucked it behind Isa's ear. "The older ones—"

With her free hand, Isa grabbed for Chia's wrist. Turned it over. A tattooed barcode. Chia had been marked like a grocery item.

Gentle with her touch, Chia pushed Isa's hand away from her wrist. "I am not hurt. But you must know, the older ones like you, they keep them drugged and sell them in the club rooms. Others, like me," she pointed to herself, "either young or from far away, we are put on the streets."

Isa brought her brows together. Shook her head so Chia would know she didn't like the sound of that.

"I have not yet been sent to work. I have only been here a few days, and it is that time in my cycle." She nodded, knowing Isa understood. "But soon, Tem will come to take me to the streets." She nodded at Isa, affirming that all her words were true. "I have heard this from the other girls."

Isa licked at her lips. "Thank you." Her voice sounded like a drunk old man, but she kept talking. "I heard voices when I was waking up. Who was in here?"

Chia's smile had a sheepish tilt to it. She touched her chest with her long, slender fingers. "It was me, for I prayed for you."

CHAPTER 38

Mike disappeared out the front door, and from the corner of his eye, Jacob, aka James, watched Londo flirt with the waitress with the long legs and long dark hair. She might have been a good two inches taller than Londo, but neither seemed to care. He'd catch her coming into the kitchen and give her backside a pat. Occasionally, he'd pull her right into him even though she had a pizza balancing in each hand. The girl would wiggle out of his grip, give him a little fake shriek, and then flash him a "naughty boy" grin.

Jacob wanted to barf.

Especially because this waitress seemed to be what kept Londo in the kitchen and Jacob unable to question Marko. Marko was, obviously, new to the Vita Morale Mafia. With Jacob joining the insiders' circle, he hoped Marko would be willing to share insider info.

He left the kitchen because … he had annoying tables to bus. Not easy work when your toe hurt, your head ached, and you had intel to collect.

His ex-fiancée Jonna used to soak her feet in peppermint essential oil after a twelve-hour nursing shift. For the first time since they'd broken up, he missed the smell, and he missed Jonna. Nobody could massage a foot like Jonna.

Clearing a table of pizza crust ends, he reminded himself not to stress over the crowded kitchen. Things had, after all, fallen into place easier than expected. So what if it cost him a toe and a couple days of waiting tables. He had a pandemic to thank for that. His research had shown that Mafia clans took advantage of Italy's shutdowns by providing everyday necessities not only to the poor in their neighborhoods, but also to the incoming immigrants and struggling businesses.

Clever Sophia. Vita Morale must have seized the opportunity and made a big move, buying loyalty from the locals and keeping small businesses afloat.

He'd never had a case that centered around a woman. Was Sophia taking a cut of the pizza action, or was she setting up to control a whole neighborhood? And where did her other interests lie? Brothels? Child labor?

For most of the day, Jacob busted his buns bussing tables, catching most of the English-speaking patrons, and trying to stay out of other employees' paths. The entire crew, save Marko, seemed annoyed by Jacob's presence. If he were a betting man, and he was, he'd say the Bambino's pizza family members were less than thrilled with the cousins and their interference with the daily operations of food service. Jacob had only added to their piling annoyances.

By late afternoon, the day took a turn.

The owner of Bambino's showed up. A barrel of a man with a ring of gray hair around his balding head, he bore drooped, tired blue eyes that said he found life discouraging. Looked like the employees weren't the only ones disgruntled with the cousins' influence.

"Who's this?" the owner asked Marko when he made the corner and found Jacob at the sink, a dirty dish in his hand.

"The new guy," Marko said and nodded at Londo, who played with his phone in the corner. The object of Londo's short attention had finally gone home after her day's work.

"Yeah, *our* new guy," Londo said, barely looking up. "That's James, Pops. He'll be here to help out for a few days, isn't that right, James?"

Jacob didn't affirm, but watched the old guy lift his shoulders in defeat and turn back for the dining room.

Life as an undercover drug smuggler was better than life as the kitchen help.

When the dining room emptied before the evening rush, Londo called it a day. "Hey, Marko, hey, James, both youse show up tomorrow morning," he called as he pushed through the front door. Then Londo slipped out into the community to annoy God knew who.

Wiping his hands on his tomato-splattered apron, Marko winked at Jacob and told him to go home. Feeling like he'd miss the chance to spend some time with Marko alone, Jacob didn't know if his feet could seriously handle another hour. Plus, he needed to make a couple of check-in calls.

He reminded himself not to rush things. Let relationships happen naturally.

Jacob threw in the apron.

Heading back to his apartment, he bought two more burner phones at an electronics store a guy on the street had recommended. At a hardware shop, he bought two chain-link locks and a door bolt plus a hammer and handful of nails.

The place hadn't carried peppermint essential oil, or he'd have brought that home, too.

At his studio, he checked the closet, tub, and safe. Today, his personal stuff had been left alone.

Not up to it, but knowing he should, Jacob secured a few things. If the apartment manager was going to let Mafia clans in and out of his living space at will, then nailing the window shut and adding locks to the doors didn't seem like a contract violation. The chains and bolt wouldn't stop anyone from getting in if they seriously wanted to, but his attempts at apartment security would send a message that he expected some privacy. At least when he was home.

Next, Jacob hid one of the two new burner phones in a sock and put it in his suitcase.

Then he called one of the guys at the embassy with the other phone and gave a brief update, letting the international squad know they couldn't call, text, or email for a while. He wrapped up the brief by promising to be in touch.

Then Jacob fell into his sofa and rubbed at his bare feet, turning the communications with Isa over and over in his head. If what Mike had read to him on his phone was true, then Isa was probably in Spain. The plan, when he first went to the coffee shop, was to have her look into migrant camps. But now that he'd scored a connection, he didn't need Isa running around Spain getting into trouble.

The woman gave him heartburn.

He got up off the sofa and limped over to the closet. Pulled several pages of documents from inside the pillow he'd cut open. Among the papers, he found his contact booklet and located Isa's cell number.

He pulled down the murphy bed, put his feet up, and looked grimly at a second blister forming on his big toe.

Jacob texted Isa.

THIS IS J. THE WORK IS OVER. GO HOME. NO QUESTIONS FOR NOW. TEXT A SIMPLE Y TO THIS NUMBER TO LET ME KNOW YOU GOT THIS. I'LL CALL IN FEW DAYS. DON'T NEED YOU NOW.

He flipped through a couple of pages in his files and located the names of bounty hunters he'd been in contact with. A couple of the guys worked international jobs exclusively. He tapped in the number of the one he'd already contacted.

Waiting for the call to connect, he decided the next time he went out, he'd buy a package of Band-Aids, which would be cheaper than new shoes.

The call went to voicemail and Jacob, against his better judgement, left a detailed message.

CHAPTER 39

Day three as a prisoner in a prostitution ring's community house, and her head finally stopped pounding. The multiple post-effects of the knock-out inhalant she'd received the night she walked herself into a kidnap situation at the Club Exótica had taken a physical and mental toll.

But now that she was inside, she memorized faces and mentally recorded every conversation she could. Though the results of her exploring Club Exóticas had landed her a hostage for the second time in her short undercover career, she'd managed to get herself inside a trafficking ring—even if her bodily functions weren't at one hundred percent.

Probably somewhere between forty-five and fifty-two percent.

Isa pulled her legs up to her chest. Glanced over at Chia who stretched across the bed across from her. They'd managed a good hour of conversation without interruption before Chia drifted off to sleep. She'd told Isa of her life's dreams—dreams of a good job and eventual education. To date, only two people in her village had gone away to college. Chia aimed to be the third.

The thought Chia might not see her dreams come to reality made Isa's heart hurt.

And still, she couldn't sleep. Goings and comings in the middle of the night needed mental filing. When she got out, she'd be giving Jacob names. She pulled the water bottle from beneath the mattress on the floor. Drank down the last of it. Got up and poured the tainted tea into the bottle. She hid it under the mattress again.

Then Isa banged on the door.

Chia stirred but went still again.

Finally, the door cracked open and the redhead with the Russian accent stuck her head in. "Bathroom?"

Isa nodded.

On her way down the hall, she noted a man she'd never seen before at Nasha's desk. He looked out of place, he wore a business suit, and Isa thought of the last James Bond movie she'd seen. Most of the men coming and going around the community house wore black hoodies and saggy pants, and they had knives shoved in their various pockets. This man in the grey fitted suit didn't belong, and she rehearsed his facial features as she made her way into the cluttered bathroom. Eye shadow containers in every color known to man littered the counter.

Escorted back to her room by the redhead, she plopped down on the mattress on the floor again, thinking through the different exits she'd seen over the last couple of days.

But Nasha and Tem rotated people about, never allowing girls to spend more than a couple of days together. Probably so they wouldn't bond. Or make plans to escape.

She and Chia had been lucky. They'd made it three days together.

Chia had shared her story. How men had come to her village and made a deal with her parents to find her work in a high-end hotel so she could save money for college. Her father had given these men money to pay for her journey to Spain.

It had all been a lie.

And now she'd lost touch with the other eleven girls.

Which seemed to be the worst of it for Chia—the other girls.

Story by story, word by word, moment by moment, Isa determined she wasn't there just to gather intel.

But she couldn't map out an exit as long as the house mother continued to execute Chinese fire drills and move everyone around.

CHAPTER 40

Isa received a new bedroom. A small single. The upside? She was on a real bed instead of the floor. The down? She was locked inside the room alone. The worst? Chia was told she'd be going out to work that night.

Pretending to be groggy, Isa hadn't put up much of a fight when Tem dragged her to the other side of the house. But mostly, she didn't want Nasha or Tem or any of the so-called house help to realize how bonded she and Chia had become. Isa knew girls were moved around, traded, and even sold to other organizations. Considering whoever had her passport and money knew her real age, it had probably taken the kidnapping crew a few days to figure out what to do with her. After abducting and drugging her, they couldn't just take her back to the club and drop her off where they found her ... like some stray dog.

Isa's guess? She'd be sold and moved out of their hair— probably to another country.

And that couldn't happen.

Because ... Chia.

Sophia Ventura would get a visit from Isa. Woman to woman, they had a couple of things to discuss. Isa had fantasized about that future conversation and what it would feel like to slap cuffs around Sophia's thin and gold-bangled wrists.

But her brain didn't camp out on the Sophia dream long because while she lay on the bed, staring off into space, she noted that the board covering her window had been nailed onto the frame. Not screwed in.

The window in the bedroom where Chia stayed had boards screwed into the windows, and unless one had a Phillip's head screwdriver, those woodscrews wouldn't be coming out.

But nails? Different story.

CHAPTER 41

The tiny bedroom must have been servant's quarters, or maybe a nursery. But being on the other side of what Isa figured to be at least a three-thousand-square-foot house, she couldn't be far from the master bedroom where Nasha was sure to be living.

Other than the bare mattress, a blanket, a lumpy yellow pillow, and chest of empty drawers, the room held nothing she could use as leverage to remove nails.

She assessed everything she knew about the house. A circa 1970s sprawling, single-story home, she'd noted the floors were less than spick-and-span, and the cluttered kitchen reeked of stale cigarette smoke. From neither of her bedrooms had Isa heard street traffic. They must be in the country or at least on the edges of a town.

But that was the extent of her current knowledge about her surroundings.

Having received more chloroform than someone her size should take, plus an injection of some knock-out serum some mad-scientist-slash-gangster-chemist concocted, she'd been out cold when they brought her in. She could be in another town, for all she knew, with no idea of the proximity of help. But with girls coming and going from work nightly, there had to be a fair-sized city nearby.

Stretched out on the bed, Isa considered more options, causing another headache. Even in the throes of taking down a drug cartel, she'd used her accounting skills to nail the bad guys by exposing a money-laundering scheme. Here, there was nothing to add or subtract.

But there were percentages to calculate.

She figured she had 0 percent of escaping when they brought her in as a rag doll. And because she had 100 percent success in escaping hostage situations thanks to her 96 Cartel experience, that put her current odds at fifty-fifty.

Not bad.

The window. That might up her odds to 60 percent.

Isa counted the nails in the boards covering the small window a full-sized man wouldn't be able to crawl through. But the small size she'd always hated being might work in her favor tonight.

Three of the window's sides held five nails each while the top only had three nails.

Gangsters and their sloppy work.

She needed a sturdy tool and she thought about a knife. But meals had been delivered with plastic utensils.

Isa got off the bed and checked the small closet. In it hung a lone wire hanger.

Tonight, Chia would be introduced to the horrors of street work. So how the heck was Isa going to manage to get out of that room and scavenge the house for the right tool?

To concoct a plan, she flopped back down on the bed.

Need a strategy.

She ran her fingers through her hair.

Now.

She balled her fists. Hit at the mattress beside her.

Then she clutched the frame beneath the mattress. Banged her head against the pillow, willing some miraculous idea to hit her brain.

CALCULATED ENCOUNTERS

The frame beneath the mattress?
Isa sat up straight.

CHAPTER 42

When Nasha returned for the new girl's dinner plate, she eyed the emptied teacup, the half-eaten dinner of macaroni and cheese with a side of American-style fries.

Foolish woman dey brought me. That woman don't know nothing about being hungry.

Nasha'd lived half her life starving in Benin.

The new woman's passport said she was American.

What dey doin' nabbin' Americans? Fools.

Now she had to contend with the mess. Keep the potential threat comatose was how she'd decided to deal with it. Until they moved that Isabella on to Asia. India, she'd heard. Where all those Middle East men flocked for weekend pleasures.

Fools. Da lot of them.

She glanced over to see the American's back slowly rise and fall with slumber.

Da sooner we get her out, da better.

Nasha pulled the bedroom door shut, locked it, then lumbered down the hall, helping herself to a couple of cold potatoes.

Dey need to throw dis one back to da river like a scrawny fish.

In the kitchen, Nasha dropped the plate off at the bar. Sauntered between the island and cabinets, pulling a fork from the cold dishwater in the sink. She wiped the fork across her bosom to dry it. Back at the plate, she pulled up a stool and sat, the cold fries, half-cooked pasta and lumpy cheese tasted just fine—good as the evening meal she'd finished off an hour ago.

Once she polished off these leftovers, she'd be taking the rest of those girls downtown to the club.

CHAPTER 43

With Nasha finally out of the room, Isa rolled away from the wet, sedative-soaked blanket wadded up between her body and the wall.

Dropping to her knees on the floor, she studied the joints of the bedframe. Click-and-slide locks. Perfect. She tugged the mattress off the frame and slid the nasty thin pad to the floor.

She got to work.

Every five minutes, or 300 counted seconds, Isa would creep over and put her ear to the door. Listen for movement. House activity levels hit the minimum during the evening hours, with girls gone and staff guards beginning their own festivities. Tonight was no different. She only heard the occasional slam of a kitchen cabinet or faint voices from somewhere on another side of the house.

Once she had the frame apart, Isa wedged the shorter rail's bent corner between the pressed nailed-in board and the window frame. She held her breath and pushed the rail toward the wall.

The screech of the nail pulling from the window frame built up some exciting anticipation. She scooted to the door. Put her ear to it. Rejoiced that she couldn't hear anything on the other side. Scooted back to the window. In went the rail again, and she gave it another shove.

A slight gap opened between the board and the window frame.

Working! She pulled her elbow to her side and made a fist. *Yes!*

Isa continued making little gaps on the two sides of the window.

With a fair amount of boldness building up, she pulled the dresser over to the window and climbed to reach the top board.

Then all that built-up boldness rushed right out.

She heard voices coming.

With the bedframe spread across the floor, the dresser under the window and its security boards hanging halfway off, there wasn't an excuse under the sun that would cover what she was up to.

If they caught her trying to escape, they'd surely put another needle to her arm. Or easier, just shoot her and get it over with.

Isa climbed down off the dresser. Made for the door and leaned against it, hearing the volume of Tem's voice grow louder.

Another voice. A male. One she hadn't heard before, with a more European accent. Italian, maybe.

The men stopped outside her door.

God, I'm so close to getting out. Please help me here.

She reached down for a frame rail. Readied herself to strike.

"This one, she is the first American, and it is for best that we do not keep her. We no tattoo her. Orders will come tomorrow. The broker in India has interest."

Isa's heart took a nosedive.

"She is the only one left in house tonight. All others have been sent out."

Chia already gone? Her plunging heart put on the brakes.

The men stopped talking.

Oh, God, no. Oh, God no. Don't let them in.

The doorknob moved to the right by a fourth of an inch. Like Tem was probably slipping a key into the lock. How many seconds would it take before the door cracked open? How many seconds would she have to knock the first one upside the head with the bedrail? She straightened to an upright position. Positioned the rail like a batter at the plate.

One, two, three ...

CHAPTER 44

Jacob cleared a couple of tables. Picking up other people's slop leaned on his raw nerves, and he wasn't sure why. He'd always managed to keep his spirits up during undercover work, knowing the end of the case would yield crime-busting results. But if he delivered one more Margarita Special pie tonight, he'd never be able to eat pizza again.

His toe didn't bother him anymore, and finally, his feet had accustomed themselves to the heavy traffic. But he still struggled with a headache at the end of each day.

This phenomenon was likely Isa's fault because he hadn't heard from his contact in Spain.

Picking up a couple of red napkins from the floor, he scolded himself, again, for bringing a woman in on a case. An international case. An international case spreading across several countries.

What had he been thinking?

And what was up with the ungrateful people tossing napkins on the floor? And the mess under that highchair? People really didn't respect the servers who could make or break their dining experiences.

I am an undercover expert, about to nail a fugitive.

Reminders helped.

A mob promotion couldn't be too much further ahead. In the last three days, he'd escorted one of the lower-ranking bosses to an evening meeting at a vacated office building on the other side of town. He'd been given a gun for the night and had it taken away when he returned the boss to Bambino's after hours.

He'd also been asked to make a delivery, and fortunately, it hadn't been drugs per se, but illegal cigarettes that were housed in a small warehouse where he'd noted a number of vehicles parked without license plates.

Looked like Sophia had added brokering stolen cars to her repertoire of businesses.

Even though he detested his current undercover role, he'd stuck to it just like the mozzarella stuck to the back of the chair he was wiping down.

The constant questions and digging for information revealed the family business had limped along slowly for the last ten years. But the looks of the warehouse activity and the fact she'd managed to control at least one restaurant in town without losing it to another gang said a lot for her management skills. Vita Morale grew faster than his sources at the embassy knew.

A young woman on her way to the bathroom stopped at his cart to ask him a question. But she asked in Italian. He shook his head harder than he needed to and said, "I don't speak Italian. Ask the hostess."

She frowned.

He went to the next empty table.

The big questions eating at him now ... Who ate vegetarian pizzas at this hour?

Fanatical late-eating, food-loving Italians, that's who.

I am an undercover expert about to nail a fugitive.

A couple of obstacles slowed down his case progress. Isa being number one. Every time he thought about Isa alone in Málaga, his gut wrenched, because that woman had a way of getting herself into trouble.

And she'd better not be in big trouble or he'd … he'd … he didn't know what he'd do and didn't like that he spent so much time thinking about her.

No. Worrying.

He wasn't thinking about her, he was *worrying* about a missing partner.

Yeah. That's it.

Jacob dumped a wine glass in his bus cart. He pushed the cart between the family at the big round table in the center of the dining room and the starry-eyed couple seated at a table for two.

And then she was there.

Of all places, coming right out of the restroom. Sophia Evelina Ricci Ventura, head high and as gorgeous as ever.

Did he really just think that?

She had her hair pulled back and sunglasses on, even though it was dark outside. Tight black dress, classic black pumps, and a gold purse at her elbow. Her accessories included a bodyguard who walked up and took her elbow while she slipped the scarf around her neck over her head.

Reminiscent of Jackie O.

Realizing he gawked, he flipped his position to the other side of the cart and guided it to the front windows. Hopefully, she hadn't noticed the busboy with his jaw on the floor. She would have recognized him immediately.

As she made her way to the front door, he kept pivoting position, keeping his backside to her, but catching glimpses to keep track. Another guard joined her and opened the front door. The hostess had made herself scarce, and Jacob could understand why. Sophia possessed a command presence. With two large men flanking her, dangerous wasn't a good enough adjective to describe the woman in obvious charge.

He wandered to the window, pretending to take someone's order, but he had his eyes on what everyone else was looking at.

How had he missed her coming in?

From the window, he watched one of her guards open the door of a black Mercedes GLE waiting in the street.

Had she stopped in to use the restroom?

Someone slapped his shoulder and every nerve in his body jumped. He flipped around, expecting she'd sent a guard back in to nab him.

But it was Marko.

"You're jumpy," he said. "Don't blame you. She has that effect on everyone."

Jacob looked back out the window. "Who was that?" he asked, hoping he sounded like he didn't know.

Marko pulled up close, ignoring the balding man in the chair who kept inching up to his table trying to make room for the rubberneckers. "That's our boss. Something, isn't she?"

"I'll say."

Sophia's car pulled down the street and Jacob repeated the license plate to himself three times. Isa would have already memorized it.

"But," Marko said, maneuvering back to the aisle between tables, "not for long."

What did that mean? Jacob tailed him, giving a nod to the perturbed man crammed up against the table. "What do you mean, *not for long*?"

"After dinner, we go to drink." Marko's brows were pulled together when he shot a glance back at Jacob. "The coffee is steeping."

Jacob got up beside him, leaving the cart in the middle of the floor. "I'm not sure what you're saying."

CALCULATED ENCOUNTERS

Marko paused between a couple of snug tables. A girl, mouth open and pizza at her lips, halted mid-bite to eye the two.

Marko tapped his head. "Something is br ... br ... brewing." His finger went to the air. "Yes, that's it. Something is brewing."

CHAPTER 45

She'd have to aim for Tem's temple, knock him down so she could take a second swing at this new guy who would enter behind him.

Muscles flexed, jaw set. Her laser-like beam might melt the doorknob before Tem unlocked it. *Four, five, six—*

A cell phone on the other side of the door buzzed.

The doorknob slipped back to its original spot.

"Yeah," Tem said. "De shipment is here? Now? ... Come with me ..." His voice and footsteps moved away from the door. "We got to check this shipment."

Cold beads of relief broke out across her forehead. She dropped her head and whispered, "Thank you, Lord, for the miracle."

He'd not only answered her prayer to keep the door shut, but he'd just sent her biggest problem to the basement.

Back at the window, she managed to pull out all thirteen nails to the point she could yank the plywood off the window with her hands.

Eureka. A glass window. She'd not seen the outdoors for days. Not that she could see the outdoors very well now—the window was smeared with something she didn't want to think about. She touched the latch. Sticky.

Ugh.

Isa pulled in a breath and flipped the latch. Shoved her palms beneath the window frame to lift the glass.

The window wouldn't budge.

Most likely nailed shut from the outside.

Dang it.

Dragging the mattress to the window, she picked up the blanket on which she'd dumped the liquid sedative earlier. She crawled up on the dresser, and with the bedrail and nails she'd just removed, she hammered the soggy blanket across the top of the window.

Deep breathing and hoping like heck the blanket would muffle the sound of shattering glass, she picked up the bedrail and pushed it against the window.

The angle didn't afford her much leverage, so she wouldn't be able to *push* the glass out. She'd have to hit the window with the rail.

With small taps at first, she feared making a racket. But when that didn't seem to work, she pulled her arms back and took a good swing.

Behind the blanket, the glass broke.

She used the rail to knock away the sharp edges around the frame.

Three and half minutes later—she knew because she'd counted—Isa had suffered only a minor scrape when she jumped out of the window and into freedom.

Almost freedom, that is.

Crouching beneath the window, she let her eyes adjust to the dark.

A yard. A stucco wall—maybe five feet high.

A dog of German Shepherd mix looked right at her.

And he was not happy to see her. Hairs on his back raised as he growled.

Quick, she glanced over at the stucco wall.

The aggravated dog inched closer. Got within ten feet or so.

A built-in stucco bench stretched along the wall at the side. Someone had begun demolition on that *banco* for obvious reasons. But there was enough of it left ...

Isa took off in full sprint.

She'd heard that you should never turn your back on an aggressive dog.

That's not how she handled it.

Legs moving at full throttle, she made for the crumbling *banco*.

At her heels, the dog took to barking.

Her legs pumped like pistons, her breath huffed like a diesel engine, but the wall wouldn't get closer.

Inconceivably, she willed more adrenaline into her legs and picked up speed.

Leaping for the *banco*, she got her hands on the wall. Pulled herself up and got a leg over in one move.

The dog went rabid—barking, jumping, jerking against the chain.

Good Lord, the beast was fastened to a chain that didn't stretch quite far enough.

Sucking some grateful air into her lungs, she thanked God again.

As Isa dropped to the other side of the wall, a light on the patio switched on.

CHAPTER 46

Isa slowed the pace when she reached the end of a narrow alley ... one that reeked of stale beer. According to the directions the elderly man outside the market had given her, she was a block and a half away from her hotel.

By her best guess—between the community house of stolen girls, the forest trek, the counting, and the Scripture review—she'd been on the run for two hours and thirty, maybe forty minutes. She pressed against the cold brick wall to stay hidden but also to look out at the street, where things were starting to take on a familiar shape.

Behind her, something rustled at the other end of the alley. Little nerve pricks ran up the back of her neck.

Isa looked back into what seemed to be a big black hole, save the overflowing trashcan. Nothing was moving. But something sure could have been in those shadows crouched and watching.

Man, I need to get out of this alley. Man, I need to get into my hotel room. Man, I need to stick with brewing beans.

She inched to the corner and looked left.

Shining like a beacon in the dark night, her hotel's sign lit up that side of the street.

And everything looked normal. No traffic-ring guys hanging around outside waiting on their American escapee.

Pulling back into the shadows, she broke out in a cold sweat—the kind you get when you sense something bad is about to happen.

She peeked back into the dim alley one ... more ... time. No one there.

But she couldn't shake the feeling that someone, or something, watched. Could be déjà vu from her past experiences of hiding in alley ways watching for drug cartel members coming and going from the biker bar. Gang members had a way of appearing out of nowhere.

It's my imagination. The safety of her hotel room was mere steps away and once in there, she'd start documenting and making calls—taking kick-butt action because Chia was out on the streets somewhere.

Plus, she needed a shower.

Even though she'd skidded down a steep hill on her backside in the cold night and trekked through a large grove of Spanish firs, the scent of her three-day ordeal wouldn't leave her. She lifted her arm to get a whiff. She didn't have to inhale to be repulsed.

She glanced, again, into the street. Isa counted the ornate lamp posts between herself and a shower.

At the hotel pull-through, a car rolled in. A man climbed out the driver's side of the red sports car. The woman got out on the passenger side and walked into the hotel lobby. Leaning against his car, the man lit a cigarette.

Isa pulled back against the brick. She couldn't trust anyone at this moment, innocent though the couple looked. With check-in procedures and blah, blah, blah speeches about security from the front desk, she figured the woman would return to her car then they would park. Maybe fifteen more minutes for the all-clear.

Isa rubbed her neck. One-one thousand, two-one thousand ...

The first and the last and everything in between.

She pulled in a breath and started again. One-one thousand, two-one thousand ...

The one who was, is, and is to come.

Scriptures had been playing through her head ever since she'd dropped on the other side of the stucco wall at the community house, dog barking major threats and patio lights flashing.

But during her getaway, something—probably Jesus— yanked the brain controls right out of her grasp. Slipping on wet pine needles, tripping over forest rubble, and avoiding headlights on the road, she'd heard Awena reading to her— not in the recesses of her mind, but near the frontal lobe where problem-solving transpired.

Weird, but helpful. Running around in unknown territory like a hunted animal, the biblical proclamations had helped keep rising panic at bay. Although they hadn't done much for her angry inner dragon who'd been knocking around for three days now. Except when both she and the dragon had been drugged by Nasha.

Before Coffee Magic had opened, while Isa scrubbed the sticky shelves, Awena had perched herself on bar stool and read Revelation from the Bible. She'd meticulously orated the words as if making a grand presentation, and she started with the declaration that both she and Isa would receive special blessings because they read this together.

Awena dwelled in a realm most humans didn't know existed, much less visited on occasion.

Jesus claimed he was the past, the present, and the future.

A chilly gust whipped through the alley, and she wrapped her arms around her waist while the neck hairs prickled again.

How bizarre that she could ponder the names of God, stuck in a dark alley, while her nervous system went haywire.

More than once, Jacob had commented on her lack of mental stability.

She swallowed, peeked around the corner again. The cigarette smoker still leaned against his car.

The first and the last.

Exasperated, Isa dropped her arms. *Think about your next move, not the names of Christ.* She could pull out her Bible once she got home.

But that's not the way Jesus worked these days. At least not in her brain. He wandered in and around her thoughts and situations, constantly whispering words of direction and words of reassurance.

Then, out of the dark alley—clarity sprang like a duck on a June bug.

Of course! If he is the one who was, and the one who is, and is the one yet to come, then he was *with her* earlier in life, was with her now, and would be in the big middle of her future.

On the worktable of her mind, pieces of a scrambled puzzle locked together.

Everything, every closet episode, every escape to church, every math class, every financial crime solved, every step, every fear, every tear—even her relationship with Mac and her friendship with Claire—had led her to this very moment.

And she smelled so bad.

With the back of her hand, she wiped at her nose.

God was in it all. All the time.

Laughter coming from the south end of the street beyond the alley yanked her to attention. Peeking out of the shadows, she saw a group of young people, possibly teens, heading up the street toward her hotel.

She stepped back to get cover.

Only she didn't step into the shadows. She'd backed right into something that hadn't been there ten seconds ago.

A person.

An arm grabbed her by the waist and a hand slapped across her mouth.

Jiminy! Someone had her in a vise grip.

Shoving both elbows into his sides, she kicked backwards, trying to locate a knee to crack.

But the man probably outweighed her by forty pounds and had a good seven or eight inches on her. With way too much ease, he slid her backwards.

Not again. And just when I'd figured everything out.

CHAPTER 47

He pushed her up against a wall, his forearm pinning her top half to the brick. His hand still covered her mouth. Isa got a whiff of aftershave. Musk something.

This accoster wasn't from the community house. She'd never seen him.

"I only want to ask a couple of questions," he said, glancing at the end of the alley.

Good English, but an accent that told her he was a local.

"Please, do not scream when I remove my hand. Okay?"

His fresh, minty breath combatted her reek and that would have been embarrassing if he wasn't accosting her.

From her days with cartel members back in New Mexico, every thug she'd encountered had a wicked case of halitosis. Not so with Mr. Clean here. Something was obviously missing.

Like the unpleasant attitudes of bad guys.

Who was this groomed and polite stalker?

"Okay?" he asked again, the plea almost negotiable.

This could *not* be a member of the trafficking ring she'd just escaped.

"I will let you go if you answer honestly."

As the group of teens moseyed past the alley, he leaned into her harder. Watched the giggling group pass.

She took the opportunity to get some leverage, pressed her foot against the wall then thrust her forearms into his chest. The push-off took everything she had.

Thank God for adrenaline.

Because rule number one in self-defense is to never take your eyes off your enemy. Her timing worked. She'd caught him off guard while he watched the teens.

He stumbled back. Lost his advantage.

Isa made a dash. Headed for the lighted street, that group of noisy teens her next cover.

But he was on her heels.

That guy was fast.

Take two. Hand over her mouth again and arm dragging her back into the alley, he had her a second time saying, "You're feistier than promised."

She kicked wildly.

"I am not paid enough."

So ... he was paid to nab her?

"This will only take a few moments, so be still."

Self-defense rule number two? Never, ever believe a kidnapper's promises. She wasn't going down that road. She had trust issues to begin with.

She bit at his Irish Spring fingers.

His sigh suggested exhaustion. Fresh Breath must have had a hard day.

"You're making this difficult."

She tried to say, *forget you,* but he pressed his hand in closer and it curled her lips up against her teeth. The teeth that hadn't been brushed in three days.

She tried yanking her upper body left then right, then left—like a tae kwon do fighter—to loosen his grip.

Didn't work. He just tightened things up.

"If you do not do this my way, I'll be forced to interrogate you elsewhere." He pulled her spine closer into his chest. "Can we talk for just one minute?"

Isa settled down. Knocked the back of her head against his chest in an aggressive *you-won't-tell-me-what-to-do …but yes* move.

"You are small, but you are scary."

Oh, brother, was he going to talk his way through this?

He cleared his throat. "I think I will try a different angle and hold on to you while I ask my question."

Already, he was breaking promises.

"I'm going to ask you your name, and I want you to give me an honest answer. You can do that, right?"

Isa let her tensed-up shoulders relax a little.

"You nod for yes. You shake your head for no."

Wait for the name, then decide the next move.

"Isabella Phillips."

She shook her head for a firm *no* while seizing her gasp mid-breath.

"Too late," he chuckled, moving his hand from her mouth. "I felt your answer. You're Isabella."

With gigantic shakes of her head, she cleared up the mistake. "I am not. I've never heard that name."

He let go of his grip around her waist.

Isa dropped to her feet, swung around, and faced him.

"Jacob Lahache," he pronounced. "Ever heard of this man?" He wiped his hands like he was done with the whole ordeal. "I am going to have to charge him extra."

CHAPTER 48

"Let me get this straight. Jacob paid *you?*" She pointed at his face, which was framed by a dark, cropped beard and hair cut short at the sides. He wore a collared shirt beneath a close-cut suit jacket.

Who was this guy?

She shook her head hoping information might tumble out of some forgotten file in her brain. "Jacob paid you to find me?"

"That is incorrect," he said, knitting his fingers patiently together. "He paid me to put you on a plane."

Isa folded her arms tight across her chest "He what?"

"Easier said than done."

"And where is this plane supposed to take me?"

"Oh, I have bought you a ticket to Albuquerque, New Mexico."

Isa's hands went to her dirty hair. "My gosh, he's one gigantic control freak."

"He said to tell you that he doesn't need you finding leads now. He has found his own."

"What else did he say?" she dropped her hands to her hips.

"That ... that without me," he hesitated a beat before finishing his sentence in an annoyingly honest manner, "you would find too much trouble."

"And who are you?"

"I'm the connection you were supposed to make. But, uh …" he scratched his head. "Something went wrong. I don't know where." He shrugged and continued, "Until he told me to pick you up, I didn't even know you were here in Málaga."

Isa stomped the dirt. "Dang Jacob."

"It is interesting, no?" He flipped his hands in the air. "He said the same about you."

Isa clamped her eyes shut. This was just too much. Too, too much to process.

"Why didn't you just ask me who I was to begin with?" She opened one eye. "You didn't have to waylay me." Then the other eye opened. "What's wrong with you? What's wrong with you *and* Jacob?"

"You were sneaking around the alley. I thought you might be a petty criminal." He flashed a wide smile of pure white pearls. "Plus, Jacob said you would prove to be difficult. I have been watching your hotel for a couple of days now."

Every muscle in her body went slack. She fizzled like a dying sparkler on the fourth of July. "I'm too tired to talk about this." She started for the end of the alley.

"Wait," he called after her. "That is not the way to the airport."

She kept walking. *Bath. Coffee. Phone.* She needed all three.

Her would-be captor caught up just as she reached the end of the alley. She didn't even stop to give the area around her hotel a decent detective survey.

"It's okay," he said as if she cared about his mission. "You probably have some things to pick up at your hotel. The plane does not leave until midnight. We have a couple of hours."

He stuck to her as they crossed the empty street.

She couldn't care less. She, without Jacob or his all-over-the-place plans, had just discovered a trafficking ring holding innocent children captive. This was her mission now.

"Where have you been, anyway?" The gentleman stalker with fresh breath asked.

"What's your name?" Isa asked, head down, eyes on the pavement.

"I am Bowen Banderas," he said as if famous.

She stepped up on the curb of the hotel's *porte cochere*, eyes on the double doors that led to a bath.

Fresh Breath kept talking. "But my close acquaintances call me 'Bowie.' I think that you should call me Bowie, as well. We will be friends. *Si*?"

"Sure," she said pushing one of the glass doors open. "We can be big buds."

Without looking his way, Isa approached the reception desk.

The young lady behind the desk eyed Isa but smiled at Bowie, who'd pulled up beside her.

"I lost my room key," Isa told her.

The receptionist frowned. Made an obvious attempt to hold her breath and talk at the same time. "Name?" she asked.

Isa didn't blame her. She could hardly handle her own scent. "Isabella Phillips."

The woman typed something into her computer. "I will need to see your ID," she took a slight, but noticeable step backwards.

Bowie interjected. "Excuse, please. We have been a ... camping. And Isabella has lost, well, everything, including her appropriate papers."

"I remember seeing you," the receptionist answered, sounding like she had no intention of prolonging the interaction. She hit her keyboard, swiped a plastic card through an encoder and stretched her arm to lay the room key in front of Isa.

"I'll see you later," Isa said glancing at Bowie and heading to the elevators. "I'm sure you'll be around."

"I am to wait for you in the lobby, yes?" he asked, following on her heels.

"No. You can go." She punched the elevator button.

"But, uh ... we are going to the airport." He made light of it all. As if he didn't have a clue.

The elevator doors opened.

He got on with her.

"I'm going to take a shower." Isa pressed the button for the third floor.

"Yes. I did not want to say something, but this is a good idea. I would not think you would want to offend the other passengers on your plane." He flashed the pearly whites again.

What a tactful and kind guy. And he couldn't be more delusional. "I'm not getting on a plane, Bowie."

The elevator doors closed.

"But if I do not deliver you, then I will not get paid," he stated. "It's a business transaction, and I am sure that you can understand that this is also for the best. Málaga has obviously not been, well ..." He chuckled. "It has not been a good experience for you." Looking her up and down, he asked the obvious question again. "But where have you been?"

Isa watched the number of the floors light up until the doors opened.

"Hmm?" he asked, brows raised expectantly. "I don't think I could have missed you. I've been an investigator for three years and have never lost a client."

She stepped out of the elevator.

Bowie stepped out of the elevator.

Isa sighed.

"I, uh think we have some things to clarify," Bowie started.

Isa flipped him a not-now palm.

Down the hall she went, Bowie shadowing her like a good private eye. At her room door, she turned to face him while swiping the new room key. "You can go home now. I'm not getting on a plane."

"But ..." he shook his head, eyes pleading with her. "... this is not an option. I have made a contract with Jacob Lahache."

Isa stepped inside her room. "I'll talk with Jacob and explain everything. But I'm not leaving Spain." She rubbed at her forehead. "At least not yet."

"But—"

Holding up her hand to stop him again, she said, "I found my own lead, followed up by visiting a gentleman's club, was kidnapped, drugged, escaped, and I now ..." unexpected emotion sprung on her, but she blinked back the tears forming. "I've fallen in love. I'm not leaving. Thank you for coming."

"Oh, no, no, no," he said getting his foot into the threshold before she could shut the door. "That is a good story." His lips parted, teeth sparkling. "I wish to hear it."

"If you hear my story, you have to help me."

He pulled his chin in looking intrigued. "I do not know what it is that I will help you with, but if I do this whatever thing, you will agree to leave, and I will fulfill my contract with Jacob?"

"My kidnappers have my passport. I can't travel. Applying for a new passport at the embassy could take what? Three days?"

He chuckled. "Passports are not a problem for me. I have connections and can have you one in twenty-four hours."

She frowned. "A fake one."

"There are some things we should not question."

Isa opened the door wide and stepped aside.

"Ah, good, then." Bowie followed.

She tossed her room key on the dresser and eased down onto the edge of the bed, the weight of her ordeal getting heavier by the second. "Bowie, here's the truth that you'll need to get through your head."

He waited, black-as-coal brows inching up his forehead. "Yes?"

"I'm not leaving without Chia."

CHAPTER 49

Bowie eyed the cute but smelly Isa sideways. "What is a Chia?"

This Isabella Phillips heaved exasperation then pulled neatly folded items from the hotel's dresser drawers, which he found intriguing. He thought he alone used the hotel amenities of deep dresser drawers instead of the wrinkle-inflicting, shallow luggage.

But what was she talking about now? He asked again, "What is this Chia?"

"It's not an it. It's a girl from Nigeria," she answered, opening the bathroom door. "You'll need to wait in the hall. I'm going to bathe now." Isa pointed to the room door.

"The hall? I will wait here. You can lock that door, you know." He gestured at the bathroom.

From beneath the folded clothes in her hand, a hairbrush appeared, and she pointed it at him. While it was a very substantial hairbrush, it was hilarious to see this disadvantaged Isabella threaten him with it. When speaking of her, Lahache had mentioned the word *feisty* more than once. "You cannot order me about with a hairbrush."

"You'd be surprised what I can do with this." She narrowed one of her bloodshot eyes.

He lifted his hands in the air. "Okay, okay. But you must promise me that you will let me back in when you have ..."

he shoved his fist to his sternum, coughed, "... when you have become presentable." He eyed her from head to toe. "And that cannot happen soon enough."

She padded on into the bathroom. Shut the door. The knob wiggled when she locked it.

Before letting himself out, he explained his mission one more time for good measure. "Jacob Lahache has paid me to deliver you to the airport, put you on a plane to Albuquerque. This is my contractual agreement for which I am bound. I am sure you understand this. I am a man of my word."

The voice coming through the bathroom door was louder than it should have been, considering her size. "A man of his word would not stand by and let a young girl kidnapped from Nigeria be forced into prostitution. So, while you're in the hall, you can get on your phone, change my flight, and add a seat."

He extracted the small roll of antacids from his front pocket, unwrapped a portion of wrapper, and popped a pink one. Head shaking, he pulled the bedroom door closed behind him and slid down the wall to sit cross-legged on the floor.

He ripped another chewable from the roll and mumbled, "This is not going to end well."

CHAPTER 50

Jacob eyed Marko as he guzzled down half of the twelve-ouncer.

Made Jacob shudder a little. Or maybe it was the chilly bar.

Wiping beer foam from his upper lip with the back of his hand, Marko said, "It is a complex situation."

"Run it by me one more time." Jacob pushed his glass of OJ to the side.

"You don't like beer?" Marko asked, motioning for the bartender to bring him another.

"I'm not drinking tonight." Jacob said, drumming the bar with his fingers. "But anyway ..."

"The question is, can I trust someone who doesn't drink with me?"

Marko, Marko, you can't trust anybody in this town and if you don't learn this now, you're going to have a very short gangster career.

"I can be trusted with a glass of orange juice same as I can be trusted with a beer," Jacob said.

Marko, his face rosy and gullible and eager as a puppy, smiled wide.

"Start over with this plan of yours," Jacob said, guilt stabbing. Or was that chest pain?

"It is not *my* plan." Marko polished off his beer. Pulled over the second glass the barkeep set on the counter. "Londo and Mike. They are the ones connected."

"Connected to an up-and-coming gang, right? That's what I heard you say?"

"I can't tell you more unless you tell me you want a piece of this most exciting action. Londo says you're risky."

"Londo couldn't find his butt with both hands and a map."

Marko shrugged. "He knows people. People who don't like this woman."

"The woman I saw in Bambino's? With the black dress and scarf?"

Marko nodded. "That woman ..." he sipped at his beer foam. "Londo says she is no match for the Ghettas."

"Ghettas?"

"A new coalition."

"A baby gang?"

Marko, growing more gullible green, asked, "What is this thing you call a baby gang?"

Jacob stifled a cough. He had no idea where Isa was. His contact in Spain hadn't returned his latest text, and frankly, the stall in intel had him second-guessing his plans. Maybe he wasn't supposed to be in Italy. Maybe he wasn't supposed to be chasing criminals anymore. Maybe he *still* wasn't sure who he was. Maybe a lot of things. "Baby gangs." He flicked his hand in the air. "You know ... young guns fighting their way into the traffic." When he pushed his hair back, the temperature almost singed his fingers. How did his hair feel hot when the bar resembled an igloo? But he kept up his game, kept talking to Marko. "Everyone knows the old-style families are on their way out. It's all about the new guys on the streets."

Man, he needed a siesta.

Marko nodded with enthusiasm. "Londo. Mike. They align with a new coalition."

"Okay. I got that. What about the woman?"

"You in?"

Jacob patted the bar. *Make it look like this is a big decision.* He rolled his head around his shoulders. "Yeah, okay. I'm in. I didn't come to Italy to serve pizza. What ya got?"

Pride lifted the edges of Marko's lips. "I have officially promoted a foot soldier. A smart one." Even his chest swelled. "That will move me up in important issues."

"Yeah, yeah. Good for you. Tell me more about the woman leader."

"Sophia Ricci something. Italians have names as long as a sentence. Too long to remember."

"Sophia Evelina Ricci Ventura?"

Marko almost dropped his beer. "You know her?"

"I've heard of her."

"Doesn't matter." He shrugged. "She'll be out of the picture."

Jacob's heart sped up, and that coupled with his body heat, he thought he might be headed to the red zone of a stroke. "What does that mean?"

"Londo and Mike. They will do the cleanup." Marko's eyes sparkled with the talk of a big takedown. "They are related to the family. Third cousins, I think."

Kill Sophia? Jacob would need to get to her first. "What's a cleanup?"

Of course, he knew. But just to confirm—

"They will bring order back to the streets."

"You're talking more than pulling cash out of Bambino's then?"

"Yes." Marko drained his second glass. "More."

Jacob let the info marinate … or stew, considering his current personal thermometer.

"This Sophia whatever, whatever will be exterminated." He gave Jacob a quick nod. "Yes, what is a woman doing in this business anyway?"

"There's a hit on Sophia, then."

"She's good as dead, that woman."

CHAPTER 51

Exhausted, Isa hadn't taken the oomph needed to get a physical study on the man who'd attacked her in the alley but whom she'd also arm-twisted into helping her. As he adjusted into the back seat of the cab, she gave him the once-over.

Okay, twice-over.

He looked more tightly wound accountant than investigator bad boy. Accountant, investigator, friend, or foe, time made the choices for her now because Chia—

The cabbie asked for a location.

Isa rattled off the street name she thought she remembered.

The cabbie stated no such street existed.

Isa tried the name again, adding the ever-popular Spanish *O* at the end.

Bingo. He said he knew the place.

Bowie said it was a bad part of town.

Hello, low-level informants don't hang out in the upscale burbs, Buddy.

Isa glanced at Bowie's shoes.

Leather oxfords.

Oh, brother.

"I don't think you know what you're doing," Bowie offered.

Probably she didn't. But saying so would be unprofessional. "Did you call Jacob?"

"Not yet. I have not called him yet."

"Doesn't he need to know we are not getting on the flight?"

"I don't want to disappoint him."

Disappointing Jacob wasn't something she'd ever concerned herself with. He forever deserved a letdown or two. "He's a big boy." Isa pressed at a wrinkle in her polo. "He won't be surprised that I've caused a hiccup."

"I'll call him once we have one."

"One what?"

"Plan." He faced her. "Excuse me, but I am not at all sure you know what we are doing."

She frowned.

He shrugged. "I am paid to observe these kinds of things."

"We're looking for an address because I'm only forty-six percent sure I can find the place where I was held hostage. That's the plan, by the way."

"I see." He patted at his jacket's inside pocket. "If you were fifty percent sure you could find the place, what would we be doing?"

"We would be proceeding to that place. But at forty-six percent, there is the chance it would waste our time. On my way back to Málaga tonight, I cut through a woody area, and I'm not sure if I turned east or west."

Bowie gave Isa a dead-eye stare.

Inside, where the dragon lived, her confidence faltered. The beast must have given up on her somewhere in the alley and gone dormant at last. At this moment in her adventures, she wasn't sure if a dormant dragon was a good thing or bad. She stared out the window, wondering if after being drugged, held hostage, and sleep-deprived, if kidnapping a girl who'd been kidnapped was doable with the overly polished and a bit stiff professional beside her.

"Now would be a good time for you to tell me about the woody area and your hostage situation. I might could get you to ..." He rolled his eyes around in his head like he didn't believe a word of her story so far. "Eighty-nine percent?"

Isa smirked. "Make fun if you want. I am an accountant and I calculate risks with percentages."

His chuckles just kept coming. "So I have heard."

What else had Mr. Jacob-always-pushing-envelopes told Bowie?

Beside her, Bowie shifted. "So, tell me."

Isa didn't face him but started the long story with Pepe and how he'd surprisingly tipped her off about the viper pit called Club Exóticas.

CHAPTER 52

Pepe peered out through a crack he'd opened in the doorway. Eyes the size of duck eggs, he let an inappropriate word in Spanish slip, then yanked the door shut.

Isa knocked again. "I need your help, Pepe."

The crack opened again. "I thought we agreed you wouldn't come back here." Pepe gave Bowie a skeptical squint. "It's the middle of the night and now you've brought the police."

What? Isa's swerved to face Bowie. "You're police?" That one hadn't occurred to her.

Bowie's palms shot to the air. "No, no, no." Head shaking, he said, "I am not the police. And we are not here to talk about me. Unless you have now pulled me into a trick which ..." He exhaled, seemingly resigned to the confusion. "Which ... I would not find surprising. Jacob warned me—"

"You look like police to me," Pepe cut in, trying to close the door.

Bowie's leather oxford had found its way into Pepe's threshold.

Indignant, Pepe eyed the obstacle.

Score a giant point for Bowie.

But this nonsensical interaction wasn't moving things along. She thought of Awena. And Maria. And how life kept dishing up peculiar characters.

She tried a redirect. "I have a couple of questions, Pepe. I've met a girl who needs our help."

Pepe's face scrunched up in anguish. Not in a he *hated-a-girl-was-in-trouble-anguish*, but like he *hated-what-he-was-about-to-do* anguish.

He opened the door.

"This can't take long." He stuck his head out, looked up and down the street. Then he motioned Isa and Bowie inside and shut and locked the door behind them. "You can't keep coming here," he said his stubby finger pointing at Isa. He sliced the finger through the air to aim at Bowie. "So, who are you?"

"I am a private investigator helping to get this Isabella Phillips out of our country." Bowie put his hand over his heart as if he had an allegiance with Pepe already. "I respectfully request your help. I think you and I both want the same thing."

Isa rolled her eyes.

Pepe shifted from one hip to the other. "If you're talking about getting her," the finger swung back in Isa's direction, "out of here, then I am in. With limitations."

Bowie glanced around at the disarray of boxes. "What business are you conducting here?"

"Knives. Mace," Isa answered hoping like heck Pepe wouldn't get antsy and throw them out.

"I smell tobacco," Bowie said.

"No, you don't," Isa answered before Pepe could.

"But I do." Bowie's minty smile appeared as he nodded with ridiculous enthusiasm.

"Well, it's none of your business what I do here, and you better get your question out before I change my mind about all this." Pepe backed for the door.

"The gang working Club Exóticas," Isa said rubbing the bridge of her nose. "Where would we find the house where their girls live?"

Pepe's little body almost deflated. "I'm going to hate myself for this," he said.

CHAPTER 53

Jacob pulled the collar of his windbreaker closer around his neck. A breeze kicked up and rain pellets spotted the pavement in front of him.

So what the heck was going on with Isa?

And how had things gotten so complicated with the cousins and Marko?

Bounty. Stick with the goal.

How would he intervene on the cousins' plans and keep Sophia alive until he could bring her in—the number one goal.

Jacob looked behind him, rubbing at his sore neck.

Something was off with his body. Had been for a couple of days now.

He rubbed at his forehead, which felt warm considering the chill that ran down his back.

He sniffed.

Shoot. He couldn't smell the rain. COVID-19 symptoms included loss of smell and taste.

That's when out of the darkness ahead, headlights swelled.

Was he seeing right?

The lights swerved right at him.

The fog that had rolled into his brain slowed his reaction, but when it occurred to him this was a car about to run him over, he slid sideways.

The vehicle jumped the sidewalk. Almost clipped him in the legs.

Trapped against a building, he knew something not so good took shape.

The back, passenger side door opened and a guy in a long raincoat, a gun pulled, stepped toward him.

Someone was at his back, a barrel poking his sore ribs.

Sore ribs?

Jacob coughed.

CHAPTER 54

Shielded by a pine that was sure to induce an allergic reaction, Isa avoided touching the tree and zeroed in on the front door of the brick country house. Frazzled and nerves raw, Bowie's verbal practicalities weren't helping.

"This is not wise," Bowie, squatted a couple of feet in front of her declared. "We should have had the cab driver wait down the hill. When you sent him away, did you think about how we would spring a hostage and get back to the city without a car?"

Isa didn't move her eyes. "Maybe I didn't think that through, okay? But I know the way on foot. I blazed a trail earlier tonight. Remember?"

"Okay, try this for a new plan. Tonight, we watch for traffic patterns. We can determine who comes and goes and when they do. We put you on a plane for Albuquerque tomorrow. Then, with a bigger gun and bigger guy, I will come and get your Chia in two … three days tops."

"I told you. I am not leaving without her. So if you want me on a plane quickly, then we'll have to grab her now."

Bowie dropped to his butt. Crossed his arms over his knees. "This is not going to turn out well." He dug around in a front pocket.

Ignoring the temptation to pick up a rock and throw it at the back of his head, Isa rubbed her eyes. Stretched her arms. Put her gaze back on the house.

The front door of the old brick house opened.

Isa leaned forward and slapped at his shoulder. "Look! Someone's coming out."

Bowie inched forward. "Oh no," he moaned, lifting back into the squat position. "You are correct." He reached around to his back side and pulled out a Glock just like the one she had back home, and now missed. She fished the third can of Mace Pepe had given her out of her jacket pocket.

"And now …" Bowie pulled up to his feet. "It rains. This is … how do you Americans say it?" His hands flew in frustration. "Perfect."

Sure enough, droplets of water peppered her head. "You melt in the rain?" she asked, realizing the man coming through the community house door was Tem.

"I melt at the thought of taking on an entire house of gang members with one gun and one can of pepper spray. But, I am a man of manners and we will get the lady what she desires this night if her Chia is, in fact, here."

Oh, brother. Everything, from the juvenile bikers stealing her first can of Mace, to getting herself kidnapped a second time, to inheriting this quirky and reluctant partner, felt sloppy. The tug to take control and start counting tree trunks hit hard.

Headlights swept across the landscape in front of them. Both ducked.

A car approached from the opposite direction, pulling into the gravel drive. It swung in close to the house.

She grabbed Bowie by the back of his suit jacket. "That's her!" Again, but louder, "That's her!"

Out of the back passenger doors crawled two girls. The one on the far side was tall and unmistakably, Chia.

She rounded the front end and started for the man on the front porch. The driver of the car stayed put and yelled, "Hey, Tem!" motioning for Tem to approach the car.

Bowie's groan expressed some reluctance on his part. "Here we go."

The next thing she knew, Bowie scooted around the tree and skidded down the hill.

Isa sprang upright and followed.

The sprinkles hadn't developed into an all-out rain.

Bowie turned when he reached the bottom of the incline. "You coming? This is your confiscation."

Isa tightened her grip on the Mace can while she gained downhill momentum. She passed Bowie, stumbling just a bit. "Let's do it." Grateful for boots and not flip flops, Isa kept going.

Bowie passed her, gun drawn, and headed for the car.

She'd forgotten to ask who would take who, so since he went for the car, she made for Tem. He didn't seem pleased to see her.

From somewhere near the car, a female squealed and let go a string of words in an unrecognizable language.

Both hands on the can, Isa aimed the Mace like a gun.

Tem scowled. Said something unkind.

Off to the right, she heard Bowie exchange pleasantries with the car driver. "You will stay in the car but give me the keys."

Tem, realizing Isa meant business, started for her, arms out like he wanted a piece of her neck.

They ran for each other like lovers in a movie. Only Tem probably didn't need a hug, and she was gonna gas him.

At about four feet of distance between them now, and maybe not close enough, Isa jammed her thumb into the nozzle of her can.

Mace magic sprayed far and wide.

Only.

The spray barely brushed Tem's really close hands and arms.

Had she not lined up the spray nozzle before blasting?

He laid siege to her wrists while she fumbled with the nozzle.

The can of Mace fell to the ground and rolled.

Isa thrust her arms upward and broke his grasp, but as if in slow motion, she watched Tem's right arm pull back like a taut bow in preparation to let his fist-arrow fly right into her jaw.

A fine mist covered her hair. Rain again?

No. The filmy substance smelled like nutmeg and copper. Like nerve-gassing, chemical-altering nutmeg and copper.

Tem let go an ear-piercing screech. Then let go of Isa, hands clawing at his own eyes.

He trembled like a volcano about to erupt then hit the gravel walkway, contorting like zombie overdosed on caffein.

Behind her, Isa heard Bowie say, "I am sorry but, now, you have to get out of the car."

She stumbled backwards. Turned for the car.

There, tall and beautiful and brave stood Chia, eyes wide and the can of pepper spray in her hand.

Isa grabbed her. Pulled her in for a colossal squeeze. *Unbelievable.* Gratitude floated up like a choir of angels entering the crescendo.

"In the car, please," Bowie urged, motioning for them to come.

The driver slouched on the driveway, sizing up Isa, then Bowie, then writhing Tem, and from the looks of his confused expression, he wasn't going to put up a fight for the car.

Bowie motioned for Isa and Chia to hurry.

Isa had Chia by the arm.

Tem continued to shriek between groans of misery.

Yanking the back door open, Isa instructed Chia to get in. Looked around for the other girl.

The petite girl was at the hood of the car, hand over her mouth.

"Come," Isa said. "Get in. We're here to rescue you."

But the girl backed away.

"No, come with us," Isa repeated.

"Yes," Chia echoed. She scooted across the seat and had her head out the window. "Come and get into the car."

But the other girl continued to back away, moving into a shadow.

Trying a direct order, Isa commanded, "You must come!"

The girl bolted for the back of the house.

Isa started after her but stopped short when Bowie loudly mentioned that people in the house might be waking up now.

Isa made for the car's passenger side. From the corner of her eye, she saw the community house's front door open and Nasha stepping, mouth open, through the threshold.

Bowie's gun made a target switch.

CHAPTER 55

As the fuzzy sense of being drawn from reality rolled over him, Jacob laid his head against the back of the leather seat.

The men on either side of him must have considered him an easy catch. He'd hardly fought. Had issued more threats than punches. But that was okay because now—slouched and barely there—he occupied a position to gather all kinds of information.

Even if he felt like death warmed over.

"So ... where are we going tonight?" He had trouble leaning into his standard and effective sarcasm which typically kept his audience unnerved. "Let me guess. We're off to the theater?"

The bigger soldier on his right chuckled. Said something in Italian to the others in the car.

The guy in the front passenger seat flipped his visor down, an expressionless face behind sunglasses.

Sunglasses at midnight.

Jacob was far removed from intimidation. Fevers and chills did that to a person.

The man in the mirror said, "It will be a show, all right, and you'll have a front-row seat."

"What time is the curtain call?" Jacob asked. "I could use a drink."

No one answered.

Jacob closed his eyes. Swallowed, which wasn't easy— his throat had thickened.

"He doesn't look so good."

Who had said that?

Jacob blinked as he lifted his head, an idea tunneling through the fog. "I got a question." His voice and brain were not lining up correctly, but he put the request out there. "Any you brothers got an aspirin?"

The gangsters on either side of him stiffened.

"Tylenol? No? I think you gentlemen just loaded a primo case of COVID into the back seat of your nice car here."

The screech of rubber grabbing asphalt split the dead-air silence. The two back doors sprang open, and Jacob's guards made a fast exit.

Nice reaction. Time to exit the car and make a run for it. But he didn't feel like running. He felt like napping. The now empty backseat looked inviting. Maybe he should catch a nap before his next move.

Moving headfirst into a welcoming, dark tunnel of oblivion, Jacob leaned, then crashed, into the back seat. He heard someone say, "Hey, Joey, I think that guy's dead ..."

CHAPTER 56

Doing eighty, Bowie jerked the wheel to the right, barely missing the oversized pothole in the slushy country road.

The car fishtailed.

From the backseat, Chia squeaked a foreign word.

Isa grabbed the dash.

He should be at home in bed, Isa on a plane, and this job finished.

He would have to reconsider accepting contracts with Americans. His last American contract had been with the CIA, and they had cut dinners at his favorite restaurant from the budget. Not to mention that the North Americans eternally wanted their contracts finished early. The rest of the world understood the finesse needed to appropriately pull a case apart, examine it, and carefully plan the execution. Not so with Americans. They wanted their lists checked off and cases closed by the dinner that was not included in the expense sheet.

Enslaved to their watches, they were.

"We should have gotten the other girl," Isa said, hanging on to the dashboard. "We had time."

He ignored that statement because if she had her way, Isa would undoubtedly make him turn around and go back to the community house. Instead, he made his own demand. "What were you *thinking* when you jumped out of the car and pounced on the large woman at the door?"

"I want to rescue them all," the bleeding-heart, all-American woman declared.

"From Nasha," Chia echoed from the backseat. "The woman is cruel."

"Well," Bowie said, shaking his head. "Thanks to Isa, this Nasha nurses a broken leg now."

When the large woman had come through the door, Isa had flown from the car, caught the woman behind the knee with her boot, and taken her to the ground alongside the man yelping from the pepper spray.

This was when the car's driver had made for the woods, and they borrowed his vehicle.

The little American in her big boots was certainly pleased with their success tonight, but this would not be the end of it. This he knew. They'd stirred a hornet's nest.

Bowie glanced at Isa's feet then back to her frown. "You should probably get boots that fit. You'll get blisters wearing shoes too big."

"Watch out!" Isa yelled.

In the middle of the country road stood a man, his shotgun aimed for the car.

"Duck!" she screamed.

He heard Chia squeal. Felt her hit the back of his seat as she dove for the floorboard.

Hand over fist, he jerked the steering wheel, shoving his foot to the brake.

The windshield shattered.

A boom reverberated.

CHAPTER 57

Their borrowed car swerving and fishtailing, Isa lifted her head to check on Bowie.

Still upright, he had a ferocious grip on the wheel.

Another gun blast, and Bowie announced, "Now, I am angry."

The car slid to a stop.

"Where's your gun?" she asked, knocking glass off her shoulder.

"Floor," he said through his teeth, throwing the car in reverse.

The guy in the road sprinted toward them. Isa went down, hands moving across the floorboard while the car zigzagged backwards.

Found the Glock.

Gripped it.

Lifted to a seated position, Glock pointed.

First shot—her hands kicked up. But she held the Glock tight.

The man, pumping his shotgun, dipped low and looking like the Hulk in fatigues, he kept coming at them.

"Yikes," Isa screeched.

Bowie threw on the brakes. "Try again!"

Second shot. Kicked up dirt close to the man's feet. He yelped.

Then Bowie shoved the car into drive and hit the gas. "More!" he yelled, barreling straight for man, the car fishtailing. "One more. And hit him this time!"

The man stopped. Aimed.

But with Mad Max Bowie at the wheel, the car became a bigger, badder weapon than a flimsy shotgun.

The man dropped his aim and started backing up.

"Are you going to fire?" Bowie inquired. "If so, please do it now."

"You're going to hit him!" Isa exclaimed. The thought of that man, shotgun or no shotgun, spread like a stomped cockroach across the car's grill sucked the air from her lungs.

Eight seconds more and the man would be a hood ornament.

She grabbed the steering wheel. Yanked it.

They nearly missed him as he dove for the ditch.

Giving her a death glance, Bowie took back control of the steering, keeping the pedal to the gas engaged.

Isa flipped around in her seat to see the man crawl up from the ditch.

Bowie rounded a curve, and she lost sight of the man in the road.

"It's over." She patted Chia on the back. "It's over."

Chia rose, eyes wide. "I think we have angered the demons of Nasha."

Isa faced front again and set Bowie's gun beside him. Of course, Nasha had demons. The entire unsafe house reeked of demonic activity. Boy, could Awena do some damage in that place. "That was close."

Bowie's laser glint could have cut through a diamond. "You grabbed my steering wheel. You should never grab another man's steering wheel."

"I couldn't stand the thought of his body on the hood."

"But I wanted him dead."

"But we got away."

"But I needed to investigate him. Get his identity papers."

"He's a gangster." She shrugged. "Probably doesn't even have legal papers."

"He wore an *Ejército de Tierra* uniform."

"A what?"

"Army."

"Like Spain is officially protecting something back there?"

Bowie pushed back into his seat but kept his eyes on the road as it widened into a main thoroughfare. "More like officials are *unofficially* protecting what goes on back there."

"You're saying that local authorities look the other way while girls are stolen and sold as goods?"

From the backseat, Chia gasped.

"Not just local but federal police," Bowie said tossing a glance back at Chia.

Isa rested her head against the seat. What was wrong with the world these days?

"And one more thing," Bowie said, pulling onto a highway.

With an open windshield, the wind, the sprinkles, and her loose hair slapped her face.

He looked over. "You are not a very good shot."

CHAPTER 58

Tree bark lined the walls of his throat. Sandbags covered his arms and legs. And who glued his eyelids shut?

From floating around in some ethereal dream, Jacob had a hard time understanding why all of a sudden, everything felt weighty and real.

"Jacob."

Jonna?

No. That was over. Thanks to Isa's insistence that he suffered from multiple personality disorder.

A still-shot of Isa in a pine tree rushed across his brain. Maybe he was back in the cartel's castle in the Sandia mountains.

Guns, and cars, and ... pizza.

Italy.

Jacob's lids popped open.

Fuzzy around the edges, two silhouettes moved around at the end of his bed. One had a long appendage off the shoulder. A tree limb? A stick?

A rifle.

He raised his head—which proved harder than it should. Looked beside him.

His heart kicked up, pumping much-needed adrenaline to his brain and limbs. Yanking at a tube, then pulling at the tape, he extracted a needle at his wrist, blood oozing. No way would he lie there like a victim while she watched.

She reached out and touched his arm. "Don't be afraid, Jay Hernandez."

Jacob knocked her hand away. *Not staying or hanging out in her mercy bed.* He pushed the sheet off to reveal missing pants.

She raised her brows.

He slid the sheet back across.

"But you're not Jay Hernandez," she said, folding her arms in her lap. "You're Jacob Lahache."

In a mustard-yellow, crushed-velvet, wing-back chair, sat Sophia Evelina Ricci Ventura. The dress snug, the legs long. She had her hair pulled back in a taut bun.

"Or is it James Hawkins?" She smiled, her face aglow in the sun stretching through a nearby window.

Play along, even though your entire body is at war with itself.

A cough pushed up from his chest and, instinctively, Jacob covered his mouth with his elbow, eyes never leaving Sophia.

"Doc said he should see improvement day or two." The voice came from the end of the bed.

Jacob checked. Yep, one of the guys who'd nabbed him on the street. He didn't recognize the other gangster in a fitted suit. Couldn't recall much of what happened after they put him in the car, either.

"You've taken ill." Sophia approached the obvious as if she were his sister. "We're trying to help you get better."

Clearing his throat wasn't easy with all the tree bark. Talking wasn't better, but he needed to manage some smack talk to locate the upper hand. "Let's ..." he tried clearing the airways again. "Let's get on with the business I'm here for."

"Good. I was about to ask you why you've come to Italy ... and why would you be working for a pizzeria that I finance?"

"To take you back to the States. You ..." he stifled a cough mid chest. "Jumped bail."

A smile chocked full of charm eased across her flawlessly made-up face. "Oh, Jacob. You do entertain me."

"Hands up," Jacob maneuvered himself up, resting his elbows. Another cough kicked but he held it down. "I'm taking you in for bail jumping ..." Wheeze. "And other crimes against humanity."

CHAPTER 59

As bullets sprayed the windshield of Isa's Corolla parked outside of Coffee Magic, Awena whispered to her from a vortex somewhere. "All things happen for a reason, my daughter."

Demons floating nearby laughed out loud.

In one smooth motion, Isa sat upright, knocking the white wool blanket and off-white dog curled up at the other end of the sofa to the floor.

The dog yipped and jumped to Chia, who still slept soundly on an air mattress on the floor three feet away.

Where was she?

"Good morning."

Isa turned her head to see Bowie coming around a kitchen island, a white coffee mug in each hand.

The fresh brew filled her depleted senses.

In a sweatshirt, jeans, standard mint-smile, and wet wavy hair, Bowie plopped down beside her. Handed her a cup. "I don't have cream."

"I'm good without it." But she'd really, really love a big dose of mocha-almond creamer. Couldn't deny she felt deprived as the images of the last 72.5 hours replayed across her brain. She shook her head at the memories, trying to file them into the appropriate boxes she'd need to open after this first cup.

Bowie pointed at the pup curled up at the back of sleeping Chia's knees. "This dog, he prefers women."

"Women come here often?" Isa asked, hating herself for such a lame and obvious question. Where was her brain this morning?

Bowie sent her quizzical glance. "My sister. She watches Luna when I work. She should take this rescue mongrel to *her* home." He swallowed some brew. "She is the one who talked me into this foster dog who takes a daily pill. I have to give the dog a pill ... like a ... like a sick old woman." He grimaced. "But my sister, she said I needed something to bond to."

Interesting.

"Good coffee," Isa said, taking another taste. "Notes of blueberry and spice."

"Exactly," he exclaimed. "The note of ripe berry is very good, no?"

She nodded. "Nice blend."

"You know your coffee."

"I own a coffee and bakery shop."

He did a double take. "I did not see *that* coming."

"Life has led me to some unexpected places."

"Jacob said you were a cop."

"I was."

Luna left sleeping Chia and jumped up next to Bowie on the sofa. As if holding a bomb about to go off, Bowie picked the dog up via the tips of his fingers and set her back on the ground. With his foot, he guided the dog back toward Chia. Luna jumped for Isa instead.

Isa rubbed the pup around the ears.

"He sheds," Bowie observed.

She grinned.

He shuddered.

But then he got back to Isa. "Ex-cop, bake shop, and so now you are a human rescue agent."

Luna nestled into Isa's lap.

"You try to reach Jacob again?" she asked, avoiding the uncomfortable subject of her past.

"Yes, but he is ... how you say ... DIA."

"MIA?"

He nodded.

"Maybe we should call the consulate in Italy," she said.

He looked over like she might have three heads.

"Yeah, okay. Right. You wouldn't want to tip everybody off."

"A cop would know this." He looked at her sideways. "I thought you were a cop."

"I was a forensic accountant."

"Oh." He made the word two syllables. "I see. Desk job. That explains why you cannot shoot."

Whatever. Isa straightened her shoulders. "I can shoot. I brought down a cartel leader with two shots to his legs."

"You are not supposed to—"

"I know, I know. Aim at center mass, and all that. I brought down a cartel leader anyway. So I was thinking—"

"Jacob told me not to let you do that."

"So, we need to make a plan," she said, the sometimes annoying eye twitch showing up. "Since my hotel room was ransacked and my suitcase is missing, I can't share any of my necessities with Chia. We'll need to buy her a few things."

"Buy? A few things? In public?" His eyes grew to the size of goose eggs. "Obviously, someone is looking for you or the girl or both. And, last night, they got too close for cozy."

"You mean too close for *comfort*?"

"I mean my place will be their next stop. We will purchase Chia a ticket today and fly you both out. And then I will find a way to clean up the mess we have, I mean *you* have, left behind."

Luna Dog rolled over on his back in hopes Isa would move the love from his ears to his belly. She complied. Rubbing the dog produced a sense—however small—of calm and gave her the wherewithal to ignore the Jacobesque, backhanded insults coming from Bowie. "What about Jacob? I'd like to get him the intel I've gathered."

Without missing a beat, Bowie's index finger shot in the air. "I have the answer," he said. "I shall pass along the information for you." He looked right at her, the glow of his idea radiating. "You can share anything you have on the trafficking ring with me now."

"Well ... I don't exactly have information to share yet." Isa rolled her bottom lip back and forth beneath her teeth. "I mean ... I know some things, like the club the traffickers use, where they keep the girls. But not the international routes used or who, exactly, is exporting these girls—"

"You alone will never untangle this knot. It is best to be left to the professionals."

"What professionals? You said last night the guy you tried to run over was with the feds. If people like you and me don't get involved, nothing is going to change."

"Nothing is going to change anyway. Except, perhaps, our living status. It is best to take your Chia and go while you can."

Isa stopped rubbing Luna long enough to gather up some of her own loose strands into her hair tie. "I was supposed to obtain detailed trafficking intel for Jacob to tie to a woman in Italy. I haven't done that yet."

"You say *yet*, like you plan to stay. That is problematic."

She glanced around the room, spotless save Chia piled upon an air mattress on the floor. Last night, after nabbing Chia and finding her hotel room ransacked, Bowie had brought them to his place but advised they not turn on lights. Now she could see how his living space mirrored his neat appearance. Sleek white lamps on clean-lined tables. Colors of charcoal and maple-toned woods back-dropped the moss-green sofa which had served as her bed.

This man had style. And probably a housekeeper. Isa recognized the telltale sign of OCD.

Took one to know one.

She studied him. Bowie looked nothing like she felt—harried and overdone already. After last night's charades, he still appeared cool as a cucumber. She mumbled, "I think so," beneath her breath.

"You think so what?" He sat up straighter.

He knew what. Had to. If Jacob had been so unkind as to give him a complete assessment of her, he should know she would want to do what she was about to do.

"Finish the job."

Bowie pressed his palm into his forehead. Looked bewildered.

"We should talk again with Pepe. Get more information. Help Jacob a little more."

"I am sorry, but I do not think we are on the same boat?"

"Page."

"I am to deliver you to an airplane. This is my contract with Jacob Lahache." Crisp little shakes of his head said one thing, but the glint in the dark eyes hinted at another.

She sensed she could win him over. He couldn't be that hard of a sell. After all, she'd talked him into helping her last night.

"Did Jacob tell you there's a bounty on the mob boss he's after?"

"Of course. I am a confidant of Jacob's. He told me everything."

"Did he tell you the price of the bounty?"

Bowie's brows formed a straight line across his forehead. "Perhaps. But what price did he tell *you*?"

"You tell me how much he told *you*."

"*You* go first."

All right already. "Two-hundred and fifty thousand."

Bowie whistled.

Chia stirred.

Luna flipped over and growled at Bowie.

So he didn't know the bounty price. That Jacob. Playing everybody. "He's offered me half if I get the information he needs."

A blast of betrayal lit up in his eyes. "Jacob Lahache has not offered me this deal."

Dangle the carrot a little lower. "I'll give it all." She leaned toward him. "All one hundred and twenty-five grand to *you*, minus a little, if you help me."

"One hundred and twenty-five thousand dollars? Minus a little? What is this minus a little?"

On her air mattress, Chia rolled over. Eyes fluttered.

Isa placed her coffee cup on the coffee table. "Minus enough to get Chia home and money for college," she whispered.

CHAPTER 60

Bowie rubbed at his chin while the Nigerian girl gracefully lifted to a cross-legged position. She stretched her arms above her head.

That's when he spotted the bar code on her right wrist. Typical traffickers. They branded their victims, letting the markets know what girl belonged to what pimps with costs attached. The thick line beneath the bar system indicated she'd been marked by a ring that brought girls from North Africa. From here in Málaga, the victims would be shipped off to various European cities. As Jacob Lahache had uncovered, many were sold or loaned to organized crime gangs in Italy. What Isa didn't understand, however, was that the network she wanted to crush expanded almost hourly.

And now he'd seen evidence of his own country's servicemen involved.

His carefully selected and expensive coffee didn't settle well in his stomach this morning. He got to his feet to fetch antacids.

"Where is Isa?" Chia asked, pulling Luna into her lap.

"Taking a shower," he answered, the tug at his heart commencing. The tug would become the inevitable wrench by which he would get involved in yet another hopeless case.

The bounty amount was a nice incentive, though.

Chia got to her feet to fold the blankets on the floor.

Bowie opened a kitchen drawer and withdrew a new pack of antacids.

CHAPTER 61

The table in Sophia's opulent dining room could rival one in a king's palace. He wasn't sure of the exact neighborhood where these digs resided, but it was a humdinger of a setting. Large house cascading off a hill with sweeping views of the Bay of Naples.

A blockhead in a sixties-style turtleneck and aviators stood by a swinging kitchen door, his arms crossed at the wrist and gun in his right hand.

Swallowing a bite of fresh melon, Jacob tried conversation again. "The eggs are a little on the hard side, wouldn't you say?"

Nothing.

"Wanna pass the salt?"

The stiff could work as one of the Queen of England's palace guards.

And speaking of the queen, she entered the breakfast scene—another tight dress, another encounter meant to mess with his head.

His temperature normal and his cough under control, he was ready this time.

"Sophia," he said, acting like he was the host instead of the prisoner. "Join me. I hate to eat alone."

She played along, gesturing her hand to the robot with the gun. Robocreep disappeared through the door.

At the buffet table, she made herself a cup of tea. Then, instead of taking the seat at the opposite end of the long, luxurious table like most mob bosses did in the movies, she sat next to him, perfume evident, smile inviting.

Sophia had come to play.

"Jacob," she started. "It is good to see you up and eating. Our medications have helped, I hear. I'm pleased." She reached for a grape on his plate. "We bring medical relief to people all over Italy." Popping the grape, she batted her lids. "I have a robust immune system. It's my intent to help others as well."

"You into pharmaceuticals now?"

"I'm not the bad person you think I am." Her eyes radiated pure virtue. "Here in Italy, organizations like ours keep entrepreneurs in business and help the poor get on their feet. We've been successful where governments fail the people. Now we're sharing the drugs that some doctors have shunned. I'm in a position to make a difference."

He leaned back in his chair. "Interesting take on crime and bloodshed. I think this makes you more loan shark than savior."

She placed her elbow on the table, cradled her chin in her palm. He had to admit, she played the alluring goddess with innocent motives very well.

"I've been propping up local, family-owned businesses during the virus wars. Without me," she said, "some entrepreneurs would have failed."

He reminded himself that inside this bleeding heart, a black widow had spun a web.

"Your own New York City is evidence," she continued. "Already, the people on the streets are rebuilding that city where the local government has bogged down progress."

"So let me get this straight," he said crossing his arms. "You offer some poor business guy money for help, but in return, he gives you his profits or he loses not only the business but his life? That's not a sweet deal for anyone but you."

"Then why do I have beggars at my door? People know I'm here to loan them what they need, including the medical help. You are an example of this."

"You nabbed me off the street. I wasn't begging at your door."

"Oh, but you were."

He pushed his chair back. Put his hands behind his head. This was going to be good. "How, exactly, do you figure that?"

She pulled on her tea like a man pulls on a bourbon—something akin to flirting. "Were you not waiting for me at Bambino's? I saw you watch me, and you did it so carefully. I imagine you thought yourself clever to be working at a restaurant I own ... or might as well own."

"So you saw me? You're a very good actress. You figured I'd come to haul you back to the states, then. Right?"

"That," she said smiling, "would be the obvious conclusion. But I know you left the FBI, and I suspect you're here for more than a simple-minded citizen's arrest. Men like you want to play around awhile. Like you did back in New Mexico with El Padrino, and that naïve Isa Phillips."

That's where she had it wrong. Men like him wanted black-and-white justice even though they played in the grey to achieve it.

"And, of course ..." She checked her blood-red nails. "I have your burner phone, and there are messages from Spain. Your supposed undercover contact there is trying hard to reach you. What are you up to in Spain?"

He laughed to keep from tensing. "Looking at how far your reach is, of course. You've been checking on me? Well, I've been checking on you, too. Looks like you've added trafficking to your list of entrepreneurial endeavors." He dropped his arms to the table. "Not cool, Sophia."

"It's not what you think, Mr. Righteous. We financed a few gentlemen's clubs. They service an unmet need."

"With stolen children."

"I have nothing to do with stealing children. I provide business for willing prostitutes. The girls make big money in Spain, in Italy, in Russia. Other places." She shrugged like she was talking about common stock market futures. "A girl's got to make a living."

"That's only a partial truth. My intel says you're part of a bigger organization that pays transports to bring *stolen* girls into Spain to disperse to areas all over the world."

She leaned forward, making her top-level form obvious. "You cannot believe everything you read or hear. Everyone knows the press is deceptive these days."

"I guess I won't know until I get a closer look at your shiny new empire."

"Jacob, your sense of justice is off. There's a new order coming into play. You should leave your boy-next-door ideals behind and follow the new progressive way."

"Is that an invitation to join you?"

Sophia reached over and picked at his fruit again. She selected a strawberry this time. Eyed it for a moment, then opened her full red lips and took a bite. Chewed in contemplation. "I'd hate to see you die when you could do so much good."

"Okay, now I can't tell if you're recruiting me or threatening me. That doesn't make you seem very trustworthy, Sophy."

"Oh, I so want you to trust me." She licked strawberry juice from her top lip. "Otherwise, I would have let you die of the virus, right? I saved you. Isn't that proof of my trustworthiness?"

This was an academy award performance. But he, *he* was the master of multiple personalities. Isa had pointed that out more than once. This was his opportunity for the showdown of a lifetime without the FBI watching his every move.

He reached across the table and pulled the half-eaten strawberry from her hand. Put it back on his plate. "I'm not that easy. You'll have to show me."

Sophia raised a brow.

"Your head's in the gutter, Sophy." He grinned and took a swig of OJ. "I want to see the inside of your organization and come to understand how you've managed to revive a dying Mafia family business."

"You think me a fool. You've already told me you've come to take me back to the States and put me in jail." The hurt in her eyes came across as real.

But it wasn't.

Elbows on the table, he said, "I think it's going to take more than a simple seduction to convince me your way of doing business is better than mine. True, I came for the reward money. But I'm willing to consider a better offer."

That's when she slowly rose from the table, her eyes never leaving his.

Jacob didn't know if she was going to get Robocreep and his gun from the kitchen or call for her finance guy to bring in the books so he could have a look.

But either way she was inching herself up for one grand purpose.

He waited. Watched the presentation.

Once up, she stepped next to his chair.

This is not going to happen, is it?

It happened.

She took his hand and placed it on her hip.

He let it rest there, knowing the moment's plan was to lure him into her sticky trap. He'd have to play along ... but he'd have to be tough.

Then Sophia Evelina Ricci Ventura bent over and laid a kiss on Jacob, trusting whatever drugs she'd filled him with were working in her favor when it came to contagions.

He resisted at first.

But that didn't last.

Sophia knew her stuff when it came to killing and ... kissing.

When she pulled back to look at him, she said, "If we're going to do business together, you'll have to shave that beard."

CHAPTER 62

"You'll be safe here." Isa rubbed Chia's arm, stopping at her wrist. She squeezed, then slipped her hand into Chia's.

The girl's hand felt warm and strong, her fingers interlacing with Isa's.

But her eyes studied the floor.

"We'll work to get her back to her village," the heavily accented woman from the agency said. She stepped back, giving Isa a moment to say goodbye.

Bowie waited outside.

During the hurried interview with the rescue agency, both Chia and Isa had recounted their horrid abduction stories. While Isa's story unfolded, the inner dragon stirred slightly, but nothing like the flame-inducing beast of the past. Maybe the therapy sessions with Kevin had made a difference.

That and prayer.

When Chia shared with the agency woman, she'd kept her eyes on her feet as she recounted the journey through hell. She'd also wept as she relived the realization she would be separated from the other Nigerian girls. Those innocent girls had been sold off "like chickens headed to the market," she'd cried.

Fingernails pressing harder into her palms, Isa had watched Chia's expressions morph from relief to fear to grief, knowing she, but not her Nigerian sisters, would return home.

It was all wrong. And twisted. And sick.

Now, with Chia's hand in hers, no words of comfort came forth. None of the Christian comforts she'd heard from Awena over the last few months seemed to fit.

So she drew Chia into her breast. "You have my email."

The girl leaned in, nodding, her tall and elegant form melting into Isa.

At the threat of tears, Isa bit her bottom lip.

"We will take good care of her," Isa heard the agency woman say from somewhere outside time and space. "We have replaced six girls to their homes this year so far. This one will be one of the lucky ones."

Did luck have anything to do with it?

Not if God was sovereign. *But how could a sovereign God allow ...*

Regal and beautiful, Chia straightened and finally lifted her gaze to meet Isa's. With a deep and wordless understanding, Chia nodded, let go, and left the room, the agency woman trailing behind her.

Old feelings of helplessness rushed at Isa. She thought about seeking the refuge of a closet. Only she was in someone else's building.

And she wasn't a little girl anymore.

CHAPTER 63

Teeth still buried in her bottom lip and her head down, Isa counted her steps out of the agency lobby, through the glass double doors, and up to Bowie, who read something on his phone.

He glanced up, flashed a smile, took a closer look at her, and for the second time since she'd known him, frowned. "Did it not go well?"

"No." Isa's shoulders sagged. "I mean yes."

"Which one?"

"I mean no, it *did* go well."

"But your face says it did not."

Crossing her arms, she decided to contemplate the street traffic which was easier than contemplating her emotions. "It's hard." She cleared her throat. "I don't have answers."

Bowie's brows lifted. "For what?"

"For anything. Nothing." She threw her hands up. "Nada."

Bowie dug around in his jacket's inner pocket and located what looked to be a hanky. He offered it.

"What's that for?" she asked.

"You have this ..." he pointed to the inner corner of his own eye, "this wetness there."

Isa snapped the offering from his hand, hating he'd noticed. She dabbed at her eye and for good measure, blew her nose. "Thanks," she said handing it back.

Bowie reached out looking like he wished he had fire tongs on hand. He took the hanky by the tip, made for a nearby trashcan. Dropped his hanky in.

Mourning for Chia's situation, feeling inadequate, and realizing her dragon had barely taken notice, Isa managed to lift one side of her mouth in a half-hearted smile. OCD Bowie. She related.

"Now," he said. "It is time we get—"

"I'm not getting on a plane." She wasn't done with human trafficking crime. "At least not yet."

"I was going to say coffee. Get coffee. We need more coffee."

She nodded. "That, we can agree on."

Bowie grabbed her elbow and herded her through the mass of cars slowing for a red traffic light. "Hurry," he urged. "Stop lights here are only recommendations."

"Oh?"

"And the yellow divider lines in the center of the roads are mere suggestions."

Another smile took shape.

"Do not be sad, Isa Phillips," Bowie said, stepping up on the curb. "You have done a good deed. We have rescued this girl, and now she will be returned to her home. We have achieved success."

She slipped out of his grip but walked beside him into a little café. Spaniards got a late start on the day, and Bowie was right. She needed to see all that had happened so far as a win. One step forward in her investigation and one very precious girl would be returned to her home. *Win.*

The familiar smell of brewing coffee and baking goods took her back to her own home. Like Coffee Magic home— where routine yielded order and QuickBooks entries yielded profits. So simple and so much easier than all the unknowns and risks of crime busting.

But she was in this now. In like her life depended on being in. Like lots of people's lives depended on her being in.

Chia depended upon her being in.

"Are *you* in?" she asked Bowie, dropping down into a chair at one of two empty tables. The cramped café had a line of Spanish zombies hunting caffeine forming at the counter.

"I know I should ask what you mean by *in*," he said, "but please, at least wait to tell me until I have more coffee." He headed to the line at the counter.

Isa rubbed the back of her neck. There had to be a way to infiltrate this grotesque underground world. She felt close, but far. Having been in the house with the girls, she'd *seen* how things operated, but hadn't *infiltrated* the operation. That was the difference between this case and the cartel bust she and Jacob had wrapped up back in New Mexico.

Only that case wasn't completely wrapped up, either, since Jacob had told her Sophia Ventura duped her into believing she was an innocent informant ... when Sophia was probably manipulating everyone and everything while she built a female-run Mafia kingdom. Isa aimed to learn the truth.

She needed to permeate this Spanish human-trafficking ring before she could tie Sophia to anything in Spain. She needed to find an insider and gather intel.

As coffee seekers continued to file in, Isa noticed Bowie held his phone to his ear. He glanced up and looked her way, waved when he saw her watching, then turned to face the wall.

Maybe he talked with Jacob.

Jacob. Even more reason to keep at this case. Something very fleshly wanted to prove something to him once more.

She made a mental assessment of the challenges:

Number one: she was in another country and out of her well-known element. Laws were different, and undercover game rules might or might not apply.

Two: she dealt with a new breed of criminal—not an overconfident drug lord, but worse—an overconfident woman.

Next list: the advantages at her fingertips. One—she had been given a unique, albeit limited, view of life as an involuntary prostitute. That had to count for something. Two—she and Bowie had rescued Chia, getting started on this venture with one huge success under their belts. Motivation counted. And then number three—God promised to be with her, always.

She looked up to see Bowie, two paper cups in hand, winding his way back through the line.

No doubt, God was in this. He'd been with her in the Sandia Mountains when, kidnapped, she'd solved the case through her own unique crime-busting, but God-given skills. It was during that case she'd somehow come to terms with her brother's overdose. It was during that case she'd found the Lord trustworthy even when people were not.

"Now." Bowie sat the cups on the table. Straightened his sports jacket and pulled out the chair. "Now you can tell me what you mean by *in*."

Isa pulled the lid off her coffee. "Where is the cream?"

"You said you didn't use cream."

"When did I say that? I love cream."

Bowie raised a brow. "In my apartment this morning." He turned for the coffee counter again, mumbling something about fickle Americans.

The word *trust* bounced around in her head some more. If the Lord was trustworthy, and he'd certainly proven himself to be so far, then how could she reconcile trust with what she'd seen in that house of horrors where the stolen girls lived? What was she supposed to do with that information? Use it? Learn from it?

An epiphany grabbed a brain cell and hung on. *Purpose it*. The recent past had taught her this very important lesson—there was purpose in all things. Every situation. Every encounter.

Bowie reappeared, setting a small pitcher of cream and a spoon in front of her.

She mentally stepped back into reality—the café, the customers, and the truth that on a scale from one to ten for starting points in an investigation, she had a little more than a zero. Maybe a one-point-seven.

Getting himself seated, Bowie asked again, "One more time. What did you mean by *am I in*?"

She poured cream. Stirred her black coffee into a lovely shade of pecan. "Could it be possible that God is in this?"

His mouth opened. Then shut.

She kept going. "I mean, there has to be a purpose in this situation if there is a purpose in everything, right?"

Bowie glanced about like he was checking to see if anyone else heard the off-kilter conversation. "So, you do not want to know if I am *in*." He paused. Took a breath. Started again. "You want to know if God is *in*."

"Both. But I think God is *in* ... so I'm asking you." She held the cup to her nose, letting the steam warm her face. "And, by the way, was that by chance Jacob on the phone?"

He wiped at some imaginary crumbs in his lap. "No. It was a ... a business call." He waved off her query. "But tell me now. What are you asking me to be in *for*?"

"In for the bounty. In for cracking this case, of course."

"I thought that's what you meant." He shook his head, but with his cup, he gave a hesitant gesture. "I am in if the bounty is even possible. But this is not a *case* as you call it. This is a giant octopus with tentacles reaching around the entire world. We are only two people, and one of us is not a very good shot."

Isa rolled her eyes.

"But if we can find a tie to the Mafia mistress Jacob wishes to take down in the next twenty-four hours, and collect a bounty, then I will offer my help with limits." He sat his cup down and leaned forward to make his next point. "Even though I have already fulfilled my obligation to you in rescuing your friend Chia."

Isa overlooked his reference to her piling-up requests. "Twenty-four hours? Why do we only have twenty-four hours?"

"Because very bad criminals are on to you, which means they are on to me, which means my future work in this town will be compromised."

Isa pondered that with another gulp. "And?" She tucked in her chin. "That's it? If we can keep your career intact and make progress in twenty-four hours, we're going to do this?"

"With limits."

"Okay, what are the limits?"

"You don't carry a gun."

She sneered.

"And I'm limited in time."

"Going somewhere?"

He glanced at the ceiling. Then back to her. With a surrendered sigh, he said, "Okay, I had plans to go to Italy."

"You're kidding."

"I wish."

"To connect with Jacob?"

"No."

"Say what you want, but I don't believe that. When do you go?"

"Day after tomorrow."

"Then we have forty-eight hours."

"No. Twenty-four. It takes me a day to pack."

"Pshaw. I'll help you pack if you give me forty-eight hours."

He looked at her sideways. "Isabella Phillips, I'm finding it increasingly difficult to resist your offers, despite Jacob's warnings and my own instincts."

Except for the backhanded insults, compared to Jacob, Bowie could prove to be a dream to work with. "I have an idea," she said.

"Of course you do."

Just as she opened her mouth, two secret-detail-looking men stepped out of the crowd and up to their table.

Bowie did a double take as the men flanked his chair. One wore a trench coat, the other a leather bomber jacket, and both wore dark shades.

Red flags started waving as her shoulders tensed.

Instinct drove Isa's hand to the side of the chair where her purse hosting her Glock should be ... only she'd stopped carrying the Glock back in Albuquerque, and only her purse had been stolen.

"*Señores*," Bowie said, first taking in Trench Coat then nervously eyeing Bomber Jacket. "Can I help you?"

Bomber Jacket nodded toward the door.

"Wait a minute," Isa warned, not liking what took shape here.

"Settle down." Trench Coat said, those sunglasses aimed at her now. "We're here on business with your friend."

"Oh, I remember." Bowie's shaky chuckle wasn't convincing. But he pushed his chair back and stood. "This is the follow-up from my last case." He gave Isa a sideways all-is-okay shake of the head. "I will be back."

Isa almost crawled up to stand on her chair so she could see above the heads in the coffee line as Bowie exited with the two. But that, she decided, wouldn't be a professional undercover maneuver.

She scooted her chair to sit beside Bowie's chair so she could watch him and the two interesting characters through the interactions of the couple seated at the small table at the window. Chewing on a wayward nail, Isa swayed right and left, peering between the animated movement of the hands of the fellow at the table as he talked about somebody's mother.

Outside, Bowie looked to be laughing, and he put his hand on Bomber Jacket's shoulder.

Her heart rate decelerated. But her teeth kept working at the nail.

For five and a half excruciating, eternal minutes, Bowie and his associates discussed their matters at the glass storefront window while the man at the table railed on.

Finally, as Isa's coffee got cold and her nail began to bleed, Bowie walked back through the café door alone and made his way back to their table.

"It was just unfinished business from a case that needed to close," he stated, as soon as he was in earshot, cutting off her opportunity to ask questions. Isa noted the little line of perspiration beads at the lip.

Adjusting into his seat, he eyeballed the woman at the next table, who stood abruptly and yanked her purse off the back of her chair.

"I think he ditched on her mother," Isa said.

"Ditched?"

"Talked about. Spoke ill of. You know, ragged on her mother."

He waved his hand about. "I will never be able to memorize or understand all the American idioms." Bowie wiped his lips with a napkin and said, "But there is never a dull moment in Málaga, heh?"

"Looks that way."

He tried a chuckle, but it didn't come off as genuine. "So, you were about to tell me your superspy idea."

Okay, okay. If that's what he wanted, she would play like whatever just happened out there on the sidewalk didn't just happen. For now. She took a quick sip of her room-temp coffee. "We need to pay Pepe another visit."

CHAPTER 64

Midday, the seedy section of Málaga appeared as different as chalk and cheese to the night before. The only signs of life in the daylight draped themselves across a bench and the hood of a parked car.

"Maybe we can find a door at the back." Isa made for the sidewalk when Pepe wouldn't answer his door.

"Maybe your friend Pepe is not here," Bowie called after her. "He made it clear he did not want you to come back, so I don't think he will talk with you."

Isa glanced back. "He will talk with me. He just didn't want *you* to think he wants to talk with me. It's part of the investigation game."

At the corner of the street Isa took a left, walked a few feet, and turned into an alley that ran directly behind the group of connected buildings that housed Pepe's whatever store.

Across the street, at the other end of the alley, a woman stumbled around in her pajamas and furry leopard house shoes.

Bowie caught up, his OCD on display as he buttoned his khaki trench and flipped the collar up. As if that would help keep the grunge of the urine-soaked alley at bay. A year ago, she would have felt the same if not for Therapist Kevin. Hard-fought psychoanalysis sessions paid off in progress dividends—managing environmental disgust and occasional disorder.

Counting off doors, she identified what should be the back door at Pepe's. The missing bottom panel of the crooked screen door said a lot about the building's upkeep. A rickety fire escape ladder hung on the wall beside the door. A haze-smeared window topped the rusty ladder.

Isa slipped her fingers through the handle, thinking the door could fall apart if she pulled too hard.

The door didn't fall apart. But the handle came off in her hand.

Bowie gave her that *see, I told you*, look and pulled his collar tighter at the throat.

She slipped the door handle, rusty wood screws protruding, into her windbreaker pocket in case she had the opportunity to screw the handle back in.

Hands on the frame, she wiggled the screen door open.

The wooden and graffitied security door to the back room stood ajar a couple of inches. Isa glanced back at Bowie who was shaking his head like *don't even think about it*.

She gave the door a slight push.

Squeaking in protest, the door opened several more inches.

Bowie scooted in close. Whispered, "Surprising little Pepe would not be a good idea. Little men carry big guns."

She cut her eyes back at him.

"I am sure you noticed he deals in illegal goods."

She figured.

"Cigarettes," he continued. "Probably hashish and marijuana, too."

Maybe she *should* make her presence known. "Pepe," she called.

Nothing stirred within earshot.

"Pepe." She said it louder, taking a step into the back room that, just like the front, was stacked with cardboard boxes.

Another step and Bowie pulled on the back of her windbreaker. "I think we should leave," he whispered.

"This is my only informant," she whispered back.

"He's not an informant. He's a seller of goods. That he knew where to send you to find girls should let you know he's one of them. Maybe selling girls himself," he murmured.

"So you think he set me up?"

Bowie kept up the hushed tone. "He likely received a payoff for sending you to that club where you were kidnapped. If you told him you were alone, you made yourself a target."

"Then why did he let you and me in here last night? Why did he tell me the address again? He knew we were out to make a rescue."

Bowie blew a low, slow breath out. "*Of course* he sent you back in. He was not helping but sending you into another sting."

"You might have mentioned this hypothesis earlier," she rebutted, neck strained. "Why are we whispering?"

"Because I don't want to frighten that scary little man. Let's go."

She shook off his hesitations. Stepped all the way into the little room. "Pepe, you here?" she called out loud.

"He's not here," Bowie said in a normal volume.

"Let's look around."

"Let's don't. I tell you what. We will leave this all behind and go to Italy to meet Jacob and start from there."

Isa headed for the front room where the knife case and a million more boxes waited. Getting around a stack she saw other stacks had been knocked down. Overturned cartons, brown paper wrapping, and Styrofoam peanuts littered the floor.

A struggle, a fight, or maybe Pepe had taken a spill off a ladder. "Pepe?" Isa slid over to an upright opened box. Looked like someone had rifled through it.

Behind her, Bowie shuffled around. "The way this is arranged," he said, picking up a wad of newspaper formed in a long roll, "it doesn't look like cigarette packing."

"Either Pepe is cleaning house, or someone's been inspecting his goods." Isa walked down another aisle.

She heard Bowie kick at a couple of downed boxes. "These are empty," he called out.

"What do you think?" she asked, pulling at her ponytail.

"Ammo, and we should not want to know. We should go."

"Ammo as in illegal arms?"

"Could be a lot of different things in here."

"Then why the store front?"

"You're the accountant. Don't you recognize money laundering when you see it?"

"Pepe?" She called again.

A motorcycle shifting gears echoed from the street outside.

She made her way around a stack of crates. A staircase opened in the back corner. "Bowie, over here."

"Where?"

"Here."

His face peeked out from behind a pile.

She pointed at the stairs. "I'm going up."

He pulled in a breath, opened his mouth, then shut it, resigned. "Okay."

With no rails, she put her hands against the grimy walls of the narrow stairwell. "Pepe?"

"I do not think he is here," Bowie repeated. Again. "And I think—"

"I know, we should go." But she mounted another step.

"You see," Bowie continued, "men dealing in underground markets do not leave their doors open. And now we are trespassing."

For a PI, he was sure into procedural etiquette.

"I just want a little look around," she said, hands still at the wall, and heart in her throat.

The stairwell landing had doors on either side. The door on the right stood open. Isa poked her head into what looked like a bedroom. Against one wall sat a single metal-frame hosting a thin mattress covered by a patchwork quilt. A dorm-room sized refrigerator leaned against an otherwise bare wall, the electrical wire stretched taunt, barely reaching the plug at the halfway point.

She heard Bowie open the door across the landing.

When Isa kicked at a pile of clothes on the floor, a mouse ran out and made for the back of the fridge.

She managed to stop the scream mid-throat.

Don't tell Bowie or he'll have a cowie ...

"Uh-oh," Bowie gasped from the other room. "This is not good."

CHAPTER 65

Isa backed out of Pepe's bedroom, eyes on the fridge. At the landing, she turned for Bowie who stood in the threshold of the door across the hall. His forearms pressed against either side of the doorframe. Isa couldn't see anything on the other side of his now-unbuttoned trench coat. She peeked under his right arm.

Uh-oh, for real.

Squeezing past Bowie, she dropped to her knees next to Pepe, who was spread-eagled on the floor. Blood pooled behind his head.

"Do not touch the body," Bowie warned, staying put.

"He might be alive," she countered.

"He is very dead. Not just mostly dead."

Isa stared at Pepe's chest because she couldn't look at his face, haloed by blood. Even though she had been a cop—a desk cop—the sight of sticky, blue-red blood made her nauseous.

She counted off eleven seconds.

No movement in Pepe's lungs.

"He *is* dead!" She sat back on her heels. "Pepe ... what happened?"

Bowie came over. Had her by the underarms lifting her to her feet.

"What happened?" she repeated, the room leaning slightly.

He tugged at her windbreaker. "Time to go."

She whirled around to face him. "I ... can't ... understand—"

"Aick!" Bowie backed away, eyes on her legs.

Jiminy! She had blood smudges on the knees. With the pooled blood on the floor, the gaping mouth on the body, the smudges on the knees proved to be the final straw. The room went slant and the bells went clang and Isa swayed into Bowie's reach.

Blood ooze syndrome hit.

"Breathe," Bowie said. "We don't have time for a faint."

Isa pulled in a breath, tasted dust, but held it for four seconds anyway. Then she let her lungs deflate. Repeated the process.

The room straightened up.

Leveling her on both feet and jiggling her shoulders, Bowie examined her eyes. "You look good now. I'll lead you down the stairs." He took her hand.

"Wait ... I got to think a second."

"There is nothing to think about. It is clear what is happening. Your hotel room was ransacked. Now Pepe is dead after you've been here not once, but twice."

"Three times," she confessed. She'd created a dangerous pattern. How had she overlooked that basic tenet of investigations? *Don't create routine. Don't be predictable. Argh!*

Bowie dug around inside his jacket. "My place will be next, or worse." He pulled out the antacids, ripped at the foil, popped two in his mouth. Chewing, he said, "It is now time to cover our tracks."

"You think this is all my doing?"

"I don't want to know. But we could be in deep, how you say—"

"I get the idea, but Pepe sells in the underworld markets. This …" Her finger pointed at Pepe, but her eyes locked on something on the other side of the room, "could be the result of a deal gone bad."

It couldn't be just about her, right? She *really, really, really* did not want Pepe's murder to be her doing. She wouldn't be able to live with herself. "There's got to be a clue, and we need to find it."

Bowie moaned, not like he was going to be sick, but like he knew things were not going to go his way. "What will it take to get us out of here?"

"The desk." She nodded toward the corner at a large, scarred, metal desk, drawers open, and contents scattered around the floor.

Bowie's hands hit the air.

Isa inched around the body and toward the desk. "Maybe we should call the police."

"They likely set this up to get you and me out of everyone's hair permanently."

She scooted a couple of the loose papers around with her boot. "This is interesting," she mumbled as she bent to get a closer look. "Bank transactions. Big ones."

"Don't touch." Bowie warned. He didn't seem interested in the papers, just the door he was glued to.

Squatting, she saw another sheet halfway beneath the desk. She couldn't quite see the bank's name, but this document had different fonts and colors typed across the page. To avoid leaving a fingerprint, she pulled the paper closer with her scabbed-over fingernail.

Banco Daviviendo. Colombia.

Transaction figures littered the page. Large amounts coming in, smaller ones going out. Daily.

Looked like real evidence that Pepe moved money.

And from the humble appearance of his digs, he moved money for someone else—someone who had a bunch of it.

Isa bent low to peer beneath the desk. Something was crammed between the desk and the wall. She slipped to her knees.

A briefcase.

On all fours, she crawled beneath the desk.

Bowie emitted exasperation louder than necessary.

Pliable leather. Forgetting about prints and dustings, and not touching evidence, she wedged her whole hand into a strap wrapped around the case and tugged.

"Isa."

"There's something here."

His octave went higher. "Isa."

"Let me get this." Another tug and she backed out. Held up her prize for Bowie to see.

"Your knees."

She glanced at her blood-stained jeans. "What?"

"Evidence." He pointed at the docs on the floor.

The gasp she inhaled was sharp and convicting. Prints. Her bloodied jeans had left knee prints across the floor plus on two of the bank statements.

A rattle echoed up from downstairs.

Like maybe the front door had opened.

Bowie put his finger to his lips.

Glancing behind her at the grubby window, she knew there was but one way out of this.

Bowie was already there.

Quietly pulling the rickety window open, he stuck his head out.

She stepped lightly across the scattered papers while securing the briefcase strap over her shoulder.

Male voices lifted from a room below. A door shut.

"Leave the case," Bowie whispered, already out the window and clinging to the fire escape ladder.

She adjusted the strap and shook her head and got to the window.

Bowie frowned but started his descent. Halfway down, the ladder shifted and screeched.

Her heart froze over, and from the look on Bowie's face, he might have just made a big mess in his pants.

Probably whoever was in Pepe's place downstairs froze, too, because what happened next was one for the *Isa's-in-over-her-head* record books.

Another agonizing shriek from the expiring fire escape and Bowie made a jump for it, only the ladder came off the wall with him.

In the alley below, Bowie held the detached ladder in his hands, blinking.

She hurried back across the room, tiptoeing past Pepe, and gently closing the door to the landing. She wiggled the slide bolt into the lock.

Repeating the tiptoe around Pepe, Isa got back to their next problem. The ladder.

But Bowie had leaned the ladder up against the wall beneath the window, forgetting she'd need another three feet of legs to reach the top rung.

"Try it," he whispered.

Briefcase snug at her hip, Isa got her legs out the window and eased down facing the wall. She pointed her boots and felt around for something to step on.

Felt nothing but stress as five precious seconds evaporated.

Needing to delete space between her feet and the ladder, she dropped lower, fingers gripping at the window frame.

"Just drop," she heard Bowie say beneath her. "Push off and drop. I'll catch you."

Just drop didn't compute. She continued reaching, searching for that saving rung with the toe of her boot. Had to be there … if she could … just reach … a little … farther. But when the door in the upper bedroom rattled, the push off happened.

Not exactly airborne, but in a free fall, she scraped her knees and jaw against the ladder. And somehow, her legs found Bowie.

She felt him collapse beneath her.

Isa had landed on top, both facing upwards.

Bowie groaned.

She rolled off.

Clambering to her feet, she sprinted for the street, briefcase banging at her back.

Bowie passed her, his trench coat waving in the breeze.

At the opening, he stopped. Isa collided into his back.

They both stumbled forward, but he took her elbow with one hand while moving his hair back into place with the other.

She straightened and they walked down the street, together. Just an ordinary couple on an ordinary walk looking very everyday ordinary.

Except for her blood-stained knees.

CHAPTER 66

Leafing through an Italian newspaper he couldn't read, Jacob made note of possible exits. A bank of windows lay on the left. The double doors he'd been ushered through opened behind him. After a half day of what she'd called recovery rest and a lunch of pasta so he'd be energized by the carbs, Sophia had sent one of her robots to bring him to her office.

He'd been waiting there for more than an hour.

Echoes of his days working undercover with the 96 Cartel bounced off Sophia's plastered walls. Drippy over-the-top chandeliers hung from the ceilings, velvet-upholstered furniture filled almost every corner, and on his way to the office, he'd passed an indoor pool with a fountain that rivaled Central Park.

All Sophia's talk of sacrifices to buoy businesses was hard to believe, considering what she must have spent on this piece of slab. The fresh flower arrangements on every table probably kept three florists propped up.

Where was all the money coming from?

He'd be sure and ask since Sophia seemed willing to share some secrets.

But ... there would be a price to be paid, and Jacob, finally feeling more like himself, was eager to hear it.

He'd watched Sophia sucker Isa into believing she wanted to turn evidence against her husband and enter a witness protection program six-something months earlier. Even though Jacob had warned her against it, Isa had paid the full price for Sophia's charades. Her witness had fled.

But not Jacob. There wasn't a play Sophia could make that he hadn't seen before. Eight hard years undercover with the FBI wasn't for nothing.

From behind him, the queen entered the room. As she came around the fuzzy red sofa, he could see she had flanked herself with not one, not two, but three bodyguards who'd gotten the memo—the day's color would be black.

Jacob rubbed at his clean-shaven face as the entourage took their place center-room. "You're wearing lots of accessories this afternoon, Sophy. Black is your color." He gestured at the men.

The flash in her eyes told him plenty.

Good. He would be able to dig beneath the surface of her attractive façade and twist a nerve or two. Irritated villains made mistakes.

She nodded at her colorless guards. Two left the room to stand outside the double doors and the one with the broad shoulders took a seat on the sofa next to Jacob.

"There's a good article on fashion trends," Jacob said, offering the stiff beside him the newspaper. "And the top five dining critiques for Naples look good. We should do dinner."

When the man sneered, opening his jacket to reveal his pistol, Jacob dropped the newspaper at the guy's feet, which, for a broad-shouldered bodyguard looked rather small. *He must be wearing shoulder pads.*

"Nice office," Jacob stated, watching Sophia move to the frilly gold desk in the center of the room. She took a seat on the cushy chair. Whatever she'd spent on that opulence was a waste. His Walmart laminate piece back in his Albuquerque apartment hadn't cost more than sixty bucks and had everything a desk needed—flat surface, four legs, and a drawer.

"You're looking better this afternoon, Jacob."

Here came the charm. Her voice oozed with it, and while she rubbed the top of the desk, he couldn't tell if she was loving the feel of the gold-leaf wood or the fact that she had him caged like a bird.

Women.

"And you're much more handsome without all the shaggy hair on your face."

"Think so?" He pulled his hands down both cheeks. "Smooth as your vibe, Sophy. You're one smooth player."

"What ever happened between you and that …" she glanced at the ceiling … "that little accountant?"

"Isa Phillips?" *Play it cool.* Hopefully the little accountant was back in the States by now. Last thing he needed was Sophia picking up on intel that pointed to Isa in Spain.

"Yes, Isa Phillips. I remember you and she had a connection. Was that part of the undercover work or was that a blossoming romance?"

"Part of the work."

"You are a good actor then. From my husband's cameras, your connection had looked very real. Where is she today? Do you still work with her?"

"Don't know. Don't care."

"My resources tell me you've left the FBI."

"Your resources are correct. I'm an independent contractor these days. Bounties offer bigger pay, and before you and I negotiate terms for me bringing you in on this bounty, I have news you're going to find interesting."

She blinked the blink of an innocent girl. What a joke. "Oh?"

"Yeah." He scooted to the edge of the sofa, discounting the stiff next him who'd reached for his gun at the move. "You've got bigger problems than me. The New Order on the streets wants to take you down, and we both know they'll be extremely messy about it."

Sophia didn't flinch. She smiled.

He pushed harder. "And there will be more. Even the old mob guys don't like the idea of a woman encroaching on established territory. But with me," he pointed at his own face, "you stand a chance. Here's how it will go. I take you in, you show good will, you get a smaller sentence, and eventually life in the good old USA as a reformed citizen. The way our government hands out cash these days, you might even get a really nice setup ... though you'd probably have to forgo the golden desk and indoor pool."

Her smile endured. "It sounds like you care."

"Of course I care. We go way back."

"Thank you for the warning—and Jacob ..." Sophia swayed to her feet. "In all honesty, this is why I've brought you here."

"I'm glad we can finally be honest with one another." Jacob patted his heart. "It means the world."

The guy next to him grunted.

Sophia came around the desk, heading his way.

Jacob's pulse kicked up a notch, wondering how many passionate kisses he could take before ...

But she didn't come that close this time. She sauntered around the desk and leaned against its front. "I've got a better plan."

CHAPTER 67

Isa dropped the briefcase on one of the two queen beds topped by fluffy white comforters. This hotel room outshined the two-star minimum box she'd checked into a couple of days earlier.

Bowie, like some of the men she'd known, had swanky ambitions.

During their short and volatile marriage, Mac had preferred steak dinners to enchiladas. She suspected Jacob had been bought off a time or two, as well, as he'd spent much of his career hanging with criminals who made six times as much money as he did as an agent in the FBI.

But Sergeant Caba—the man who'd been as much of a father as a boss—he'd always lived life in simple mode. Back when she worked at HPD, she counted him wearing the same shirt three times in one week.

So here she was, in a hotel room she would never be able to afford and feeling self-conscious about it. But Bowie had not wanted the illegally obtained files of the dead man in his own apartment, and so they'd checked into a hotel he thought would provide a safe interim space before their flight to Italy.

And Bowie hadn't wanted to put their temporary hideout on his traceable credit card.

Isa had gawked at the wad of bills in hand when he paid cash for the room. PI work in Málaga must pay well. No wonder he didn't wish to jeopardize his vocation.

She plopped on the bed beside the briefcase. "Should we be concerned that we've not heard from Jacob?"

Bowie mumbled something unintelligible from the window where he watched a parking lot four stories below. Paranoid and antsy, he wasn't convinced they'd not been followed.

But Isa had a strategy. She figured if she could sniff out a trail to bank fraud, and she could tie that fraud to the human trafficking ring Pepe had probably sold her out to, she and Bowie could turn evidence over to the local police. Bowie would be the hero of the day, and maybe they'd find some loose end that led to human trafficking channels to Italy. Then she'd fly to Italy with Bowie, meet up with Jacob, and together, the three could connect the dots to Sophia and collect the bounty. Chia would go to college, Coffee Magic would be pulled back into order, and sessions with Therapist Kevin would move from weekly to twice per month.

Like the old days as lead HPD forensic accountant, the sense that she'd found the trail to a financial *gotcha* had her looking down the road of justice for all.

When she pulled copies of passports, driver's licenses, and bank deposit slips from the briefcase, she knew that she knew what she knew.

Money laundering by identity theft.

Long after identity-theft victims had learned their accounts had been compromised and had changed their numbers and passwords, the original thieves would sell the stolen identities to money-laundering criminals who opened new accounts in victims' names. The game would move fast, jumping from an account in one bank to other new accounts in other banks.

Nail the banker and you could close the laundry lanes.

"I should have grabbed the transaction papers with my knee prints on them," she said out loud while opening a stained blue folder. "Oh! Here's one." She held it to the light. Six hundred thousand deposited in a bank in Brazil and nine withdrawals emptying the account a week later, all in the name of a Bruna Silva. Isa flipped through the file of fake passports, looking for the unsuspecting Bruna's credentials.

"What are you finding?" Bowie asked. Satisfied the coast was clear, he had finally left the window to make himself a coffee with the Nespresso machine.

The hotel room she'd rented when she arrived had hosted a plug-in hot water carafe with packets of instant coffee. No creamer.

"Identity theft, and I want one of those." She pointed at the Nespresso.

He grumbled. But obliged.

Isa riffled through more papers.

Carefully balancing the cup on the saucer, Bowie brought her an afternoon fix. "Identity theft, then? I'm not surprised at all. An illegal cigarette smuggler like your friend Pepe is bound to follow current crime trends."

"It is not just identity theft. It's big guns money laundering." She tossed a passport atop the blue folder. "Here's the deal. Under stolen names and social security numbers, smurfs conduct bank transactions, moving money from one account to another."

Bowie sat down on the bed opposite of her, cramming his thick index finger into the dainty cup's handle. "What is a smurf?"

"In laundering schemes, there's often a designated person—a smurf—used to spread small financial transactions over many different bank accounts, keeping exchanges under regulatory reporting guidelines. Illegal monies flow through diverse accounts under names of people who've had their identity stolen. But these people have no idea this is happening in their name because, the transactions are under regulatory amounts, being made in foreign countries. Of course, nothing is ever reported."

He looked as confused as Jacob had looked when she explained the deed transactions El Padrino and his crew used through Quitclaims.

"The problem isn't just the lowly smurfs like Pepe." She knew she geeked out on this stuff but couldn't help herself. "There's some greedy bank CEOs having their palms greased and looking the other way. When you can bring down the big guns at the bank, that's when you have a chance at stopping it all. The guys in suits behind the desks don't think like criminals and never have a backup plan if caught. They spend their greedy careers believing they'll stop before their next transaction or believing they're too clever to be caught. But once these executives are arrested, they usually sing like canaries to get a plea."

"Sing like canaries?"

"Spill the beans."

"Spill beans?"

"Talk. Turn over evidence to get a lighter sentence."

He saluted her with his cup. "I understand. So Pepe was a smurf, and now we can dispose of the bag before we're taken in as suspects to his murder."

He sounded like Mr. Rogers explaining a beautiful day in the neighborhood, only they talked about murder and crime and stolen children. She waved his factual coolness off, studying a deposit slip in Amad Salenger's name. "I can't figure why Pepe made copies of all of this when he should have kept electronic files."

"I didn't see a computer in his place when we were there."

"Unless the murderer took it." She looked at the ceiling, urging her brain to connect dots. "Or …" She rubbed at her chin. "He might have made copies and hidden this physical evidence, knowing one day he'd use it for blackmail purposes."

"The little man had big ambitions."

Getting back to her piles on the bed, she said, "Looks like he did. But I'm not done yet. I'm looking for connections to Italy. To the mob Jacob is trying to penetrate."

"It's a long shot, Isa. You and I stumbled on a murder. Now we look guilty. That's not what I signed up for. I was only going to help you gather information."

Isa looked past Bowie to the gold-framed picture on the wall—a bullfighter with a red cape teasing a very large, horned, and black beast. "We should turn this over to the police when I'm done. I'm sure there's lots in here they'd like to have hold of."

"Considering the man who tried to gun us down at the traffickers' home was a federal officer, I—a simple bystander who lives locally—should not be the one turning over incriminating evidence. Here in Spain, police look the other way when it comes to prostitution, if you hadn't noticed. It is best for me that I am not viewed as a threat to this international octopus that involves corruption at the police level. If I am considered involved, I will never work in Málaga again. Or I could be …" He sliced his index finger across his neck.

She got the picture. And he had a point. Only once in her forensic accounting career had she worked with a PI. A law firm had hired him to investigate a CEO at a credit union. The PI had been a great source of info, but not necessarily ethics. Private investigators garnered from the bad guys because they didn't turn the bad guys over to the authorities. PIs were often the deal makers moving information, not people, into the right hands.

"Okay, then, we won't hand this information directly to police. But we can make sure it's found, right?" There was more than one way to get these files to the police.

"I can agree to leave it somewhere obvious," he concurred.

Isa held out her palm. "So give me your phone."

"For what do you need my phone?"

She pointed to the evidence spread across the bed. "To take pictures."

His knee-jerk reaction made him lose his grip on the dainty cup, and black coffee splattered across his shirt and pure, white bed comforter.

CHAPTER 68

Jacob sloped back into the sofa next to the stiff with the gun. Eyed Sophia and her shoulders-back posture with her backside against the fancy desk. "I figured you weren't going to be that easy," he said.

"Easy? I'm never easy, but I am flexible." Her look said he might be on the menu for dinner.

"Okay, let's have your plan, then. You've obviously healed me with your illegal pharmacy trades for a reason. What has your malicious mind got in store now, Sophy?"

Gesturing toward the door, Sophia signaled for her sofa guard with the shoulder pads and little feet to leave.

The reluctant guard adjusted the gun he'd almost drawn a couple of times and gave Jacob the stink eye. But he left as his queen had directed.

Then, not surprisingly, Sophia made her second move of the day. Her chosen seat on the sofa was one-third into Jacob's seat on the sofa.

She must've liked to share her secrets up close where her perfume and her curves were notable.

She slipped her arm around his.

On the inside, he shored up the gut that wanted to quiver.

On the outside, he let her melt into him.

He'd play along. Whatever it took to get Sophia to tell him her plan.

CHAPTER 69

Watching Bowie rub at the coffee stains on his shirt, Isa pulled in a patience-seeking breath. Why he couldn't see this evidence could be mined like gold itself, she didn't know. They could leave the hard copies behind, but she was taking the information nuggets with her.

Bowie squawked some more. "I don't think taking pictures of this evidence is a good idea. Can't you remember these names and numbers?"

"I don't happen to have a photographic memory."

"It's out of the question. My career will be over with this financial evidence on my phone. The president's bank account information is probably in that death pile on your bed."

"What kind of detective are you anyway? Aren't you supposed to work with the authorities and care about justice?"

Lips pursed, rag in hand, he glared.

She returned the scowl.

In a posh hotel in the upper-class quarter of Malága, an America versus Spain standoff commenced. She'd win. No one, *no one* could beat her at this game. The silent treatment had been her vibe for years—working alone behind a desk in a little corner office at HPD. Stare-offs were just another form of hushed torture.

Of course, Bowie broke. He dropped down on the bed and went to work on coffee droplets sprinkled across the white comforter. "Here in Málaga, if you wish to live, you do not poke around in police activity. Even if their activity appears suspicious."

"Corruption needs to be exposed, Bowie."

Not missing a beat, he pulled his own trigger. "If that's the way you feel, then take your justice to America. There's plenty of corruption in authorities there."

Ouch. Mac came to mind. Claire came to mind. Milly Washington making suggestions about Todd Wilson came to mind. Truth was, when oddities and hunches and those little red flags waving had pointed to a few things, she'd managed to look the other way plenty. Like Mac's work schedule never quite lining up with the hours he spent away. And Claire's letting Isa in only so far before quietly closing personal doors. And currently Milly Washington's dreaded box of Claire's diaries.

Now she'd have to take a serious look into Milly's box and see if she could string some clues together.

While conviction wormed its way through her heart, Bowie returned the rag to the bathroom.

Back into the bedroom, Bowie made for the window again. "Here's how my work goes," he said, opening the curtain a couple of inches and peering at the parking lot below. "I am hired by jealous wives to follow faithless husbands. Or an employer to follow an employee who cheats insurance companies. I agreed to help you get Chia and I agreed to help you find a trail of information, but now ..." He turned, tilted his head to one side and shook it like he wanted to rid his brain of the ideas she proposed. "Now there is a murder, and we could be suspects one and two."

"I know finding Pepe dead changes things a little—"

"A little?" He shook his finger at her and her pile. "No, no, no. I have contracted with Jacob Lahache to ensure your safety. I will not in good conscience let you put yourself in further danger. It's over. We pack up tonight, I go on my vacation to Italy, and you go home."

So now he wanted to make this about her and not his own safety.

Figures.

"Okay, then." She pulled at her ponytail. "If you'll give me a couple of days to sort through this evidence, then we'll stash the case where the right people will find it, and then, we will book it for Naples."

"We?" Bowie stomped to the Nespresso machine. "I am the one going to Italy, and you are going home." He reached inside his pocket. Pulled out the antacids.

She watched, biting her lip and knowing he wasted his breath and esophagus on this tirade.

Before he popped the green chewable, the realization of what she said hit. "Wait a minute. Did you say Naples?"

Isa lifted a page from the top of the file. "This bank ..." She wagged the paper at him. "This one has several accounts moving money around right in the heart of the Forcella neighborhood, which happens to be the biggest gang area of Naples."

"Did I tell you I was going to Naples? I only said Italy, correct?"

"I'm not a newbie at this game, Bowie. The call at the café this morning, the weird way you've been acting ... I figured you've been talking to Jacob and the two of you are scheming something without me." She slid off the bed and stretched her arms overhead. "I plan to be there when that something erupts. Look at it this way," she said, leaning over and picking up the document which had to lead to trafficking exchanges right where Jacob was supposed to be. She shook the paper again. "All this is no coincidence. God has lined up every detail for us."

Bowie scrunched his face when he swallowed down his chewables. "But has God covered the detail of your passport yet?"

"Now you're being snarky," she answered, rubbing her tired eyes. *Bowie might have as many personalities as Jacob. Men.*

But the Lord *had* lined up every detail. Including the mother lode of evidence spreading across the white comforter before her—the white comforter with little spots of brown from her blood-stained knees.

Oops.

CHAPTER 70

In the elevator, Bowie popped two more antacids.

His already raw throat had caught fire when Isa said she suspected he'd talked to Jacob earlier.

Ignoring her comments hadn't dowsed the flames.

Now, the situation had taken an unexpected pivot, and he headed somewhere he didn't want to go. And he didn't want it to take this long. Now Isa had talked him into another day of sorting through Pepe's files. He'd be changing his flight and adding her to the itinerary.

And why did she have to keep bringing God into this?

He made a mental note to call his sister, tell her he'd be out of town for a few days, and have her pick up the dog. And then he'd instruct her to get out of town too, because if he didn't deliver to this new connection in Naples, and he didn't play his cards perfectly once there, the repercussions would be deep and wide.

The elevator doors opened, and Bowie set his jaw. Other than moving to Costa Rica, there was no backing out now.

But he could fix it all. And he would.

CHAPTER 71

Spooning at her Greek yogurt, Isa eyed the airport crowd.

Baggage and virus warnings reminded her that every space—no matter how far removed she could manage her thoughts—posed danger of one kind or another. From the corner of her eye, she saw Bowie lower his newspaper to eye level, conduct a quick survey, then lift the paper back over his face.

Like the nights back at home. In those old days, she'd somehow thought that flimsy bedsheet pulled over her head would keep her hidden from her stepfather's intentions.

Bowie. Who'd thought he'd turn out to be such a help but also such a pain. Not as headstrong or aggressive as Jacob, but every bit as problematic. Why did men oppose every idea a woman offered when it came to finding solutions to major issues?

Insecurity?

That thought hadn't occurred before and was one she'd need to roll around in her head once she was back home and baking muffins.

But Bowie had stepped up in unexpected ways. He'd not only paid for but seen to it that a, *ahem*, passport, was delivered to her room along with a new pair of jeans and a white blouse. He'd thought to include a toothbrush and paste, and a couple of unmentionables that were a size too large. The jeans had fit. The blouse hung loose. Thankfully, her navy nylon jacket fit snug and kept her from looking like a teenager in her mother's shirt.

Bowie also had on new attire.

When they had left the briefcase at the driver's side wheel of an official but parked *Guardia Civil* car near a shopping mall, he'd confirmed they were out of security camera's views. When found, Pepe's briefcase would look like someone *wanted* it to be found. She and Bowie had agreed on that much. They had also concurred that alerting local police would be smarter than the national authorities since the guy they'd run off the road three nights earlier had looked to be federal.

The security announcements started again, and Isa slapped at Bowie's newspaper. "You talk to Jacob yet?"

Without lowering the paper, he said, "No."

He'd mentioned more than once, that just in case his cell phone had been hacked, he didn't think it wise to try and contact Jacob until they were in Italy.

"But you know where he is in Naples, right?"

He snapped his paper, lowered it, and glared. "We've been through this. I don't have an exact address, but an apartment name."

She tossed her ponytail. "Just making sure we stay on the same page." While she had his eyes locked on hers, she promised, "I'll pay you back for the clothes."

He snapped the paper. "It was no problem."

"But I will," Isa retorted, and pushed up the sleeves covering her left arm. After painstakingly writing bank names, account numbers, and transfers down her arm—and okay, both thighs as well—she wanted to make sure her clothing didn't smear the hard work. The process had been a bit messy, because she hadn't taken the time to construct spreadsheet-type cells. Body parts as worksheets had limitations.

Bowie glanced over, made *tsk* sounds, and again, buried his mug behind the day-old news, his coffee untouched.

Both helpful *and* reluctant, Bowie had turned out to be her biggest male enigma encounter to date.

CHAPTER 72

Waiting outside for Bambino's to open for the lunch-run prep, Jacob stared at the keypad screen, willing his mind to remember Isa's number. Until now, he'd transferred information from one burner phone to another, but since Sophia had confiscated the latest temp phone, and his head had been deprogrammed by the nasty virus, he had trouble pulling some details from the memory banks.

He'd heard that was a short-term side effect of COVID-19.

He had no idea if his connection in Spain had found Isa and sent her packing back to the States. The whole idea of having her join him in this mission had been a bad idea.

Giving up on the mental exercise, he shoved the phone back into his pants pocket.

He'd lost track of her. He should have known that would happen the first time he put the unrealistic thoughts of sending her to Spain on paper.

He rubbed at his jaw where stubble used to be.

But oh, how Sophia had scored the night she nabbed him. He'd never been taken against his will before, and he blamed the ill-timed COVID virus for that miscalculated error.

Fatigue slipped up on him, and he sighed, defeat threatening. Never, ever had his mental pistons refused to fire on cue.

Maybe he should find a cup of coffee. Which only made him think of Isa again.

Dang that woman.

He waved off thoughts of Isa, promising to revisit that problem later in the day.

But now ... now he was back at Bambino's, working for Sophia as an undercover stooge.

He'd play along because, at the end of all the insanity, he wanted the female boss fugitive next to him on a plane back to the States.

Jacob had been bounced around like a ping pong ball in a match played by greedy mobsters who happened to prop up failing businesses and offer hard-to-find medications to the poor. Jacob ran his fingers through his hair, got them stuck in the unbrushed tangles, then dropped his hands to his side.

Go figure.

Where were the good old days when criminals were criminals and not society saviors?

His weary shoulders drooped as his dreaded day began. The door to the pizzeria opened from the inside.

"Pick your jaw up, Marko." Jacob walked past the naïve and unsuspecting gang member. "I'm back."

Making his way around the empty tables, Jacob added, "I had the virus. Couldn't call for a couple of days." At the kitchen door he stopped. "Londo and Mike been around?"

Marko, brows low and having trouble pulling all Jacob implied into a cohesive thought, just nodded.

"Well?" Jacob asked. "What's the latest?"

"The cousins ... they looked for you. They said you were not in your studio."

"They were right. For security reasons, I stayed in a motel. When you're flirting with gangs, you don't want to be caught sick in bed."

Marko nodded, buying every word of it.

Jacob flipped on the kitchen lights and went for the silverware. "Set up tables?"

The cook stumbled in the back kitchen door and stopped short when he saw Jacob. He looked to Marko, a giant question mark in his eyes.

"He is back," Marko suggested, hands up and shoulders high. "He's been sick."

The cook backed out the door he'd come in.

"I'm no longer contagious," Jacob called after him as the door shut. "Is everybody going to make this a big deal?" He glanced back at Marko. "You going to make this a big deal? I'm back, okay? I'm well and ready to work ... on all fronts."

With the tips of his fingers, Marko wiped at his forehead. "But there is a setup already."

Jacob caught a quick breath but kept moving. Pulled a stack of cloth napkins from a bin. "That so?"

Marko nodded, getting comfortable with Jacob again. "Setup for the woman. The Sophia woman." He opened his jacket slightly, revealing a Smith and Wesson 19 tucked into his waistband.

Jacob moved his sights from the gun back to Marko's face. "Oh?"

"Londo and Mike, they have a ... pop ... ordered."

"I'm listening." He put a handful of napkins on the stainless-steel bar.

"When the woman comes here, I'm to ... well, we are to ..." he looked over his shoulder at the back door, the one the cook had backed out of. "We are to exit there. They're popping her right here at the pizzeria."

This wasn't good news. "How are they going to know when she's coming in? Those two lug heads got a gunman waiting outside 24/7? Or are you the popper?"

Marko snickered. Walked over and smacked Jacob on the shoulder. "Not me. No. Some of her men have joined the Ghettas. They say even her driver is in. I'm not the shooter." He patted his jacket. "This is for protection."

Jacob's lungs tightened, and he thought the virus might try a comeback. Then out of the nowhere, Isa's heart-shaped face and dark eyes flew onto his mental screen.

Why, God, why, am I dealing with focus issues at a time like this?

"That woman, Sophia, her guards and driver will let us know when she is coming here, to this pizzeria. She drops in often."

Jacob shut his eyes. Told himself to concentrate. "What about the customers? They getting popped, too?

"We're to clear everything before she arrives, saying there's a fire in the kitchen. You know, get the customers off the street then give her driver the signal to bring her over. That's when her own people follow her in and nail her."

What kind of messy message were these new guys sending? True, the up-and-coming baby gangs ruled by leaders from other countries didn't have the loyalty to the locals that the old, established mobsters did, but shooting up a business in broad daylight?

Finally, a brain piston fired. The Ghettas planned an excessive move for notoriety. "Why not gun her down in her car?"

Marko's answer proved him right. "Publicity. The Ghettas want to let everyone in Naples know they are now in charge."

Marko swam deep waters with deadly sharks, and the thought of the kid getting hurt squeezed at Jacob's already out-of-whack heart. "Look, kid, you sure you want to be part of this? Man, if innocent people get hurt, you'll be a wanted man."

The naïve immigrant shrugged. "To make it here, you got to show the allegiance."

Marko would likely get his allegiant head blown off his body. This mess of idiots calling themselves Ghettas would create one heck of a war zone.

Whether it was post-virus lethargy, or maybe his crime-fighting days were coming to an end, the enthusiasm he'd had back in the States when pulling this job together was on the decline. The motivation flatline had probably started the day his mother broke the news ...

Maybe he should check out Isa's therapist when he got back to the States.

But he was in this mob war now and needed to finish what he'd come to do. "The kissing cousins around today?" he asked.

More snickering from clueless Marko. "They won't be around till the job is done." He beamed misguided light. "I've been assigned as lookout."

Sophia had planned for Jacob to meet with one of her stooges every night and download intel, six blocks over at one of the busier bars.

That's what she'd said when she and her driver dropped him off this morning three blocks away.

Tonight, he'd go to the bar and send her the message that she shouldn't be seen around any of her propped-up enterprises for a few days. Her enemies' plans were moving quicker than she'd expected. And from there? He might have to get her alone, hog-tie her, and put her on a plane—get this big mess over with before the Ghettas discovered his triple bounty-hunter, gang-member, Sophia-stooge play.

Because Sophia had hired Jacob to gather intel about the Ghettas.

CHAPTER 73

Isa scooted out of the cab and stepped up on the curb next to Bowie. He reached out and took her by the arm. "There." He gestured with his head at a corner café. "Coffee."

"Now?"

"I found the airport coffee lacking."

"I thought we were going to walk around this neighborhood and look for Jacob's apartment building?"

"First, coffee." He reached in his pocket for his hourly antacid fix.

She watched him pull the little tablet from the roll. "You've got major issues. And we need to find Jacob."

He chewed. Swallowed with eyes clamped shut. "We cannot start this without the motivation of a decent cup of brew."

Isa glanced around. "Really? We're just getting started and you want a break already?"

Bowie tugged at her arm. "We need to settle in."

"You're procrastinating."

"I'm fueling my motivations."

When he turned for the café, she threw her free hand into the air but let him guide her to a small wrought-iron table for two on the sidewalk.

The green-aproned waiter didn't bring a menu but stepped up to their table expectant.

Anticipating dragon fury, Isa pulled in a breath. Reminded herself that working with partners meant compromise. Mostly. Maybe. Okay, this might be the first time for compromise, but it was a good start.

Bowie ordered two shots of espresso.

"Try Jacob," Isa said, nodding at his phone. "Let's call him."

His thick upper lip stiff, he pulled out his cell. Pressed at his screen and put the phone to his ear.

Compromise working.

She agreed to coffee. He agreed to the phone call.

"Let me talk to him," Isa said laying out her palm. "I'll get to the point quicker than you."

Bowie leaned back out of reach. Shook his head.

As their waiter set the espressos on the table, Bowie pulled the phone from his ear. Said, "No answer," without making eye contact. He commenced to reading something but tilted the phone at an angle that Isa couldn't see if it was a text or maybe an article on ten ways to ditch bossy partners.

Could Jacob have another phone? Could Jacob be working so deep undercover, he couldn't find a moment to connect? Could Jacob be dead? If Bowie cared, it didn't show.

Isa pulled at her cheeks, elbows on the table, watching him disconnect from their mission. What had happened?

"When you're done, might we discuss our plans?"

He slapped the phone, screen down, on top of the table. "We have discussed the plans. In the hotel. At the airport. In the cab." He shot his hand up and counted off his fingers. "We will walk the neighborhood, find the apartment building, talk to an apartment manager, or knock on doors." His jaw jutted forward. "*Caramba*, Isa. What else is there to discuss?"

Isa threw her hands up like he held a gun on her, which he sort of did. With only the poorly copied fake ID he'd managed to secure before they flew, she had nothing. No money, no phone, no connection in Naples except Jacob, who was probably incapacitated or dead.

Bowie made his *tsk* sound and picked up his phone again, his face red. He'd sighed and heaved and popped his antacids at the Naples customs, and when he'd called for the cab, he'd turned and looked back at the airport like he wanted to rush in and make a U-turn for Spain.

She gazed into her only support at the table—her espresso.

Help me.

As a rule, coffee consumption helped most everything.

In the spirit of compromise, she should be honest with herself. Her nerves were on edge like Bowie's. Only she'd had therapy sessions and knew how to control hers.

Questions circled through her brain while Bowie read whatever. Would Jacob blow his Captain America coolness when he discovered she'd come? Would he resist helping her find the Italian bank and the CEO who hid the dirty profits from human trafficking?

And was that why she'd come? Or ...

Or had she come to face Sophia in revenge?

Or had she come for the opportunity to work beside Jacob again?

That thought provoked a bothersome airlift of untimely butterflies inside.

"So ... what is next?" She hadn't meant for those thoughts to take verbal form, but they did.

Bowie, thank goodness, pretended not to hear her. His thumbs moved across the bottom of his screen. He glanced at a street sign then back at his coffee.

Isa looked out at the skinny, bricked streets instead of asking Bowie if he was finished with his espresso already.

Excruciating minutes passed.

Finally, their gazes crossed paths again. That's when she saw something in those dark eyes that hadn't been there before. Bowie, the OCD, minty-breathed, infidelity PI whose biggest fault was his politeness, held a shadow of something in his eyes. Maybe it was the espresso he'd downed. Maybe it was the sun peeking over the buildings. Or maybe a plan brewed there after all. Only it didn't look like it would be an honorable plan.

What's happening to Bowie? The PI who owns a fuzzy dog, helped me rescue a girl from human trafficking, and bought me clean clothes?

"You hungry?"

He asked like he might have a poison apple in his pocket.

"Sure," she said, wanting to ignore the strange glint in his eye. In the spirit of compromise, of course.

"There's a pizza place a few blocks away." He pointed up the street and slipped his phone into his pocket. Standing, he held out his hand, jaw set tight and telling.

Isa hesitated for a beat but got to her feet and took his hand.

"I think I know where Jacob is."

Isa stomach did a back flip. "You ...you ... *what?*"

CHAPTER 74

Isa stepped through the front door of Bambino's Pizzeria, unprepared. Yeah, yeah, Bowie had just said Jacob would be there—and that must have come from the mystery read on his phone—but she hadn't primed her heart for the impact.

All sensory organs jumped into overdrive when she saw him. The garlic permeating the air. Old-time Italian music. Red vino on white tablecloths. Aproned waiters slipping around tables, pizza platters in hand.

And through the kitchen door stepped Jacob Lahache, thin and pale and mouth open as he locked those fierce blue eyes on hers.

When Jacob marched toward her, Bowie melted into the background behind her. The tables of customers blurred and heartbeat thumps echoed in her ears.

But when he grabbed her by the elbow, voices, music, and the clatter of plates filled the airways again.

His first greeting could have been: *How awesome that you're alive*, or even *Hey, welcome to Italy*. But no. The first words out of Jacob Lahache's mouth were, "You need to leave."

Even with emotions and sensory glands scrambling in different directions, Isa had the super sleuth instincts to note Jacob's slitty eyes and glued-together teeth. He'd lost his grip on his distinctive Lahache cool. She pulled her elbow away, uncomfortably aware of the stares as a vision of him and her on a dance floor at the Drake's Horn materialized from the medial temporal lobe of her brain.

She thought she'd locked those memories away for good.

Along with the emerging memory came a more inconvenient recollection. He'd kissed her that night on the dance floor, pretending ...

Her awkward, "Hi Jacob," didn't mask over any of the stuff running amuck in her head and heart.

And making things worse? An apron-clad young man ogled from the kitchen's swinging door. His interest obvious, Isa set aside all the untimely nostalgia, realizing they might have walked into a troublesome situation.

Thanks to Bowie.

What the heck.

"It's nice to see you, too." She plastered her best infomercial smile across her face.

"It's not nice to see you." His frown stretched low. He glanced at Bowie. "And who is that chump?"

From somewhere far away behind her, Bowie moved back into the scene and stuck out his hand. "I'm your Spanish Connection. Bowen Banderas."

Jacob's frown twisted in confusion. He didn't reciprocate Bowie's hand-shake gesture. "What are you doing? You were supposed to put her on a plane."

Pulling his hand back, Bowie, acting like himself again, made his case. "I could not reach you, so we came to find you. I've sent several messages to your phone."

Through clamped teeth, Jacob said, "You're about to blow my cover."

Smile still mortared on and trying not to move her lips, Isa said, "You're the one overreacting here."

Jacob looked from Isa to Bowie and back.

He'd shaved his beard. Lost maybe ten pounds.

"Look, we were worried. A whole lot happened in Spain. But I do have a money trail." Not that her current information had opened any lanes to Sophia, but she had bona fide bank names and account numbers temporarily tattooed on her body. That counted for something.

Jacob pulled in a sharp breath and let go of Isa's arm. "I'll meet you at Fuga, a bar two blocks over. 4:15. After my shift."

The old, in-control Jacob showed up. He squared his shoulders. Laughed like he'd heard the funniest joke ever, and said, "Sorry for the mix-up, friends. We'll have to do lunch another day." Then his face went serious. He mouthed the word *go* and gestured at Bambino's front door.

Because Isa was now an experienced undercover agent able to read between the lines, she winked at Jacob. Said "Okay. We will see you later." She turned, grabbing Bowie by the lapel, and made for Bambino's door.

Outside on the sidewalk, she took a hunk of Bowie's arm flesh between her fingers and squeezed.

"Ouch," he said pulling from her pinch. "I know it looks like I haven't been completely honest—"

"You didn't *think* Jacob worked in there. You *knew* he worked there."

Enough. No more compromise. No more trust. She would figure this out on her own.

Only ... she couldn't.

She still needed Bowie.

"Come on." Isa spun around and started up the street.

CHAPTER 75

Jacob got to the table of onlookers who'd finally put their eyes back on their menus. Not feeling the waiter role or the double-double agent role either, he growled instead of greeted, "What will it be?"

The woman with the pink hair frowned. Said something in Italian.

Good. He would go get one of the native speakers in the kitchen to handle this table.

Maybe he should feign sickness and head out for the day. Only ... with Sophia in town, and a mob war about to go down ... he needed to be at the connection point. "I'll get someone else," he told the pink-headed frowner and headed for the kitchen.

Marko met him at the kitchen door. "You knew those Americans?" he asked. Marko eyed him sideways, a light bulb flickering above his head. Things were not lining up in Marko's naïve brain.

"Not for long." Jacob's answer didn't sound near as casual as he wanted. "Met the woman a couple nights ago. Had a thing. Didn't know she would stalk me. She probably gave me the virus." He rubbed his neck, feeling like it might be getting sore again. "But now she shows up with a boyfriend and ... ya know, Marko ..." he tried to put a thoughtful look on his face. "I just don't get women."

Marko's tense shoulders relaxed. "Me neither."

But it was Londo standing in the back of the kitchen cleaning his nails with a steak knife that gave Jacob the idea he might not have pulled off the scene with Isa in the dining room.

"Who's the babe?" Londo ask, examining the end of his blade. "Looks familiar."

Isa. Why had he gone beastly at the sight of her?

Because she shouldn't be there. Because she'd stepped onto ground zero. Because seeing her had stirred something inside that he didn't have time for.

"I picked her up a couple nights back. An American, so you wouldn't know her." Jacob wanted to flatten Londo's nose, but he held his flailing emotions intact and turned for a cabinet of silverware instead. He pulled a drawer open.

"I know a lot of things," Londo said, getting off his wall and inching up behind Jacob. "And I'll know a lot more about you before this day is over."

CHAPTER 76

"We're ... I mean, *I* am going to need Mace," Isa said, two steps ahead of Bowie. He had a hard time keeping up, even though his legs were probably a foot longer than hers.

Naples teemed with activity. Little Italian cars honked and passed at breakneck speeds in the streets. A man sat on a bench playing *O Sole Mio* on the accordion. Scooters drove up on the sidewalk to get around the honking cars.

She must have been in a delusional fog in Spain, thinking she could put faith in a man. Bowie, like every other male, couldn't be trusted.

Only that wasn't true for the sarge back in Houston. She longed to talk this case over with him now.

"I will explain," Bowie called after her. She'd almost forgotten her latest traitor was behind her.

A Madonna look-alike driving a lime-green scooter had to swerve when Isa stopped short in the flow of foot-and-scooter traffic. The middle-aged guy on the back of Madonna's scooter lost his bread sack, loaves scattering across the pavement. Before he gathered them up, he gave Isa a few derisive gestures. Isa picked up two loaves and handed them to the man as he boarded the scooter again. "Sorry," she said.

Bowie picked up a loaf and handed it to Madonna before she hit the scooter gas.

"We need to find a place for me to explain," Bowie said as the man on the scooter turned to glare.

"No more talk. No more long, drawn-out coffee sessions. I need answers, and I need Mace."

"You do not need to gas me." Bowie said, his voice small.

"Really?" she asked, hands on her hips. "I don't think I know you anymore."

"You know me. We've spent the last two days together. You met my dog."

"You set me up for something back there. Why?"

He said nothing but stood there, his face twisting up in anguish.

An empty bench, flanked by dead plants wrapped with Christmas lights, sat next to a headless mannequin sporting a red leather jacket. Isa walked to the bench. She plopped down, arms crossed.

Bowie scooted over, his eyes drooping from either guilt or exasperation—it was hard to tell.

"Tell me what just happened back there," she said, looking up to see if it was Bowie or a demon standing before her.

He eased down tentatively beside her and adjusted his jacket. "Jacob had mentioned he got a job at the pizzeria when he asked me to find you. But when he did not answer my texts or calls, I didn't know what to do with you."

"Why didn't you just say so? Why be secretive?"

"It wasn't a secret. It was protection."

"Explain."

"Jacob warned you would be difficult to convince." He shrugged, his palms up. "And Pepe is dead."

"That wasn't my fault."

His chest caved a little. "You have to admit you can be reckless. Nothing I said would convince you to go home. So I thought I needed to protect you, and knowing you wanted to come to Naples, I decided to give up my vacation and help you. And when I brought you here, I got ... how you say ... fowl heart."

"Chicken-hearted."

"That is what happened."

Isa sucked in a convicting breath. Said, "Okay, so I made it hard. I'm sorry." She shifted to face him. "But we've made great strides. If I didn't push, Chia wouldn't be free."

He nodded. "True."

"But you're not telling me everything. I sensed it back at the coffee café."

"Okay," he said, following with a sigh. "You are a good observer."

She shot him an impatient glance.

"I got here and realized that I would be following you through Naples looking at banks, interviewing bankers, looking for Jacob, finding dead people ..."

Isa cleared her throat.

"When I realized how close we were to Jacob, I wanted to hand you over to him and be done. So I decided to just take you there and leave you with him."

"Wow." Isa blinked.

He held up his palm. "But now, we have found Jacob. He is alive, and he is safe."

Isa shifted on the bench as more conviction stabbed. "You can go," she whispered. "I'm sorry I dragged you into this. I can fend for myself from here. I'll meet Jacob at the bar this afternoon, and he and I will figure the rest of this out." She sniffed. "You deserve your vacation."

Bowie slumped back against the wall. "You Americans are intense."

Isa pulled at her ponytail. "Really. You've been a huge help and I'll never forget it. Thank you for everything."

"Okay," Bowie said, patting the inside of his jacket. "I had a moment of doubt, I admit, but I am still with you."

"No, you don't have to—"

"Yes, I want to."

"You've done enough."

He sat up straight and faced her. "Where is determined Isa? We need her now."

A sheepish grin inched onto her face.

"What do you want to do?"

Bowie. Of course, he'd been torn with what to do as she dragged him deeper into the miry pits of human trafficking. He'd had to deal with orders from Jacob and appeals from her. Poor guy.

But Jacob hadn't looked so good, and his actions indicated he was in a tight spot.

But she absolutely, one hundred percent, hated using Bowie's cash for her mission-related needs, especially when his heart wasn't in it.

"Write down your address," she said.

"For what?" he asked.

"I'm going to send you every single cent you've spent on me after I get home."

One of his thick eyebrows pushed against the other, forming a single, bushy line. "If I am still in this, then I am still getting bounty reward money."

"I don't want to force you into anything you don't want to do."

"I had a moment of doubt. But I am back now."

Was he? Was she? Were they making headway or making a mess? But sitting on this bench waiting for Jacob to get off work seemed like a colossal waste of time and energy. "First, ammo," she whispered. Self-defense tools were a good place to start. Rule number six ... or was it seven? Probably it was nine, and probably it was from some

TV show like NCIS and not official police protocols. But someone somewhere said one should never be caught without a knife or some form of self-protection.

"Can you manage to find something we can use for self-defense and let me borrow a few bucks to buy a phone?"

"Are we not looking for these things together?"

"I'm going back to execute reconnaissance at the pizza joint until it's time to meet Jacob at the bar. You go look for armaments. I can meet you outside Bambino's."

"Armaments. Yes, of course. But I am going to need more of these." Bowie pulled an empty wrapper from inside his jacket pocket.

CHAPTER 77

After picking up a burner phone at what looked to be a tiny, street-side flea market, Isa texted Bowie that two seedy-looking characters had entered Bambino's.

It took him thirty minutes to respond. When he did, his texted reply said seedy people were known to eat pizza, and to not get the idea that she could follow seedy people through the streets of Naples. He politely asked her to stay put.

Bowie's mission? Find Mace, or a knife, or even a heavy-duty wrench in case they needed to perform backup for Jacob for whatever he had developing inside Bambino's. If Jacob had gone silent during the two days Bowie attempted contact, then Jacob, she knew, felt threatened and wouldn't risk communicating with outsiders.

Something was up. It reeked of danger.

Thank God, truly, that she and Bowie were back in sync.

Now, she'd positioned herself across the street from Bambino's, poised to help Jacob should he need it. But the hard and flat architectural cement block outside the store made her butt numb.

With the Euros Bowie had loaned her, she'd also bought a baguette from a street vendor and a magazine from the wine-slash-bookstore. She'd nabbed the block seat after the previous occupier had gotten up to accompany the woman with a brown sack coming out of the store. The sack had the English words *Drink and Read* printed on the front. Wiggling herself into some form of comfort, she'd opened the magazine and pretended to read. But the photos of lasagna, tomato sauce, and oozing mozzarella had her sights on the page almost more than the street.

She held the Italian cuisine magazine at the bridge of her nose, fighting to keep her eyes glued to Bambino's. Good thing the magazine had been written in Italian, because after an hour and twenty minutes of staring at Bambino's front door, she might have been tempted to start reading how the best pizza needed to be cooked with *fuoco*. She'd figured out the article topic from the glossy picture of a bubbling cheese pizza on a paddle coming out of a *fuoco* ... fire.

She flipped the page to the next article. The photo of tiramisu layers made her mouth water, so she thumbed back to the content page, removing foodie distractions.

While her spying eyes continued with the recon heavy lifting, her mind had the bandwidth to think about other urgencies at hand. Like whether Chia had made it home to Nigeria yet. And Coffee Magic and what kind of shape it would be in when she got back. And the box Milly Washington had sent and how Awena had probably analyzed her way through it, already solving the mystery of how and why Claire Washington had turned bad cop. Back when she met her, Milly had seemed convinced someone had pushed Claire into becoming a turncoat.

After digging around in deadly European human trafficking rings, she knew she wouldn't likely be up for digging around in Claire's HPD bad-cop history. But as Bowie had gone above and beyond for her, she needed to go above and beyond for Claire.

CALCULATED ENCOUNTERS

Isa pulled the burner from her windbreaker. At this point in the precarious game of uncovering and identifying trafficking lanes, she probably shouldn't make contact with anyone, lest more people end up like Pepe.

Pepe. He'd been kind. And helpful. And relocating dollars for the scum of the earth. *What a shame.* Those at the bottom of the greed chain were the ones who paid the hefty price. Those at the top, like Sophia, were the ones who reaped the benefits of the workers at the bottom.

God did not intend for the economy to work this way.

She fired off a message to Awena stating that this was her new temporary number, she was safe, would likely be tied up in Italy for a few days. She added she'd like Awena to please call Milly Washington and let her know she'd be able to look through the box soon.

Meanwhile, the steady stream of eclectic customers testified to Bambino's popularity. The pizzeria must have stayed at occupant capacity the entire afternoon.

Jacob wouldn't be waiting tables at a busy restaurant unless he looked for something or someone associated to the pizzeria. He had to be on Sophia's trail.

Probably a mob-occupied room existed somewhere behind the kitchen.

After she polished off the baguette, her brain threatened to join her numb back end. Twisting the magazine into a roll, Isa took twelve deep breaths. This got the blood flowing again. Which was good because otherwise, she might not have noticed that the customers who'd gone in to dine at Bambino's all filed out at once.

With strained looks on their faces.

Isa stood, grip tightening around the magazine roll.

The pace of the pizzeria mass exit picked up. A couple of people got shoved.

Next thing she knew, she was weaving through traffic and elbowing her way against the flow of people spilling out of Bambino's.

Getting to Bambino's door, she squeezed past a family with small kids and heard the word, *"Fuoco!"*

But Isa didn't smell any smoke.

Oh goodness, was she losing her sense of smell? She couldn't get COVID now.

She told herself to get a grip.

Inside the three-quarters-empty dining room, a large fellow shoved pizza slices into a box, and the hostess in the black dress urged him to hurry. Isa thought she heard the hostess say something about a stove in the kitchen.

Jacob wasn't in the dining room.

She whirled around. Maybe he'd gotten caught up in the exit crowd.

Through the window and people rushing down the sidewalk, she saw a black SUV pull up to the curb.

She lifted to her tiptoes, unconsciously rubbing at her coming-back-to-life backside.

The back door of the black SUV opened. A high heel and long leg slipped out.

Trouble. Immense bright red warning flags waved around in her head.

Isa made for the swinging kitchen door.

CHAPTER 78

"Now?" Jacob feared his blood pressure's sudden thrust might push right through the top of his head like an oil rig hitting pay dirt. With no Sophia stooge in proximity, he had no way to warn her of what was about to take place. "She's coming here?" He glared at Marko. "*Now?*"

Marko pulled a Smith and Wesson from his waist like he expected a showdown.

Not good. Not good.

Why would Sophia circle back to Bambino's when she had set him up to meet with her guys at a bar later? Why was he not able to pull all the pieces together on this job?

The cook moved around quick, turning off ovens and with a pizza to-go box tucked beneath his arm. He shot Jacob an *oh well* look, and scrambled for the back door, grabbing the tiramisu off the counter as he passed.

Marko cracked the swinging dining room door to peek at the action. "The car is here!" he exclaimed. "As promised!"

Why, oh why, do women never do what they say they will do?

Jacob commenced to ransacking the kitchen drawers looking for a knife. If he was going to blow his secondary cover by getting Sophia out of the building, he'd need some form of weapon. He got his hand on a big old cleaver at the back of a chopping block's drawer. Wouldn't be able to stab that flattened stainless-steel directly into flesh but could possibly remove a head with a calculated swing. Jacob gave it a practice swipe.

At the swinging door, Marko slipped further to the dark side. "I want to see the boss woman squirm." A nervous, bizarre chuckle followed his declaration.

As Marko tried to push through the door, someone pushed from the other side, banging against his gun arm. He lost his grip and the Smith and Wesson dropped to the floor.

Jacob rubbed his eyes with the back of his hand, wishing what he looked at was a mirage. Inopportune Isa Phillips stood inside the door, and she eyed Marko's gun on the floor.

She had something rolled up in her hand.

Marko looked back at Jacob and then at Isa, hesitant and not sure of his next move.

But not Isa. Her eyes darted from Jacob's cleaver to Marko's gun, and she made an instant move. Jacob's stomach went sour as he watched her make a dive for the Smith and Wesson.

She executed a near-perfect a tuck and roll. Which was hard to believe. She came up with the gun pointed at Marko and broadcasted to anyone within ear shot that she was, indeed, a trained professional. All covers blown. All lies exposed.

Thank you, Isa Phillips.

Marko glanced at Jacob in confusion.

"Get out now. Things are about to get out of control," Jacob said, pointing his cleaver at Marko.

Flustered and awkward, Marko pushed past Isa and the pointed gun and stormed out the back door.

Even an idiot could figure Isa was there on some official business with her show-off move. But he'd have to worry about how to explain her away later because right now, he had a criminal to rescue and a bounty to secure.

"What is happening here?" Isa lowered her aim and glanced around the empty dining room. "There's no fire."

"No, Nancy Drew, there is no fire." He took hold of her arm, guiding her out the swinging door and around the tables of half-eaten pizzas to a framed window near the bathrooms. "And you've got to get out. With Ghettas at the back door, you're going out this window. Here, you take the cleaver and give me the gun."

"But—"

He shook his head, taking the Smith and Wesson from her. "No time to explain." He placed the cleaver into Isa's opened palm.

"But, Jacob …"

That little bell that rang every time a customer came through the front door … rang.

In perfect unison, their heads swerved to the sound.

The first one through the door was the guard who'd sat on the sofa with Jacob in Sophia's office. Sophia followed in pseudo-disguise of scarf and big sunglasses, Louis Vuitton bag across her shoulder. Behind her came a guard Jacob had never seen. And two seconds later, in walked Bowie.

"Isa," Bowie exclaimed, passing Sophia and her confused-looking guard. "I could not find you at the book and wine store."

"Isabella Phillips," Sophia exclaimed, lowering her sunglasses. "You're finally here."

At Sophia's greeting, her men in black tucked themselves in close.

Looking exasperated, Isa raised her meat cleaver like a blackboard pointer and said, "The restaurant has been evacuated because there's a fire. Only there isn't." She pointed the tip of the cleaver at Sophia. "Nice to see you, Sophia."

Jacob wanted to pull his hair out by the roots. Or Isa's.

How nice that the conversation is going well. Why don't we all grab a table, finish off a pizza, and make polite arrangements?

Outside the front windows, Jacob saw Sophia's driver exit the car.

"Hey," he said.

The driver went to the rear bumper and popped open the back door.

Bowie turned to face Sophia. "Who are you?"

Jacob got louder. "Heeeey!"

Another guy crawled out of the back of the SUV.

Sophia tucked her chin to her shoulder. "Me? I'm the owner of this enterprise. But why," she asked, looking around, "has everyone left?"

"Everybody down." Jacob said, moving in on Isa. Nobody else in the dining room seemed to be putting Jacob's dots together. "This is happening."

Looking over her shoulder, the lights finally blinked on for Sophia. Her mouth opened wide like she wanted to scream, but no sound came.

Outside, a hooded and masked gangster, gun unashamedly public, stepped up to the other two at the SUV.

Jacob watched the driver hoist a big, audacious machine gun.

Outside, somebody screamed.

Then all the noise in the universe hushed, waiting for the inevitable blast.

"Everybody down," Jacob cried, pushing Isa into Bowie then leaping for Sophia. Like a scene from *The Matrix*, in slow motion, Jacob flew through the air, as Sophia's hand reached for her mouth and her guards reached for their guns.

Behind him, Isa and Bowie knocked against tables.

While in flight, he prayed those two would hit the floor and make it to the back of the dining room or bathrooms.

Time sped up again when he landed on Sophia, the mechanical reverberation of rapid fire and shattering glass blasting through the air.

Outside, more screams. He imagined people ducking behind cars and stampeding shops.

Beneath him, Sophia shifted. He couldn't hear it but felt a moan escape her chest.

Seconds of loud gun fire and breaking glass seemed to last forever.

Then the air stilled again.

He heard shuffling at the back of the dining room. Isa and Bowie—moving for the bathrooms.

Keeping his head low and with Sophia groaning beneath him, he surveyed the floor. Dough, tomato sauce, and glass everywhere. Sophia's dead guards were crumpled on either side of him.

He got to his knees. Lifted high enough to peer at the door.

The door wasn't there. Just hinges.

Weird anticipatory silence followed.

Jacob scanned every window and exit, looking for the next threat.

Marko stepped into the dining room. "Oh, my—"

Bullets sprayed.

Hands on top of his head, Jacob flattened atop Sophia again, knocking any air she'd pulled in right back out again.

Poor Marko.

Sirens. Italian sirens in the distance.

CHAPTER 79

Backs against the narrow hall with the bathroom doors shut, Isa counted the seconds. She guessed she'd get to 120 before risking a look at the dining room.

But at count 98, Bowie crawled over her and stuck his head out.

"Y'all good?" she heard Jacob ask.

Bowie gave him a thumbs-up.

The sirens weren't getting closer.

"They're gone," Jacob yelled. "Maybe in the back, 'cause the car is still out front."

Bowie scrambled to his feet. Isa did the same. They stood side-by-side, stunned at the commotion. She'd never seen a crime scene post-machine gun. Three bodies on the floor, and Jacob squatted next to Sophia. Other than that, everything else was unrecognizable.

Was Sophia hit?

A blast from the kitchen and Isa sank back into the hall. Another blast and she covered her head. The scent of burned chemicals hit the air.

My gosh, they're going to burn the building down before the cops can enter.

"We got to get her out of here," Isa heard Jacob shout. "Mollies coming in through the back door!"

Molotov cocktails?

A third blast and Bowie had his arm around her.

She heard the distinctive whoosh of fire catching hold. That sound put her into first gear, motor gassed.

She passed Bowie doing a hundred miles an hour. Got to Jacob, who had Sophia on her feet.

Blood streamed down Sophia's leg.

"Take her where?" Isa asked, getting an arm under Sophia's shoulder, the one with the designer bag still hanging from it. "Outside?"

Sophia rolled her head toward Jacob.

Isa caught a glimpse of a knowing look that passed between Sophia and Jacob. Looked like this wasn't Jacob and Sophia's first connection since he'd arrived in Naples.

"Get me out," Sophia gasped. "I'll help you, just get me out!"

So Jacob and Sophia were making deals? Making nice? Making like ... what?

But Isa hung with them as Jacob, arm at Sophia's other shoulder, dragged her to what was once the front door.

Smoke billowed from the kitchen.

Through the shattered windows, Isa saw two of the assassins appear, hustling their way back to the SUV. One glanced her way. He stopped, confusion shadowing his eyes, like he had not expected them to be alive. The assassin's hesitation gave Jacob just enough time to push Sophia onto Isa. He pulled Marko's Smith and Wesson from his pants and stormed the two bad guys, the gun engaged and bullets flying.

Both men went down.

The hooded number three assassin was nowhere to be seen.

Jacob hustled back to Isa and Sophia. "In the car," he ordered.

Stunned by his swift and precise kill, they didn't argue.

CALCULATED ENCOUNTERS

Trying to maneuver Sophia into the back seat of the SUV wasn't easy. The woman's long legs wouldn't cooperate. With a final shove at Sophia's curvy hip, Isa strapped her into the back seat, but her tight dress had slipped up around her hips. Isa tugged. Heaved. Got the dress under Sophia's backside. She started to close the door but went back in again. Pulled until she got the dress down to the thigh. She needed both Jacob's and Bowie's heads in the game—it was the moral thing to do.

Closing the door, Isa located Jacob, who had his gun high, sweeping, and letting anyone who even thought about approaching know the consequences. "We should wait on the police," she hollered. As if on cue, an explosion erupted down the street. Two parked cars lifted into the air as automobiles and landed on the pavement as balls of fire.

"I don't think the police are going to make it today. Stalling is probably part of the plan," he said, going for the driver's seat. "Get in."

Isa scrambled for the front passenger door, the meat cleaver somehow and miraculously still in her grip. "Wait. Bowie."

Bowie emerged from the smoke, making for the car. He got hold of the handle and had the back door open before Jacob put the car in gear.

Isa glanced at the back seat. Sophia, looking like she wasn't aware her own people wanted her dead, groaned.

Bowie slammed the door, and the four took off down the skinny streets of Naples, the forgotten rear door of the SUV bouncing up and down.

CHAPTER 80

"Where will we go?" Isa asked, one hand pressing into the dashboard and the other gripping the back of Jacob's seat. "What's the plan here?"

"Take me ... to the villa," Sophia wailed from the back seat.

Jacob adjusted the rearview mirror, then put his sights back on the road.

Made a sharp left turn and all occupants swung right.

Isa checked the back seat again.

She found Bowie shirtless. He had taken the top half of his clothes off, ripping the shirt into strips. Then he tied off the blood flow at Sophia's wound.

"Maybe we should find a hospital," Isa said, looking back to Jacob.

"No hospital," Sophia gasped. With Bowie working on her leg, she'd come back to life.

Figures.

"You'll bleed to death," Isa stated.

"She won't bleed to death," Jacob snapped, rolling his eyes at Isa.

Thank you, Jacob, for your unyielding support. She hadn't forgotten the looky-look that had passed between him and Sophia back at Bambino's. Or how he'd half-heartedly tossed Isa into Bowie, while leaping like a ballet dancer upon tender Sophia.

"She needs a doctor." Bowie broke in.

Isa glanced back again.

Bowie continued to wrap his shirt around that long leg. How could the woman's leg still look so good stained with blood and a shirt wrapped about her thigh? And she wished Bowie had worn a T-shirt under his dress shirt, because now, the unforeseen picture of his pectoral muscles in the raw would be forever embedded in her brain. She hadn't expected Bowie to look so ... so ... fit.

How could she consider such matters in this breakout, run-from-the-bad-guys moment?

Because some things will never go unnoticed, she decided, and turned her sights back to Jacob and the familiar—his stone-like jaw.

"I'm thinking the hospital or the police station. Maybe the police will get her to a doctor," she said.

"Bounty," he answered, his lips barely moving. He cracked his neck with a sideways tilt and said, "We have to get her on a plane to the US. The Italians take possession, she'll never be extradited. She's wanted for crimes here, and we ..." He paused as if in deep, contemplative thought. "We wouldn't get paid if that happens."

"I can ... I can ..." Sophia winced when Bowie tied the knot. "I'll pay you the bounty prize ... I have a doctor ... I must call him."

"Of course you have a doctor," Jacob retorted. "You're probably paying three or four of them to get those meds you store up. But no can do, Princess. The Ghettas have infiltrated your operation and will be waiting for you. You can't go home."

Isa choked on that one. Cleared her throat. "Like we'd take her home."

She turned to see Sophia open her purse and commence to digging.

"Whoa," Isa said, reaching back for the bag. "Bowie, make sure she's not packing."

With a pitiful pout, Sophia slipped the Louis off her shoulder and willingly passed it to Bowie. "Check for yourself. I was looking … for my phone to call … the doctor."

Bowie slipped his jacket back on over his bare upper body then opened Sophia's purse.

"So, police," Isa said, redirecting again. "We should find a station. I might get GPS on this burner phone." She reached for her back pocket.

"Not if we want the US bounty money," Jacob answered.

"This is about money?" Isa braced her palms on the dashboard as they took a sharp curve.

"It's about the goal. It's what I came for."

"It's what you came for, too, Isa," Bowie echoed, being no help at all.

"How did you plan to get her to the States?" Everyone in the car had gone mad. She was the only person with brain intact.

"Airplane. Only she'll need a passport."

Isa pulled the visor down, eyeing Sophia in the mirror. "Sophia, mind if we stop by the house and pick up your papers? Maybe you could pack a bag. Grab a snack."

"No need to get snarky," Jacob said.

"Her papers are here." Bowie held up Sophia's passport.

"Well, that's convenient. Maybe we should drive to the airport. Only, let's see … the woman is wounded." Isa drew out the word *wounded*. "I think airlines frown on bleeding passengers."

"Thank you, Isa." Sophia said.

Isa rolled her eyes and pushed back into her seat. *Why me*, she mouthed to the scenery flashing by.

"We could charter a plane." Jacob nodded at his own idea.

Sophia leaned forward, hands on Jacob's headrest.

Isa eyed the woman, suspecting the worst but also thinking Jacob deserved the worst.

"I have another place ... west of Naples," Sophia announced. "I can send for my doctor." She winced then added, "And send assassins for those who tried to take me out today."

"It *was* your own family that tried to take you out." Jacob let go a heavy sigh. "You knew you had blood enemies." He looked over at Isa. "I hate how hard to explain this is going to be."

"Explain," Isa said.

"Yes," Sophia confirmed. "Explain it to us."

Things couldn't get more bizarre. With a bloody wound, in a getaway car with the good guys, Sophia had become a part of "us."

At a hard right, the four inside the SUV swayed left. Jacob ran up on a curb and they all bounced, but not as big as the back hatch door.

Jacob directed the SUV for the hills west of Naples.

Isa braced. Not for the next bump, but for the next wrong move on Jacob's part.

CHAPTER 81

If this had been vacation, Isa would have inhaled pure ecstasy. The cottage tucked into a wooded slope couldn't be more charming.

But this wasn't vacation.

And Sophia wasn't their friend.

Both Jacob and Bowie had seemed to forget this fact.

Helping her out of the car, Bowie took Sophia's phone from her hand and slipped it into his pocket. Which meant, at some point in their drive to her secondary or possibly third or fourth home, he'd let Sophia have her phone.

Dadgum Bowie. She knew she couldn't trust him.

Jacob, on the other hand, had spent the last half hour in the car explaining to Sophia how he hadn't given her the full picture when they were together at her villa.

At her villa?

He told Sophia the Ghettas were further along in their plans than he'd revealed to her earlier. And she shouldn't trust anyone in her family.

Like he had experience in blood-related dysfunction. Compared to Isa's family history, Jacob's family dynamics were probably more like the Cosby Show where the Huxtables, Cliff and Claire, proved to be perfect, loving parents.

Sophia had not acted surprised by the news her third cousins Mike and Londo had joined a new breed of gangs seeking to push the old families out of Naples. That's why she'd asked Jacob to work as her spy, gathering intel behind the family's back. Her own father, she'd said between grimaces, had been taken out by a rival gang member who was married to her fourth cousin's sister-in-law.

Fourth cousins? Isa had met her mother's sister and kids exactly twice. That side of the family had moved back to Mexico to take care of the grandmother Isa had never known.

Why she let anything Sophia had to say affect her thoughts remained a mystery. The woman had suckered her in once, making Isa believe Sophia was the victim of an abusive husband. But Sophia desired Isa to be her stooge, not her hero—a patsy, a way to get her cartel and evil husband out of her ambitious way.

Sophia had continued to sucker Bowie and Jacob now. She'd groaned on about her leg but managed to give Jacob directions to her winter cottage. Though Isa had protested the idea, here they were in the late afternoon pulling into a what was sure to be a booby trap.

A beautiful, scenic booby trap, of course.

Back in Coffee Magic Jacob had all but made fun of Isa for letting Sophia dupe her in the cartel caper. Who duped who now?

Out of the SUV, the rear hatch door finally shut, the four stood in front of the arched door that looked like it belonged in the Hobbit's Shire. This day, this scene, this moment ... unbelievable. How beautiful and vulnerable Sophia looked leaning against Jacob, her face brave, her dress tight with her attendant Bowie removing her burden of finding her cottage key by digging through the Louis Vuitton for her.

Oh, brother.

A gangster army probably waited on the other side of that fairytale door.

Good thing Isa still gripped the meat cleaver.

Bowie's hand finally emerged from Sophia's fashion-statement purse with a single key secured between his thumb and forefinger. "Just like she promised. In the inner pocket," he exclaimed, as if trying to convince everyone Sophia was now trustworthy.

He probably had the hots for her. Jacob probably had the hots for her.

They were probably going to die before either man proposed.

Jacob transferred Sophia to Bowie, took the key and positioned it at the deadbolt above the twisted iron handle.

"Wait," Isa whispered, reaching to touch his hand. She wished to reason some logic into the thought columns of his brain—which currently, seemed to accommodate more than a few empty cells. "I've learned the hard way. We shouldn't trust her." Isa kept her voice light, her eyes wide.

On cue, Sophia groaned.

Bowie stiffened.

Jacob, for the first time since she'd sat by his hospital bed some six months ago—with him recovering from a bullet wound and exposing a wee ounce of vulnerability—looked at her with a pensive shadow hanging out in the eyes.

Could he? Would he listen to her for once?

"Why believe anything she says now?" Isa reasoned. "She's obviously used her phone and who knows who she called." Then Isa added, "Thanks to Bowie here." She shot Bowie a couple of eye daggers.

Suspended in thought, Jacob hung there, key at the keyhole, his tired eyes locked on hers. She might, finally, drill through his formerly impenetrable cranium. Miracles happened.

But Bowie. But Bowie intervened. "My friends, this woman needs a doctor. But at a hospital, she will be arrested."

"I'm okay with that," Isa said.

From the peripheral, she could see Bowie still had one arm around Sophia, but with his free hand, he hit the air. "We would forfeit the reward you promised. Have you forgotten our agreement, Isa Phillips?"

"At this point, it's about right and wrong, not the money."

"Yes, yes," Bowie agreed. "I am for the right thing as you say, but the *federales* often look the other way when it comes to economic crimes. If arrested, she could be released before you are able to leave the country." Bowie sounded like a stupid law professor.

"Hand her over to the authorities." Isa looked back to Jacob, still frozen at the door. "It's the right thing."

Bowie tried harder. "She will be protected. Have you forgotten the federal officer we almost ran over in España?"

Sophia made a couple of fake, shallow coughs and said, "Take me down and you take down the common people I serve."

Oh, so here at the cottage door, Sophia revealed the *why* to her madness. The common people. Like her husband jailed in the States, Sophia saw herself as a savior of the disadvantaged. What a scam criminals sold themselves while raking in the big dough. Isa wanted to throw up, but she wrapped her fingers around Jacob's wrist. "Don't listen to that nonsense, Jacob. We turn her in to the police now and we still win."

Jacob blinked.

Slow and low, Isa gave him more reason. "We get back in that car and we take her in."

Jacob blinked again.

Almost convinced.

But then ... Jacob pulled from her grip, shoved the key into the deadbolt, and unlocked the door.

Even her dragon's heart sank.

CHAPTER 82

Isa called it intuition. Awena called it the Holy Spirit. Jacob called it training. Call it what you will, but that second sense that tells you things are not going to go as planned ... well, that happened.

Behind Jacob, Isa hesitated before going in. But choices were nonexistent unless she wanted to get in the SUV and drive herself back to town, find a police station, give directions, and hope like heck law enforcement would show up at the cottage before her traitor partners and Sophia had moved on to the next phase of Jacob's make-it-up-as-you-go plan.

Pushing dread to the side, Isa followed Jacob into the front room.

Dust particles floated through the filtered rays of light that had managed to slip around the sides of the drawn roman shades. The earthy smell of trapped mold assaulted her nostrils. She felt like she might have her first-in-life asthma attack.

Isa tucked her nose into the collar of what was once her white shirt. "You don't come here often, do you?"

Sophia didn't answer but hopped, with Bowie's help, to the sheet-covered sofa in the open front room.

Gun drawn, Jacob glanced down the hall and at the kitchen on the right.

"Check the bedrooms." Isa said, placing her cleaver on the side table and pulling at the shade cords.

Jacob ignored her, stuffed the gun in the back of his pants, and sat on the sheet-covered chair next to the sofa. Pointed at Bowie. "Give me her phone."

Bowie pulled Sophia's phone from his pocket and tossed it to Jacob.

Sophia, back of her hand at her forehead, leaned into the arm of the sofa with an exasperated sigh.

Oh, brother. Isa got back to work on the stubborn cords.

"Okay, Sophia," Jacob said tapping at her phone. "Give me your doc's contact information. I'll get the negotiations started."

Finally, the shade pleated upwards. Light streamed in on the situation, revealing green mold on the cobblestone floors.

"No need to call."

Wait.

That voice didn't belong to any of the four.

That voice came from the hall.

Isa jerked around to see two guns. One pointed at Jacob. One pointed at Bowie.

From the end of the hall where the bedrooms had been left unchecked, two men entered the scene. Ruger Max 9 in one hand and medical bag in the other, the short, balding one with the grey goatee said, "I am the doctor."

Isa recognized the Ruger. Mac had carried the same gun when he was alive.

The taller one with the James Bond vibe gave Jacob instructions. "On your feet with your hands up." The heavy Italian accent added an edge of sophistication to his demand. But his good looks and debonair flair didn't stop Isa from inching toward the end table where her trusty cleaver lay.

"Gian," Sophia gasped, then rattled off some desperate-sounding Italian.

Sighing and heaving himself out of the chair, Jacob got to his feet, hands in the air.

Stepping to Sophia, Gian kept his weapon aimed on Jacob. He smoothed her hair, and Italian sentiment flowed. Sophia gave Gian that look ... the same *that look* she'd given Jacob before the Ghettas burned down Bambino's.

How many men could give *that look* to one woman in one day?

"Have you a weapon?" the doctor asked Bowie.

Isa tensed. Had Bowie secured the Mace? The heavy-duty wrench?

Bowie shook his head, hands still the air.

The doctor accepted that answer and joined Gian and Sophia at the sofa. He placed his medical bag on the dusty coffee table, opened it, and stuck his Ruger in among what looked to be medical supplies.

Gian straightened to full height. Asked Jacob if *he* had a weapon.

A vision slammed Isa's memory banks while Jacob tried Bowie's move and shook his head. "No weapon here."

But Gian didn't buy Jacob's lie. "Drop it there." He gestured toward the dusty table that now had sterile medical supplies scattered across the top.

True, Sophia didn't deserve anyone's sympathy, but Isa cringed at the thought of the doc performing medical maneuvers amongst the fungus and grime.

As she watched the action around the coffee table, she remembered the sophisticated man at Nasha's desk back at the community house in Málaga.

Gian.

Gian had been at the community house.

But what really got to her, what really struck a nerve?

Jacob obliged the debonair gangster and pulled his gun from his backside. From the tired look on his face and from the deep breath followed by a cough, Jacob must have decided to raise the white flag, give up, and go to bed.

CHAPTER 83

Somewhere between bending to surrender and placing the gun on the coffee table, Jacob dropped to a crouch, yanked up the side of the table and pushed it over onto the doc and Gian, surprising Sophia.

The doc's gun, medical bag of tricks, and dust particles flew. As did all the various medicinal gadgets.

Gian fell back on Sophia's head.

A muffled scream escaped the flailing wad of gangsters.

The doc, who'd been in the process of unwrapping her shirt-bandage, dropped Sophia's leg and hit the floor, hands over his head.

So much for the Hippocratic Oath.

Isa, realizing their moment had arrived, dove for the doc's gun. She couldn't perform her favorite tuck and roll move because the table and bodies blocked her path, but she managed to secure the Ruger, get up to her knees, and with the help of a sofa arm, pull herself to full 5'4" height, weapon drawn.

The scene had taken a drastic change.

Bowie.

Bowie had a gun. And he had that gun shoved against Jacob's head.

Isa stared, mouth open and collecting dust. Guess Bowie found more than a can of Mace when he went for armament.

A traitor. A double-crossing liar. She should have known better than to make friends. So far in Isa's history, friends and loved ones rarely worked out.

"Drop the gun," Bowie told Jacob.

Jacob, shrugging at Isa, obeyed.

At the tangle of confusion at the sofa, Gian pushed the table away, straightened his black blazer, reached for his gun on the floor then aimed it at Isa.

"Drop your gun, too."

She set the doc's gun on the side table, next to her cleaver.

CHAPTER 84

For good measure, Gian had Bowie use zip-ties out of the doc's medical bag to secure Isa and Jacob's hands behind their backs. They'd been ordered to sit on the cold, moldy, stone floor against a wall while the doc finished up with Sophia's leg. The bullet had gone clean through, missed the femoral artery, and other than a nasty scar left by seven stitches, both sides, Sophia would recover.

Sophia complained about possible scarring. But giving her a grace break, Isa thought the pain meds might have had something to do with Sophia's lack of focus on the real issues.

The bad guys did most of their exchanges in whispered Italian until Bowie spoke up and asked, "What are we doing with these guys?" He'd pointed his gun at Isa and Jacob.

That's when Sophia, looking inebriated, exhaled some drama and said, "I suppose they'll have to die."

Gian looked to be okay with the idea.

But Jacob tilted his head in question. "Die? Really? Just when we were getting close."

Isa thought she might barf, but Sophia, who clearly liked to play emotional games, said, "Unless you convince me you are worth the trouble to keep around."

"I thought we had a worth-it time yesterday. You seemed to like it."

Gian, who'd put the cottage living area back in order, snapped to attention. He narrowed his eyes at Jacob, dark and deadly.

"The kiiiisssss?" Sophia asked. She rubbed her lips with her finger as she recalled the moment. "In my bedroom? Yes, I did like it."

Once Isa got her jaw back into place, she asked Jacob the question everyone wanted an answer to. "You were in her bedroom?"

He shrugged. "All in a day's work."

In the sheet-covered chair, Bowie sat stiff, looking uncomfortable with the conversation. Maybe he thought Sophia would free Jacob and that could mean Jacob would wreak havoc on Bowie's head. Or maybe he'd been kissing Sophia, too. Had every man in the room had a taste of Sophia?

"Because I think smart is sexy ..." Jacob relaxed against the wall finding his undercover slick-talk personality. "Tell me, Sophy, when did you buy our friend Bowie off?"

The doc packed up his bag, gun included, and went to the kitchen.

"Stop talking," Gian ordered.

"No, I like the talk," Sophia said, sitting higher in the sofa. Sophia on pain meds made for a frisky mob boss, and Jacob went for it.

But smack talk made Isa's stomach churn. There was absolutely no honesty happening in this room. Only games.

Jacob asked, "So what *did* you promise this low-level private investigator?"

"Hey," Bowie protested.

"Shut up," Gian ordered.

Shaking her head at him, Sophia said, "Jay, I mean James, oh, how could I forget ..." she pulled her shoulders up in a suggestive manner. "It's Jacob. It's three men in one."

On that, Isa could almost agree.

"I absconded your phone, remember? I found a lot of little texts from our private investigator Bowie, and those messages were about a friend of yours that he was to deliver back to America."

Bare chest gleaming from beneath his wool jacket, Bowie's shrug didn't do much for his credibility. "Yes, I texted you. I did not know this woman had your phone, Jacob."

The smile of satisfaction spread across Sophia's face. "A few inquiries later, and I discovered brave Isa snooping her way through *Málaga* and rescuing prostitutes."

Isa's stomach roiled. "You ordered the hit on Pepe."

Sophia tried to imitate Isa's Houston, Texas, accent, saying, "No, I did not order the hit on Pepe." She twisted her head to the side, and Isa thought it might completely rotate. The woman was a demon.

"That little smurf upset some big and important men at the top of the food chain in Málaga. Everyone knows sex trade is a thriving tourist business there." Sophia rubbed the back of her neck. "It's a growing import making a lot of people rich."

"That's sick," Isa said. "You're a disgrace to the female population."

"I thought we were friends, Isa." Sophia's incredulous pout gave Isa's stomach more reason to keep churning.

Jacob, not liking Isa's honesty, redirected the conversation. "Sophia, you and me, we are the ones with a budding friendship."

"You toy with the Americans," Gian told Sophia. "And they will talk you into a corner." Poor Gian. He couldn't get everyone to quiet down.

Sophia waved him off. "We go way back, don't we, Jacob?"

The doctor appeared in the doorway. Said something in Italian.

"It's time for me to go," Sophia announced.

Jacob didn't miss a beat. "Where are we headed?"

As Gian helped her up off the sofa, she answered. "Unfortunately, and I do mean *unfortunately*, I'll be leaving you behind. Killing does not come as easy for me as some may think."

Isa got a whiff of oil … kerosene.

Jacob must have smelled it too. He maneuvered up to his knees. "Whoa, wait. Is that gas? You blazing us, Sophia?"

Gian told Bowie to help Sophia, and then Gian stepped over to Isa. With one pull under her arm, he lifted Isa to her feet.

There had to be a way to slow down what was about to happen. Honest Isa gave the smack talk a shot. "I saw you in Málaga. You and Sophia are trafficking. And you have an inside banker in Naples. Oh, yeah. I've got dirt."

She sensed Jacob's unimpressed stare from behind.

She leaned around Gian and scowled at Bowie. "The authorities already have account information, and it will be a matter of hours before the whole ring comes crashing down."

Bowie shook his head, a signal, she guessed, that he didn't think she should go there.

"Shut up." Gian repeated. The guy was all looks and no brains.

But Sophia, drugged up and making mistakes, said, "How could you know that?"

For Isa, those words were a good as an HPD interrogation room confession. "I've got all the proof and have already handed it over. You need to turn yourself in. That's the best way out. For you and for Luca."

"How do you know anything? And keep my son out of this."

"It's too late. You're busted."

"I'm not busted. I am going to burn this cottage down with you in it," Sophia said, words slurred and eyes glassy.

Bowie put a supportive arm around the mob boss as she hopped past the coffee table, unaffected by Isa's claims.

Jacob smirked at Isa. "I bet that didn't go as planned."

CHAPTER 85

From his knees, Jacob inched his way to his feet. Addressed Sophia as she hopped past. "I see." His breathing sounded shallow. "The fuel, a kitchen fire, and you're looking innocent."

"You broke into my property," Sophia answered. "After you lured me into Bambino's, attempted to gun me down, and stole my car."

Isa wiggled around trying to break Gian's grip, but he drew her toward the hall.

Jacob's scrunched-up brows expressed a hint of desperation. "This won't work. These ties," he tossed his head back, "aren't going to burn. It'll be obvious you set this up. Why not cut me loose? Come on, Sophia. Take a chance. I'm the only one who can get you out of this. Not Bowie and certainly not empty-headed Gian."

Empty-headed Gian hissed at Jacob's remark but pulled Isa into the hall.

From behind, she heard the door slam. Guess Sophia didn't take Jacob up on his offer.

"You're going down, Sophia," Jacob yelled.

Gian pulled Isa into a cave-like bedroom with heavy boards bolted across the window. He took a thin nylon rope lying conspicuously on the single bed and tied Isa's arms to the bed's footrail. She tried to kick him. She even went for a bite at his arm. But Gian, like Bond, was nimble and ducking her every move.

Planned. The mobsters plus Bowie had planned this getaway well. "Why not just shoot me?" she asked, giving up on the physical defense and trying some mental tactics. "A fire's an inhumane way to go."

"Less evidence," he muttered and reached around her waist to pull the cell phone from her back pocket. He patted her butt for good measure.

Animal.

She heard a scuffle break out in the living room. Leaving the doctor to guard Jacob probably wasn't Gian's best idea. Jacob could still save the situation, save the day. Even if *she* couldn't figure out how he could.

Hearing the ruckus, Gian rushed out of the room.

More scuffles.

At an awkward angle on her knees and her back to the foot of the bed, Isa pulled against the rope.

It didn't budge.

She should scream. Maybe the house they passed two kilometers away would hear.

Who was she kidding?

She tried getting to her feet, but her last backbend had been some twenty years ago in an elementary school gym class.

She slipped back to her knees.

Jacob appeared with Gian close behind, a gun in Jacob's back.

He hadn't saved the day.

Gian told Jacob to get to his knees.

And Jacob did. And got himself tied up beside Isa. Both on their knees. Both with hands tied behind their backs to a low footrail.

Great.

Where was the old Jacob?

They watched Gian slip out the door.

"Why didn't you fight?" Isa asked, scooting around on her knees.

"Why didn't you?"

"I thought you were going to talk them to death. I didn't see a need."

"I couldn't take a chance at getting shot with you tied up in a bedroom. Someone was going to have to rescue you."

"Not much of a rescue when you're tied up just like me."

Jacob yanked at the rope, which made the bed scoot. Which made Isa lose her balance. Which hurt her arms. "Seriously," she said, getting her knees underneath her again. "How are we getting out of this?"

The smoky scent of fire twisted through the air.

"They lit the kitchen on their way out."

"We could pray," Isa offered.

"I agree with that assessment."

"You go. I've never prayed out loud."

Jacob shook his head. "I haven't done that in years."

"Prayed, or prayed out loud?"

"Either."

"Okay. I'll do it." Isa licked her drying lips. "Lord, like Awena always says, you are in control of all things. Show us your path and help us out of here. In Jesus's name, amen."

"That's how Awena prays?"

"Something like that. She keeps it simple."

"That's not how the Baptist preachers prayed in my day. If we prayed like those guys, we'd be at it until the house burned down." He chuckled. "I think I like keeping prayer simple."

Only Jacob could chuckle with fire blazing in a nearby room.

Isa looked around, hoping to see something they could use to cut the ropes and ties at their hands. She felt ninety-nine percent sure they'd find a way out. Leaving them alive had provided an opening, just like in movies when the criminally insane enjoyed the game of leaving an escape option for their victims. She and Jacob had options, if they could just identify what they were.

Jacob coughed.

"You're sick. COVID?"

"Yeah." He said. "Sophia gave me meds."

"Sounded like she gave you more than meds."

Jacob wiggled his fingers around, reaching for the rope at his wrist. "It wasn't what you think. I played along to keep her guessing, so she'd keep me in her loop. I didn't make myself an easy catch."

Smoke seeped beneath the bedroom door.

"When are we making our move to get out of here?" Isa asked, her one percent of doubt increasing to the ten percent level. "We can't let my evidence burn."

He jerked at the rail again.

Prepared this time, Isa steadied her knees.

"What evidence are you talking about?" he asked. "I thought you were bluffing back there."

"I'll have to show you when we get out."

"Where is it?" He tried rubbing his hands up and down the rail to loosen the rope.

"On my arm."

He stopped rubbing and looked at her, forehead wrinkled in question.

"Thighs, too."

His brows went sky high.

CHAPTER 86

From Bowie's vantage point at the back of the line, Gian struggled to keep Sophia balanced in his arms as they made their way through tall grass and around trees.

The pain meds had done quite the number on Sophia. She'd passed out five minutes after they left the drive.

He wondered if that had been the doctor's purpose.

He couldn't say he was sad about her unconsciousness. The last ten minutes of nonsensical talk between Sophia and Jacob had been unnerving.

Hurried to get this blip in his career over with, Bowie wanted his payoff from Sophia for delivering Isa and to get back to Spain, where he could forget he'd gotten himself tied up with Americans and their superhero ambitions.

He'd like to forget he'd been bought off by a Mafia member, too. A female at that.

What the heck was he doing in the back woods of Italy? He needed a shirt. He needed antacids.

Bowie patted at the gun in his jacket pocket.

He also needed to get over the God-guilt Isa had placed in his head.

But he *wasn't* getting over the God-guilt, and with every step through the high brush, the remorse knife stabbed deeper.

"How much farther to the car?" he asked, his esophagus on fire.

"One-half kilometer," the doc answered.

"Why did you park so far away?"

"Shut up," answered Gian.

The doc, looking as tired of the affair as Bowie felt, trudged through a patch of sticky mud. "Gian said no one should see the car."

"Shut up." Gian's limited vocabulary leaned against the last nerve Bowie had standing.

Bowie pushed his fist into his sternum.

He just couldn't do this.

While Gian adjusted Sophia in his arms, and the doc cradled his bag to his chest, Bowie slipped the gun he'd bought off the street in Naples from his pocket. Aimed and pulled back the hammer.

"Drop her," Bowie ordered. "Then hands in the air."

Gian whirled around to glare at Bowie.

"Drop her."

As directed, Gian dropped Sophia ... in the mud. But he didn't put his hands in the air.

CHAPTER 87

Isa's doubt-slash-confidence index went to fifty-fifty when on their knees, the two had scooted the iron bed around until they faced the door. Using his feet, Jacob pushed and kicked until he got his hiking boots off. Then using impressive toe maneuvers, off came the socks. The plan—he would use his bare feet to turn the doorknob. This idea fell into the unconventional escape category, but at least they were at the door—the only exit option in the room.

"What's with the Band-Aids?" Isa asked, seeing one wrapped around a big toe and another on the side of his other foot. "You can't grip a knob with a bandaged toe."

"You ... never mind."

Pulling the bed closer to the door, he slid his butt low and got his big feet up and on the knob.

This position had to be killing his arms.

"I hope this door isn't locked," he grumbled.

If he could make this work, she'd ... she'd ... do something and it was probably best she *not* think about that something right now. Near-death regrets had her wishing she'd been in Sophia's shoes when Sophia kissed Jacob.

The crackle of wood splitting in the heat of a fire told her Jacob's feet did not move fast enough. Her doubt index shifted from forty percent they escape to sixty percent the fire would win.

Trying not to breathe in more smoke, she declared, "We can do this."

"Hello!"

They gawked at each other. *Was that ...?*

Unmistakable. Someone had called.

"Hello? Where are you?" the man shouted, getting closer to the door.

Her doubt index moved back to forty—as long as it wasn't Gian out in the hall.

The doorknob twisted.

"Scoot, scoot." Jacob urged, dropping his feet to the floor. "Give the door room to open."

"Okay, okay," Isa shot back.

Quicker than he'd been all day, he pushed against the bed, scooting it away from the door and dragging her with him.

They could join a circus if this crazy undercover work didn't pan out.

The thumb latch at the door twisted.

The door opened to the smoky hallway.

Bowie!

Meat cleaver in hand, Bowie, shirtless and muddy, rushed over to Isa and started sawing at the nylon rope and ties.

CHAPTER 88

Isa wiggled out of the other bedroom's window. Small, but big enough for the three to squeeze through, one at a time, they landed on the grassy lawn at the back of the house. Jacob coughing. Isa thanking God. And Bowie topless and apologizing for his little hiccup in character.

Isa and Bowie sprinted for the front. Jacob's bare feet slowed him down, but he caught up with them at the SUV.

"Oh my gosh, your shoes are in the fire," Isa exclaimed when Jacob made for the driver's side door.

"And I'm okay with that," he answered, pushing the ignition button.

Rubbing at her wrists, Isa scrambled into the front passenger seat.

From the back seat, Sophia mumbled and rolled to her side, Bowie's jacket draped across her chest.

Looked like Bowie had secured her arms with sawed off seat belts.

Jacob backed the SUV up to a safe distance a hundred yards away. Bowie trotted along.

Wild flames engulfed the charmed little cottage in the twilight.

Isa opened the front passenger door and got out, stood beside Bowie, and watched the cottage burn.

"How did you do it, Bowie?" she asked.

"When I shot Gian, the doctor dropped his bag and ran."

"Is Gian dead?" Isa asked.

Bowie nodded.

"You carried Sophia back here?" Jacob asked leaning against the steering wheel, the light from the blaze flickering across his face.

Bowie peered around Isa to address Jacob. "Yeah. She's heavier than she looks."

Isa smiled. *Curves come at a price.* "I'm surprised she didn't fight you."

"With the amount of pain medication I took from the doctor's bag, she won't be fighting anything for a while."

"How did you convince her to take more meds?"

"There was no convincing, just doing."

Jacob looked at Bowie sideways.

"Same as my dog." He pointed at his throat. "At the back of the tongue."

"Gian was in Málaga," Isa said, still watching the cottage crumble. "In the community house where I met Chia."

"Chia?" Jacob asked.

"Yeah." She wrapped her arms around her waist. "Gian is the proof. I saw him there. Sophia probably bought girls from the very house I'd been in."

"I saw him, too. At Sophia's villa. When I was sick, he was at the end of my bed." Jacob scratched his chin. "The guy got around."

"What a coincidence," Bowie said.

The cottage roof collapsed with a burst of sparks and the roar of an airplane. Bowie and Isa took a step back.

"It's not a coincidence," Isa whispered. "It's the Lord."

The whirl of fire truck alarms reached up to the hills. "They are coming," Bowie said, shoving his hands into his pant pockets.

That Bowie. Half-naked and he didn't even shiver in the cold. He'd almost left her and Jacob to toast like marshmallows. She glanced over at Jacob then back at Bowie. What was she doing between these two psychotic males?

In a few minutes, the cottage would be surrounded. The police would come, and there would be no way one or two corrupt officials could sweep this under their Italian rugs. With the burning cottage, Sophia admitting her bank fraud, and Gian spotted in human trafficking activity, the female mob boss wouldn't skate away from this arrest like she skated from the US witness program.

"So the evidence ..." Jacob eyed Isa. "Where did you say it was?"

She rolled up a sleeve. "Right. Here. And a couple of other places."

CHAPTER 89

By the time the overhead announcements rambled through three languages, Jacob had moved from bank fraud on to another subject—food.

Two days with multiple translators in multiple offices, and Sophia Evalina Ricci Ventura of the Vita Morale Family Mafia would be bound for jail. For now, she lay handcuffed to a hospital bed under heavy anti-Mafia guard.

The shadow of a few days' growth covered Jacob's upper lip and chin. His hair was messier than ever, the rusty color of Colorado's rocky hills burned into his cheeks.

The FBI agent turned bounty hunter turned ... who knew where Jacob's multi-personality issues would take him next.

"The problem," he said, pointing at the overhead menu, "Is that I've not had enough meat and grease. Nothing but basil and tomatoes and white cheese. That's all I ate for days."

Astonishing that they could have a normal conversation. In their entire relationship existence, exchanges had been about her incompetence or his ego issues. "You craving a burger?"

In the airport hum of people rushing and overhead announcements blasting, keeping it light felt good.

"Yes. If I'd had some real Texas meat, I would have beat the virus two days sooner."

Pizza in tow, they grabbed the last empty table, a two-seater in the middle of the heavy foot-traffic lanes. "See," he said lifting the slice from the paper plate. "Only three pepperonis."

Isa checked the time on the expensive cell phone she'd picked up in the gift shop and vowed to resell on Ebay after getting home.

Only a half hour before he would board his flight. He flew Delta to Dallas to Albuquerque. She flew American to Chicago to Houston to Albuquerque. As usual, they followed different paths to the same destination.

"So tell me about this girl you rescued in Spain." He took a swig of his Pellegrino water. Minimalist Jacob opting for designer water had caught her a little off guard. Maybe some things Italian had rubbed off on the tough-guy bounty hunter.

Isa finished chewing her bite of classic margherita pie. "She's full of possibilities and she's captured my heart." Isa swallowed, wiped at her lips with the paper napkin. "From Nigeria. She has the typical story. Her parents gave the traffickers money, believing the slime balls would take their daughter to work in Spain so she could save up for college." A smile busted across her face with talk of Chia. Thoughts of that girl brought goodness and hope and grace. "She wants to be a doctor. Isn't that the greatest?"

"Isn't that always the story?" Mozzarella stretched from his slice to his mouth. Expertly, he wound his finger through the cheese strings and slipped the excess through his lips.

"She'll make it, though." Isa looked off into the crowd. That girl was one in a hundred. One in a thousand. "She's smart and ... I don't know ... focused. I believe she not only deserves a chance, but if given that chance, she'll make a difference in the world."

"You just met her."

"I intend to make her goal a reality."

His bows shot up. "Oh?"

"I promised Bowie if he'd help me rescue her, I'd give him my half of the bounty less college tuition for Chia. My high school trigonometry teacher helped me apply for scholarships to college. Even pitched in on my first year's tuition. I want to pay it forward and help Chia."

"But I never agreed to half the bounty. We had a deal for a sixty-forty split."

"It was fifty-fifty." Isa smirked. "Anyway, we won't be collecting the big bucks now."

His lips dipped in a frown. "We won't be collecting anything."

"I'm okay with it. We did the right thing. I'll figure out how to get the money for Chia somehow."

Jacob changed the subject. "How's the coffee shop hanging without you?"

Isa chuckled. "Probably won't recognize the place when I get back. Awena and Maria are independent thinkers."

"You hired Maria? El Padrino's cook?"

"I did."

"And the spiritual sage, Awena?"

Isa nodded. "Yeah. She's ..." the sudden desire to see her best friend and mentor hit hard. "She is ... perfect."

"With short prayers."

Isa laughed out loud. "That's a funny thing to remember from our life-threatening episode in the burning cottage."

"I've been thinking about what you said and your short prayer. I figure the Lord's prayer can't take more than thirty seconds to repeat. If it worked for Jesus, I guess it should work for anybody."

The Lord's Prayer? She'd have to ask Awena where to find that in the Bible.

Then out of the blue, in classic Jacob personality switch, the nonchalant curve of his mouth slipped into a serious line. His eyes darkened. "I'm not sure what's next."

Isa let his statement hang there unsure, also. Unsure of just about everything.

And in the count of four seconds, the shadow passed, and his eyes twinkled. "Maybe I'll pick up the guitar."

He pulled his napkin from his lap and reached across the table with it. "Let me get that." He pressed the napkin at the corner of her lips. "Cheese."

She laughed. And he laughed. And Isa didn't want the moment to end.

But time moved at a faster pace than her desires.

When he finished his slice, he stood. Stretched his arms. "I guess we better get going. Walk me to the gate."

CHAPTER 90

The gate attendant called for first class. Somehow, Jacob had scored an upgrade.

Her last-minute flight booking put her at the back of the plane. Middle seat.

Jacob awkwardly draped his arm around her shoulder and gave her the same side squeeze she received from P-Joe at the Cleansed By Jesus washateria church on Sunday mornings.

It was one move short of tousling the hair on top of her head.

He let go and stepped back.

She half-waved. "See ya."

"Yeah," he said, hoisting his new backpack up to his shoulder. "See ya in Albuquerque sometime."

Dang those emotions commencing a gut grip.

After the gate attendant scanned Jacob's phone, he turned and waved again. Then Jacob walked, slower than he needed to, down the jetway.

Isa moved over to the gate window and studied the tarmac. Nothing out there looked especially interesting— except maybe the baggage truck that pulled up. It hosted six hot pink suitcases, three purple, four red ... and who cared.

She thought about crying. But decided that would be dumb. Granted, things felt unfinished, and there wouldn't be any bounty payments. But authorities held Sophia in custody again. That counted for something.

If Awena was around, she would ask her favorite question.

What have you learned, Isa Phillips?

If I can't trust my own feelings, then I've learned that I am not ready to trust the feelings that belong to someone else. Emotions are overrated.

"Isa."

She rolled her bottom lip under her teeth. Not sure what to expect, she turned to face him.

Jacob, without his backpack, stood there looking humble, lost, and gorgeous.

His shrug said it all.

The gate attendant called another row of passengers.

If this had been a romantic comedy, he would have run to her, catching her up in his arms and kissing her.

But this was Jacob and Isa in an airport.

Her mouth went dry as she expected him to tell her he had a girlfriend. Or that he and Jonna were back on. Or his third personality didn't think they were any good for each another.

He walked up to her nose to nose.

Whatever she came up with to say or do would be the wrong thing. So she stood there, void and depleted.

Jacob studied her face. Then he wrapped both arms around her shoulders. Quiet and knowing, he embraced her with a tenderness she didn't know existed.

She lifted her arms beneath his and reciprocated. It didn't take more than three seconds for the unnatural affection to slip into supernatural. She might be in heaven.

He lifted his head and kissed her at that special place—her hairline.

He smelled of woods and musk, and she could have stayed right there until time to board her own plane.

But he let go and grasped her by the shoulders, intensity in his eyes. "I'm damaged goods."

"So am I." *Two broken peas in a dysfunctional pod.*

He let go and put his finger in her face. Something he hadn't done in a very long time. "I need you to know that I really don't know who I am. You nailed that about me day one."

"I'm sorry, I—"

"I found out my father isn't my father. My mother and ... well, now he's my stepfather ... they've lied to me all my life. I'm not the son of a decorated police officer. I'm the son of a one-hit rock-n-roll wonder who fizzled before his career got started."

She swallowed hard. Hearing other people confess anything other than bank fraud didn't fall under her life experiences.

"My mother confessed to a fling with a rocker before she married my supposed dad. She told me right before Jonna and I were to be married. Thought it was time, I guess. I haven't spoken to her since. I've got to find a way to accept it."

"Okay." It was the only word she could locate.

He looked over her head at nothing. "He's a deadbeat rocker named Guthrie Rollins. Turns out I'm the only kid he ever had, and he doesn't know I'm alive."

Passengers for business class were summoned.

"I better go." He started to look like he regretted what he'd just done.

"Wh ... wait," Isa stammered. If he'd just thrown out some vulnerability, she'd better be a safe place for it to land. She grabbed him by the shirt collar, guessing he must want something of substance from her. "I met my real father only two times. Two times! Birth fathers don't matter." She shook him. "It's the people you have in your life now that matter."

Jacob's brows dropped low. She'd struck a nerve.

"Listen to me. DNA means nothing."

He blinked a few times. Gave her an iffy thumbs up. "Maybe."

She let go his shirt collar.

He shook his shaggy head. Said, "I'll think on it." Then Jacob walked back to board his plane bound for Dallas.

Beneath her breath, she said it again. "It's the people you have in your life now that matter."

CHAPTER 91

Once the plane hit the magical altitude of fifteen thousand feet, Isa pushed her seat back, plugged her earbuds in for some tunes from way back. She closed her eyes. *Surreal.*

Her thoughts meandered through her short-term brain files. In a year, she'd gone from obsessive-compulsive accountant to undercover narcotics work with a Mexican cartel to entrepreneurial baker and coffee brewer to child trafficking rescuer. And to think that in the first six years of her career, she'd sat at one old metal HPD desk, her nose in electronic spreadsheets.

Just goes to show, you never know where God is taking you, but he sure is taking you somewhere.

Lots had changed. Even her dragon. He slept more these days. Thanks to Kevin.

A casino advertisement played through her buds, promoting the old-time rock band Journey. The song *Don't Stop Believing* faded with the ad. Journey still toured and Isa guessed they'd be rocking it to sell-out geriatric crowds long after they'd taken to the stage on walkers.

Guthrie.

One eye popped open.

Rollins.

Every muscle contracted when she jolted upright in her seat. *Guthrie Rollins. Whaaaat?* The rocker Blue T. Booker had asked her to go see was ... Jacob's father.

Isa dug through the plastic bag she'd picked up at the airport. She pulled out her airport purchases—two granola bars, a mini packet of Kleenex, a nail file, a Twix bar, and finally, her ultra-expensive cell phone.

Connecting to the plane's Wi-Fi, she counted off thirty-two long, long, agonizing seconds.

Connection made and Isa's thumbs flew across the screen's keyboard.

GUTHRIE ROLLINS.

Black-and-white photos of a lean young man with shoulder-length blond hair and guitar at his hip downloaded. Beneath one of the photos, the caption read, "Rollins plays 'Cry Regina.'"

CHAPTER 92

Isa spread fresh New Mexico honey across the decadent blue corn muffin, reading the last entry in Claire's most recent diary.

She glanced down at the crumbs scattered on and around her plate. Returned her eyes to the diary.

For two days, she had read and reread the chronicles of Claire. The Claire she'd laughed with and loved emerged there between the pages of struggles. Though she couldn't believe Claire had dropped her Christian morals in exchange for a piece of the cartel financial pie, after reading through the journals and notes, Isa physically felt the pressure someone within the HPD had laid upon Claire.

Nausea had struck when Claire mentioned having a beer with Mac. But that was the only time she cited a connection to Isa's husband.

In her early journals, Claire wrote verses and prayers to God. These had been the writings Milly Washington had mentioned on that fateful visit to the coffee shop.

But in the last couple of years, no doubt, Claire had come under threat. She'd considered an offer from Todd Wilson—an unspecified offer that would provide for her granny's medical needs. Granny Milly Washington, Isa suspected.

"What will you do now, Isa Padilla?"

Isa glanced up. She hadn't seen Awena step up to the counter. Awena had a way of materializing out of thin air.

"Now?"

"With the sacred writings of this woman who loved God but chose poorly. It is a story of human nature, is it not?"

"Are you saying I should publish this?"

Awena rolled her eyes. "No, Isa. I say you must learn from it."

"Oh. Got it." Isa studied Awena's leathered face and silky grey braids hanging over both shoulders. What had she done to deserve this wise woman in her life? In Awena, God had provided the wisdom and unconditional love of a mother.

And through her ex-sergeant, God had provided an example of work ethics—something an absent father could never do.

Isa lacked nothing.

Except, maybe, a civil relationship with Jacob Lahache.

"Great blue corn muffins," she said, eyes still lingering on her mentor.

"Sales doubled with those babies." Awena said, grabbing a towel and wiping up Isa's crumbs. "Maria's sopapillas outsold the green tea cranberry, too."

Isa took another bite of baked blue corn.

"The fancy latte this and mocha that did not tell our story, Isa. We are New Mexican."

Isa tilted her head. "And blue corn and sopapillas tell our story?"

Awena nodded once, her typical affirmation. "People of diversity. People who thrive regardless of their challenges."

"Hmm ... I didn't get that from baked corn and fried flour, but I'll ponder further."

"Cultures colliding to end in harmony through food."

Awena, in all her spiritual mastery, was a foodie at the core. Isa closed Claire's journal.

"And now you are faced with your choice, Isa. What will you do for Milly Washington?"

Isa ran her index finger around the plate, picking up the last crumbs. "I'm going to get Todd Wilson arrested."

"Like you did El Padrino?"

Isa nodded.

"Like you have now done with Sophia the mob boss?"

Isa rocked her head back and forth. "We hope that one sticks. I hear the Italians are still unraveling the financial information I gave them and trying to pin her with several crimes. But equally important, four crooked bankers in Europe have been arrested, and the human trafficking's money laundering schemes have been disrupted. Follow the money trail and you'll find the criminals. I hope they pull that awful business down."

"It is evil."

"Yes."

"Are you sure you cannot go to the Thursday night bring-a-dish?" Awena padded over to the coat hooks. Removed her tattered coat.

"No. I have to catch up on book work." Awena and Maria were keen in the kitchen but hadn't done much in the record-keeping department during Isa's absence.

"I'll walk you to the bus station," Isa slid off her stool.

"Blue T. Booker will take me."

Isa nearly choked. "To church?"

Awena looked at her like she had not one inch of faith in her entire body. "Of course to church. He comes to Cleansed By Jesus now. He's playing Joseph in the Christmas play next week."

Good heavens.

"Well, if he's becoming an honest Christ-follower, I'll need to get his taxes done pronto."

"He mentioned that."

Isa shook her head to get all the incoming information into the right slots. "Awena, how will he take you? He doesn't have a car."

"We ride his motorcycle." She made fists in the air like she had a double grip on handlebars. "Vroom, vroom."

CHAPTER 93

Isa said a silent prayer for Sergeant Caba. On the other end of the call, he repeated what he'd said three times already. "I should have seen it."

Considering that after El Padrino's incarceration, three HPD officers had been arrested, the idea of a high-level someone blackmailing lower-ranking officers was solid in her mind. And now that Claire had clearly mentioned Todd Wilson as applying pressure about some vague choice, it seemed time to plant seeds in Caba's garden of investigative prowess.

"You could come back here and help me investigate. I'd graduate you from the desk," he said, sounding more serious than she wanted him to. "Put you undercover."

"It's a tempting offer, but ..."

"Though I don't have any one quick as you in financial fraud. Sure you can't come on back to Houston?"

"Sarge, I don't think I could return to a desk and spreadsheets. And I don't think I'm all that good at undercover."

"For a bean counter and baker, I'd say you're doing pretty good. You've gone international now." He paused. "Claire wrote the cryptic note and put it in your car, didn't she?"

A burning sensation started in her throat and made its way down to her chest. "It looks like it." This conversation brought on painful memories and probably some healing, too. Those two things, unfortunately, journeyed side by side. "Claire and her grandmother exchanged verses on cards as a secret form of communication for fun when she was young. Looks like she followed the idea, hoping I'd uncover some things and rush in to pull her out of the mess she was in." An unexpected grip caught Isa by the throat. "But ... I ... I was too late."

Caba waited patiently.

Isa wiped her nose with her sleeve. Pulled in a shaky breath. "Everything went south for Claire."

"I'll stop Wilson if he's guilty. He plans to run for Houston City Council, and we'll get to the truth before that happens."

"For Claire?" Isa's nose wouldn't stop leaking.

"For Claire," he said.

CHAPTER 94

Isa picked her phone up. Put it back on the counter. Picked it up again.

The only thing on her screen was Awena's text from three hours ago. She'd made it to her cousin's home in Arizona.

Isa ambled to the front of the shop. Turned out the dining room lights. Locked the deadbolt on the door.

Stopping at table four, she adjusted the lid on the box of Blue's finished taxes. He'd said he would pick them up day after Christmas, but with the huge success of his new church acting career, he'd been in demand. He had to stop over at the ex-prostitute's apartment to help her finish her tree. And there were the food bank ladies that needed him to aid in organizing all the end-of-year canned donations. And several of the church members had requested tattoos. Spiritual ones, of course.

Christmas would arrive at sunrise, and Isa hadn't decided on her plans yet. There were just so many options.

Not.

She meandered back to her phone to make sure she hadn't missed a text in the long journey to the front door and back.

Nope.

She rested her chin in her hand, scrolling through Pinterest recipes. Why, she didn't know. Between Awena and Maria, their menu had taken on a true New Mexican vibe, and sales were up. Tourists seemed to prefer the unique blend of fare that made New Mexico a food destination.

She opened her email to find a short greeting from Bowie. His sister had permanently adopted Luna, and he was on holiday in Germany. Seemed he didn't want to stick around Málaga for more than a few days at a time. When all the financial chips fell from Pepe's exposé briefcase, he didn't want to be the one to explain how those papers made it into the authorities' hands.

She scrolled through a couple of promotional emails but stopped at one that had an unusual return address. Ese dot Nigeria dot something.

She sat up straight. Clicked on the email.

GREETINGS TO YOU MY LOVELY ISABELLA PHILLIPS. I HAVE GOOD NEWS FOR YOU TODAY. I AM GOING TO COLLEGE. NEXT SEMESTER, I WILL BE IN THE UNITED STATES TO ATTEND SCHOOL. A SPONSOR HAS SECURED ME ENROLLMENT INTO THE UNIVERSITY OF NEW MEXICO. WHERE DO YOU LIVE IN THE US? I HOPE I CAN TRAVEL TO SEE YOU WHILE I AM THERE. THANK YOU FOR SAVING ME, CHIAZOPAN ESE

Could not be real.

She reread the email three times.

The news sent her thoughts soaring. God gave yet another miracle.

She drained the carafe of the last of the French roast and read the email one more time.

Then she fired off three responses—after she hit send on the first one, she made a lap around her dining room, came back to her phone, and wrote email number two to Chia, asking more questions.

Another vigorous lap with dancing this time, and Isa penned the third set of questions.

Chia, in Albuquerque? *What? How? Who?*

God is good. God is good.

Things could have turned out very differently for Chia. But God.

What a way to spend Christmas eve and day. She'd probably bake another dozen muffins tonight and eat 'em all in the car on her way home.

And she should make that call.

For three days, she'd planned to call him but had chickened out when her hands got shaky and her voice got breathy. No way she'd grant him the satisfaction of knowing he made her nervous.

But the great news needed to be heralded or she might combust.

Two more laps around the dining room and she stopped at her phone on the counter. Clicked through contacts.

Called.

He picked up after two rings.

"Hello."

"Hi. It's me. Isa."

"I know."

"You do?"

"Yes. You're in my contacts."

"It wasn't easy getting my number back after, you know, my purse and I got absconded."

That deep and spicy chuckle of his sent goose bumps down her arms. "I was going to call you tomorrow," he said, "and wish you a Merry Christmas."

She bit into her lip.

"You there?"

"Yeah." She sucked in some nerve. "I hope I'm not interrupting anything."

"You're fine."

"I wanted to call and tell you that I have a Christmas present for you." Instantly, she regretted sharing that info, and she slapped her forehead. *Lame, lame, lame.*

"Oh?"

"Well ... wait. Let me start over. I wanted to tell you about a miracle."

"Okay. Let's hear it."

"Chia ... you remember ..." She studied a nail, thinking it needed a good chew. If only she didn't sound so nervous, and if only she could get her breath under control, and if only she could talk to him as if they were really friends. "She's coming to Albuquerque, to go to school."

She heard him pull in a breath. "Really?"

"Yes, I got an email from her. She didn't explain the details yet, but isn't that the greatest?"

"Pretty incredible news, Isa."

"Well, anyway, I wanted to share that with you."

"What about the present?"

"The what?"

"You said you had a present for me. When do I get it?"

Isa pulled the phone from her ear, looked at the screen. Yup, she was talking to bulldoze-to-the-point Jacob. She pushed the phone back and gave him her most honest answer. "I don't know."

"What are you doing now?"

"Just closing the shop. Then heading home."

"Can I come over for a mocha, cranberry, caramel something?"

CHAPTER 95

Isa searched her desk drawer for the eyeliner Maria's thirteen-year-old granddaughter had left on the counter after a shopping spree at Dollar King. Not one to wear makeup much, but it certainly didn't hurt to add a little oomph to her lids since it was the holidays and all.

But the sound of loud voices coming from outside stopped the eyelid-enhancer hunt.

Isa got up and hustled past the kitchen sinks, into the dining room, and around the counter. Through the full windows in front, she saw the orange-haired girl she'd met right before her trip to Spain. Her name, it turned out, was Jeston Jordan. Awena had not only had her own experience with Jeston monitoring the streets but had employed the teen to keep an eye on Coffee Magic's front door during the twilight hours. Now Jeston had her finger stuck in a man's face. Didn't really look like Jacob—the man was heavier and wore his hair shorter—but it probably was Jacob. *What now?*

As Isa unlocked and opened the door, Jeston said, "You're that freaked-out cop. I remember you."

"What's going on?" Isa asked.

Jacob looked over at Isa. "You tell me. This girl says I can't wait outside your door, and that I have to keep moving."

Jeston, with freshly dyed orange hair and a new tattoo on her neck, said, "He's the guy I told you about before you left town, Isa. This is *that* freak. He's dangerous and I don't want him hanging around."

Jacob shot his hands in the air. "Who put you in charge?"

Isa closed her eyes, shaking her head. "Wait. No. There's a misunderstanding." She drew in a quick breath and looked at Jacob. "Jeston here keeps an eye on our store while we're closed during evening hours." She moved her sights over to Jeston. "Jeston, this is my friend. His name is Jacob."

"She's a security guard?" Jacob stifled a laughed.

"I don't like him," Jeston said crossing her arms. "He's dangerous."

"Okay," Isa reasoned. "So this is the man who pulled a gun on your dad in the parking lot a few weeks back?"

Jeston nodded.

Jacob's eyes went wide. "Is she talking about Spiderman? Spiderman is your dad? I should have recognized you. And by the way, I was trying to help you. Your dad was in the process of beating your mother."

"Was not." Jeston stuck her chin out.

"Was, too." Jacob returned the gesture.

"That's just how they are," Jeston retorted.

Isa pulled at her ponytail. "Okay, okay. I realize there's some confusion here, but let's try to move on." She faced Jacob. "Awena hired Jeston when I was with you in Italy. Awena felt someone needed to keep an eye on the place. It's one of those Awena-decisions she made in my absence."

"Awena doesn't know who she hired." Jacob tucked his chin back in. "That girl packing?"

"Of course not. She just knows who belongs and who doesn't, and she is to call me or Awena if there's trouble."

Isa touched Jeston on the shoulder. "You did a great job, Jeston. But he's here to see me."

Jeston said, "Fine by me," and backed herself into the shadows of the building next door. But not before calling Jacob a creep again.

Opening the door for Jacob, Isa said, "After you."

Jacob stepped in. Put both hands in his pockets. "Albuquerque."

With the new crew cut, he looked more like the Captain America she'd first met. Isa locked the door, wondering if they could really manage a personal conversation for more than six and a half minutes.

She made the first attempt. "You've put some weight back on. You look go … odly."

"Godly?" He took off his Carhartt jacket and slung it across a table. "I think you were going to say I look *good*."

Oh, here we go. He was well over his COVID-in-Italy episode and back to his egomaniac self.

Isa headed for the counter. "I brewed fresh coffee. And, I have blue corn muffins and the cranberry things you mentioned."

"Hm," he said rubbing his hands together. "Blue corn muffin."

"With piñon butter?"

"You have just made my Christmas Eve."

She got the plates. The cups. The carafe. Napkins. Forks. Scooted his across the counter to set in front of him and she stood on the backside, pouring the Sumatra. "I'm surprised you don't have plans tonight."

"Ah." He nodded but cast his eyes somewhere behind her. "The family and I are not really back to normal."

"Yeah?"

"The father thing. I'm having … a … I told you. At the Naples airport."

"Yes." She rearranged her muffin on the plate. Rearranged the plate on the counter. "And I told you about mine."

She looked up to find him staring at her. Their eyes latched for a second.

Isa broke the spell. "Dig in," she said, scooting her muffin around the plate again.

"I thought you might pray or something."

That ... she didn't expect. But she went with it. Bowed her head and said, "Lord, thank you for every good and perfect gift, for giving Chia the opportunity to ..." She had trouble getting the next words past the untimely lump forming in her throat. "To, uh ..."

Then a breath-sucking sob racked her chest.

All indicators pointed to the onset of an ugly cry—including the deep maroon burn in Jacob's cheeks.

Did he not close his stupid eyes when he prayed? Just great. Just great.

Now, he looked to feel sorry for her.

She dabbed the napkin at her eyes while holding her breath and stifling sob number two.

His stare steady on her, he, surprisingly, finished up the prayer. "Thank you, Lord, for giving Chia the opportunity to have an education. And thank you that you used Isa to save her. Amen."

They gaped at each other for an uncomfortable, static five seconds, while inside her, all kinds of commotion commenced. Seemed her organs had joined a circus act.

He finally deflected by picking up the muffin. Looked it over.

She managed a solid, smooth breath once he said, "*Yum.*"

He bit into the muffin. With eyes rolling back in his head, he muttered, "Oh, that's good."

Score bigtime for Awena.

Isa, willing some dignified composure, used her fork to take a bite of the third blue corn muffin she'd eaten that day. The first two had been hands-on. But at least the ugly cry was gone, and Jacob's face back to its regular ruddy color.

Jacob studied the muffin at eye level again and asked, "So ... where's my Christmas present?"

She cleared her throat on that one. "Never mind," she said. "I was teasing."

"I don't think you were."

"I was."

"You sounded serious on the phone."

"Okay, I had an idea, but it was dumb, and you'll probably make me feel stupid for doing it. So let's forget about it."

"Maybe if I tell you what I got *you* for Christmas, you'll come clean with your gift."

She choked when the muffin got stuck on the lump in her throat that continued to hang around. "Oh. You have a present for me?"

Jacob put his elbows on the counter. Leaned in. "I do. Only it looks like you got word of it before I could tell you. I wanted to wish you a Merry Christmas with the news."

She frowned. "Got word of it. What are you talking about?"

He shook his head. "You can string financial clues together like a master, but when it comes to personal stuff, you can't find a clue. You can't find clue to a clue."

Annoyed at the insult, she put her hands on her hips. "Okay, I'm clueless."

"Chia—the sponsorship, a partial scholarship, and flights here—I arranged that."

Did she hear that right? Wait. Nah, couldn't be. "No-o."

"Yes."

"How did you ... what did you ... you?" She crossed her arms then uncrossed them. "*You*?"

Brows inching up, he asked, "Is that so unbelievable?"

The circus of emotions started up again, only this time, the tears didn't just leak out, they discharged like a firehose.

Blubbering and without thought of what he'd think, or how she'd look doing it, she sprinted around the counter and crashed into Jacob. And the bar stool.

Who cared that she'd probably cracked her kneecap?

She squeezed him around the waist, bear-hug style. Jacob Lahache had a heart after all. A big, fleshy, compassionate heart. She pulled back, wiped her nose with the back of one hand and then the other, then put those snotty hands on his shoulders. "Oh, my gosh! You didn't. I mean you did. I mean wow. Thank you." She beamed. "Thank you."

Satisfaction spread across his mug. He seemed to love that he'd taken her by surprise.

"It's hard to believe," she said more to herself than to him. "This calls for a celebration." She visualized the bottle of sparkling apple cider someone had left in the under-counter fridge.

But before she could turn away, he reached up and grabbed both her wrists. Tightened the grip.

The inner circus act froze.

He drew her in, slipping her arms around his neck then placing his hands flat on her lower back.

A hesitation.

Is he going to do this?

He did. He pressed his lips into hers.

She caught her breath. Held it.

Sweet and gentle, everything around her evaporated. She and Jacob kissed for real. *For real.*

Then.

Then, Jacob leaned into that kiss.

Like the fourth of July instead of Christmas, her senses lit up like fireworks.

And she kissed him back. And she knew that he knew that they both knew, this was the kiss of all kisses—like Buttercup and Westley of *The Princess Bride* rolling down the hill of fate to find each other's doubting lips at last.

Who knew how long it lasted? She wasn't counting the seconds or the minutes. She lost herself to him. Time had no significance.

When their lips finally parted, her hair was down with his hands tangled in it.

Wowza.

"Was that my Christmas present?" he asked, jiggling her shoulders. "If it was, that was the best gift I've gotten so far."

She straightened her polo. "Actually, I do have something for you."

"And then we get to do that again?"

She batted her eyes. Seriously. It came naturally, though she'd never eye-batted in her entire life. "Stay right there. I'll be right back."

Eyes still on him, she ran into the edge of the counter, grimaced, then made for the kitchen door.

Out of her desk drawer, she pulled an envelope that had the words *Trust Me* written across the front.

When she came back through the kitchen door, he'd gotten back to his muffin.

Slipping up beside him again, he visually explored her physique. "Isa Phillips."

"Jacob Lahache." She held the envelope by the corners. Rocked it back and forth.

"What's this?" he took the envelope, giving her a sideways glance. "Now I get a mystery note?"

"Open it."

Jacob lifted the flap and pulled out two printed E-tickets.

He flipped one of the pages over and back again. "You bought tickets to a Guthrie Rollins concert?"

"Yes," she said, pulling one of the sheets from his hands. "It's in Denver. Next month. Small venue."

His forehead pleated. "I don't know what to ... um ... say."

"Say you'll go. We'll go together."

Jacob frowned. "I don't think I want to meet this guy."

She touched his arm. "Not to meet him, but just to see his talent. I read he's considered the best guitarist of his time. Just never made the pop charts."

Jacob took the paper from her. Slid both tickets and the envelope to the counter, his posture stiffening. "You read about my father? So you're saying you researched him." He gave her the old *Jay Hernandez from the cartel days is not happy with his partner* glare.

Uh-oh.

That might have been their first *and* last kiss.

Cautious, she nodded. "I ... I always wanted to know more about my dad, but I can't find him. So, I looked for yours."

He rubbed his chin. Closed his eyes and opened them again.

Then, the tough-guy Jacob Lahache facade dissipated. "You did that?"

She nodded.

"This is crazy."

"I know." Isa's heart felt like a muffin right out of the oven—hot and gooey. She pressed her forehead into his. "But we've done crazier things than this."

His arms wrapped around her. The moment hung vulnerable and perfect.

Outside, a car playing "Deck the Halls" calypso-style, volume set at mega loud, pulled up to the curb. Steel drums blaring, it seemed the explanation point on their always-quirky connection.

Jacob said, "Okay. I'm in."

She squeezed him then crawled up on the stool next to him. Pulled her plate over. "It'll be easier than the last two cases we've worked together."

He eyed her sideways. "Speaking of cases, I got a lead on another one. Stateside this time. Something's going down in a mid-sized town south of Dallas. I was tracking a fugitive, but there's more there."

"What's that got to do with anything?"

"If I'm in with concerts, you have to be in with cases."

"So whatever this is between us ..." She made quotation marks with her fingers. "It's about guns, sleazy people, and solving crime cases?"

"Sounds like our vibe."

Oh, really? "Our common denominator is crime?"

Jacob looked up at the ceiling for a couple of beats then shrugged. "Could be worse," he finally said. "Could be dancing or sci-fi movies."

"You don't dance, and sci-fi movies would be a stretch for me. I don't own a TV these days."

"I guess our connection is justice, then."

Isa ran her fingers through her hair again. "Look, I know you haven't noticed, but I bake. I brew—"

"Yeah, I don't like the risky moves you pull when we're on a case together," he said, ignoring her current career path. "But you're a heck-of-a kisser."

Isa pulled in a deep breath and blew it out again. Some things with Jacob would never change. "I called Houston today. Talked to Sergeant Caba."

"And?"

"He needs help."

Jacob picked up his coffee and threw the Sumatra back like a cowboy downing whiskey. "You and me, Isa," he said, slamming his mug back down on the counter. "Looks like the Lone Star state is in our future."

ABOUT THE AUTHOR

Award-winning author L. G. Westlake writes fun, action-packed suspense with characters who are clever, fearless, and sometimes quirky, but always heroes. Her debut novel, *Quest for the Life Tree*, received recognition as one of the publisher's top eight books of the year and she has been writing suspense novels and encouraging blogs ever since.

L. G. and her husband originally hail from Texas where she served as founding director of a Crisis Pregnancy Center. Since that time, she and her husband have served in short and long-term missions in seven countries, and now live in the Land of Enchantment where L. G. works as the marketing manager for a ministry that shares God's Word with the world. She also enjoys cooking, gardening, and hanging out with hubby on her patio overlooking the city of Albuquerque. But the thing that gives L. G. her biggest thrill is inspiring readers to unearth their God-given gifts and become superheroes for the Lord. She and her husband have three grown children and four grandchildren (superheroes in the making).

Check out L. G.'s blogs and books at LaurieGreenWestlake. com

If you enjoyed *Calculated Encounters*, you'll want to read the book that started it all, *Calculated Risk*.

L. G. WESTLAKE

CALCULATED

RISK

GRIEVING WIDOW | DISILLUSIONED COP
SEARCHING FOR ANSWERS